Praise for 43 Light Street from Romantic Times BOOKreviews

NEVER TOO LATE

"Twisting and turning with dazzling originality, the latest venture into 43 LIGHT STREET territory offers the perfect escape for lucky readers!"

MIDNIGHT CALLER

"Take a walk on the wild side with Rebecca York in a mind-bending tale of sizzling suspense and irresistible romance."

SHATTERED LULLABY

"Chilling excitement…exquisitely tender romance… the very best in romantic suspense."

NOWHERE MAN

"…a to-die-for hero, chilling suspense and an unforgettable love story."

FATHER AND CHILD

"Great, one-sitting romantic suspense that will keep readers on the edge of their seats from start to finish."

FOR YOUR EYES ONLY

"Few write suspense like Rebecca York."

FACE TO FACE

"Harlequin's first lady of suspense…a marvelous storyteller, Ms. York cleverly develops an intricately plotted romance to challenge our imaginations and warm our hearts."

REBECCA YORK

USA TODAY bestselling author Ruth Glick published her one hundredth book, *Crimson Moon*, a Berkley Sensation, in January 2005. Her latest 43 Light Street book is *The Secret Night*, published in April 2006. In October she launches the Harlequin Intrigue continuity series SECURITY BREACH with *Chain Reaction*.

Ruth's many honors include two RITA Award finalist books. She has two Career Achievement Awards from *Romantic Times BOOKreviews* for Series Romantic Suspense and Series Romantic Mystery. *Nowhere Man* was the *Romantic Times BOOKreviews* Best Intrigue of 1998 and is one of their "all-time favorite 400 romances." Ruth's *Killing Moon* and *Witching Moon* both won the New Jersey Romance Writers Golden Leaf Award for Paranormal.

Michael Dirda of *Washington Post Book World* says, "Her books...deliver what they promise—excitement, mystery, romance."

Since 1997 she has been writing on her own as Rebecca York. Between 1990 and 1997 she wrote the Light Street series with Eileen Buckholtz. You can contact Ruth at rglick@capaccess.org or visit her Web site at www.rebeccayork.com.

43 LIGHT STREET

REBECCA YORK
Amanda's Child

RUTH GLICK WRITING AS REBECCA YORK

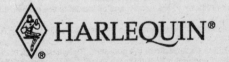

HARLEQUIN®

TORONTO • NEW YORK • LONDON
AMSTERDAM • PARIS • SYDNEY • HAMBURG
STOCKHOLM • ATHENS • TOKYO • MILAN • MADRID
PRAGUE • WARSAW • BUDAPEST • AUCKLAND

ISBN-13: 978-0-373-36072-7
ISBN-10:   0-373-36072-X

AMANDA'S CHILD

Directory

4 3   L I G H T   S T R E E T

	Room
ADVENTURES IN TRAVEL	204
ABIGAIL FRANKLIN, Ph.D. KATHRYN KELLEY, Ph.D. 　Clinical Psychology	509
BIRTH DATA, INC.	322
INNER HARBOR PRODUCTIONS	404
THE LIGHT STREET FOUNDATION	322
KATHRYN MARTIN-McQUADE, M.D. 　Branch Office, Medizone Labs	515
THE LIGHT STREET 　Detective Agency	520
LAURA ROSWELL, LL.B. 　Attorney-at-Law	311
SABRINA'S FANCY	Lobby
RANDOLPH SECURITY, 　Branch Office	407
NOEL ZACHARIAS 　Paralegal Service	311
L. ROSSINI 　Superintendent	Lower Level

CAST OF CHARACTERS

Amanda Barnwell—Pregnant and in more trouble than she realized.

Matthew Forester—Compelled by a terrible secret from his past to help Amanda.

Roy Logan—He was determined to take away Amanda's baby, using any methods he could.

Colin Logan—Roy's son was dead, but Roy was convinced that Amanda carried Colin's child.

Bud Logan—Roy's brother had his own plans for Amanda and her baby.

Al Hewitt—He'd do any dirty job Roy Logan assigned him.

Ed Stanton—Amanda's foreman wanted to keep her from making a bad decision.

Tim Francetti—He supplied Roy Logan with crucial information—for a price.

Will Marbella—One of a group of Las Vegas businessmen, but did they have all their cards on the table?

Dexter Perkins—He'd been Colin's partner in some dirty dealings; what was he up to now?

Hunter Kelley—He was supposed to be Matt's friend, but whose side was he on?

Jerry Tucker—He offered to help Matt, but could he be trusted?

Chapter One

Matthew Forester had done some things he wasn't proud of. Eavesdropping on a client wasn't one of them—until he'd tuned in the bellowing voice coming from Roy Logan's private office.

Matt had arrived at Logan's Wyoming ranch to install a state-of-the-art security system. A month ago, he'd wondered why a Western cattleman needed such stringent protection. After twenty-four hours on the ranch, it was obvious why Logan lived in an armed camp.

If Matt had been asked to pick a few choice words to describe Logan, it would have been "millionaire son of a bitch." But not out loud, since he was always respectful of Randolph Security's clients.

He'd been looking forward to finishing the job and flying home, until Logan had demanded that he stay on to do a detailed analysis of future security needs over the next twenty-five years. Off the top of his head, Matt had named a fee for the additional services that he thought was outrageous, but Logan hadn't blinked. And after conferring with headquarters, Matt had accepted the job, telling himself he could take another two weeks on the ranch.

But he didn't like the arrogant, barrel-chested Logan—didn't trust him further than he could throw a yearling steer. And when he heard the name Amanda Barnwell mentioned in the same breath as Roy's recently deceased son, Colin, he froze in place.

Am image of Amanda rose in his mind, complete with poetic words and phrases startlingly foreign to his usual form of expression. Eyes the fathomless blue of mountain lakes. Hair sparkling with sunshine. A body with generous curves that she invariably hid under loose-fitting shirts. And a voice that felt like warm honey sliding over his skin.

She wasn't his usual type. Yet he'd found her the most appealing woman he'd met in Crowfoot, Wyoming.

Crowfoot was hardly more than a wide place in the road, but he'd needed to escape from the claustrophobic atmosphere of the Logan Ranch by driving into town when he could. And he'd had the good luck to run into Amanda several times. The first had been at the post office, when she'd captured his attention as she'd accepted a couple of boxes of books from the plump little postmistress.

A shadow crossed Mrs. Hastings's face. "That girl deserves better," she said as she watched Amanda climb into her Jeep Cherokee. "She stayed at home to take care of her dad when he got too sick to do for himself. Now he's gone, and she's past thirty—and too prickly with men to catch herself a husband."

"Past thirty? You're putting me on."

"No indeed." The denial had been the prelude to a fifteen-minute earful of fascinating tidbits about Amanda Barnwell—from her upset win in the Fourth of July horse race to her quilting skills, showcased at the school fund-raiser last year. Matt emerged into the afternoon light wishing he could get to know the intriguing Miss Amanda a whole lot better—and wondering which details Mrs. Hastings was leaving out.

The desire to connect with Amanda had strengthened after he'd wolfed down a couple of her chocolate brownies at the church bake sale. He'd toyed with the idea of asking her out to dinner. Then he'd told himself there was no way a ranch-raised girl was going to get involved with a hard-bitten ex-spy who was going back to Baltimore in a couple of weeks, anyway.

Matt's attention was snapped back into focus by Roy's raspy voice. Easing sideways against the wall, he saw the tip of a snakeskin boot and knew Roy was talking to his foreman, Al Hewitt, the weasel-face guy who did the boss's dirty work.

"She's carrying my boy Colin's child," Roy growled. "And I want that baby.'

Carrying Colin's child? Matt's dark eyes narrowed. A woman like Amanda had been mixed up with Roy's low-life son?

The notion was ludicrous, and Matt's muscles tensed as he pictured himself bursting into the office, taking Roy by the shirtfront and shaking some sense into him. But there was just enough rational thought left in his brain to keep him planted where he was.

"You can't just go snatching a baby away from its mother," Hewitt objected.

"Anyone can be bought. If I offer her enough money, she'll be glad to let me take the responsibility off her hands. What's she going to do with a kid anyway—a woman alone?"

The imperious question made Matt's large hands ball into fists at his sides.

"She don't need the money," Hewitt clipped out. "Old man Barnwell left her with plenty of assets when he kicked the bucket."

"That kid is the only thing I have left of Colin. The way I see it, I'm entitled to my progeny."

"Roy, this isn't the Old West. You can't just steal that gal's baby."

"Who's gonna stop me?" the lord of Logan Ranch shot back. "Since her papa died, there's nobody around here I can't buy. I damn well own Crowfoot—the real estate *and* the sheriff's department. They'll look the other way if she disappears. And maybe it won't come to that. Go out to her ranch and make her an offer she can't refuse."

"Are you sure Colin is the father?" Hewitt asked.

"Do you doubt my source of information?" Roy growled. "No."

Matt heard papers shuffling. "This is the preliminary report from the detective I hired. Tim Francetti. He's the best. I only hire the best, remember. That's why I have a security guy out here from Baltimore. And that's why I went to Francetti. When he digs up a little more dirt, I can nail the bastards who killed Colin."

"We can avenge Colin. That's no problem," Hewitt agreed. "But the girl is another matter. I don't think she's gonna play ball with you. She's got more guts than you give her credit for."

"Listen, with her parents gone, she's just another unprotected female. If we can't buy her, we wait for the kid to be born, then arrange for her to have an accident. Anything it takes."

Acid churned in Matt's stomach as he tried to wrap his mind around what he was hearing—even from a man like Logan.

"If you lean on her too hard, she might just skip town."

"Oh, yeah?" Roy's chair creaked, and Matt imagined him easing forward. "I think you'd better arrange to scoop her up and bring her out here where we can keep an eye on her."

There was a moment of silence behind the office door, then Hewitt cleared his throat. "Not a good idea. Not with that Forester fellow around. The way I read him, he might not like to see you putting pressure on the girl."

"Write him an official letter telling him the deal is off. And keep the little mother in one of the line cabins until you can send him packing."

Matt heard a chair scrape back, then the sound of someone dialing the phone.

"Give me some privacy," Logan growled.

Without making a sound, Matt eased away from the office door, knowing that he had to get to Amanda Barnwell before Al Hewitt beat him to the punch.

AMANDA STOOD at the kitchen window. She'd started off washing dishes, but the wet sponge in her hand had been forgotten as she'd gazed across the high plateau toward the Bighorn Mountains, rising like a natural fortress against the navy blue of the evening summer sky. She'd lived all her life in the shadow of those mighty peaks, and they had always been a symbol of strength for her.

She was going to need that strength, she thought as her hand drifted to her middle, covering the child growing within her.

Her child. Hers alone. Wouldn't *that* be grist for the town gossip mill!

Her hand clenched as she tried to wipe away painful memories—of whispers and giggles behind her back. And worse. Now she mostly ignored them, because that was the way she'd learned to survive—by turning away and tightening her heart a little more each year.

Still, in the end, the need for someone to love had won over pride or dignity. She longed for a child of her own, someone to share her life, and so she'd gone about making that dream a reality.

Quickly finishing the dishes and drying her hands, she wandered into the cozy den with its tan corduroy couch and the easy chair where her father had read his subscription copy of the *New York Times* every evening.

The room was full of her handiwork—the woven hangings on the walls, the flowered pillows on the couch, even the rag rug. Settling in here for the evening usually made her feel peaceful, but she was still feeling unsettled as she pulled out her box of books and thumbed through the pregnancy manuals she'd ordered from an Internet company. She'd bought everything she could find, because control and knowledge always increased her comfort level.

That was the practical Amanda. There was another Amanda, as well. One who allowed herself to daydream. Of course, some of her dreams had fallen by the wayside under the onslaught of reality. But not the baby, because she'd decided you didn't need to be married to bear a child. And once she'd made that decision, she hadn't let convention or morality stand in her way.

She rarely thought about the actual circumstance that had resulted in conception. Yet lately she'd found herself indulging in one secret fantasy. There was an intriguing man whom she'd seen in town over the past month. Mrs. Hastings at the post office had told her his name was Matthew Forester, and he was working for Roy Logan.

She'd been put off by that at first, since she knew enough about Logan to despise the rancher who thought he was king of this part of Wyoming. Yet Forester hadn't seemed like Logan's usual sort of employee, which was the consensus among the women of Crowfoot.

The ladies had done considerable gossiping about the man—at the post office, the grocery store, the Methodist Church, the feed store and the Blossom Café. She hadn't participated, of course. But she'd told herself there was no harm in listening.

The new men who came to town were likely to be cowboys hired on at the nearby ranches. Forester had been immediately pegged as something else. It had been a minor triumph to establish that he was a security expert hired from back east.

Even before they'd pegged his occupation, they'd catalogued his physical attributes. They'd remarked on his hard, lean body and estimated his height at just over six feet. They'd admired his broad, well-muscled shoulders and his hard butt. They'd enumerated his chiseled features—from his firm jaw to the dark eyes set under thick brows that might not have been attractive if his bone structure hadn't been up to carrying the effect.

The bolder women had even talked about the generous masculine bulge behind the fly of his well-washed jeans.

Some of the talk had made the heat rise in Amanda's cheeks. But it hadn't stopped her from taking it all in, even though she'd given up thinking she could hold her own in a relationship with a man like that—or any man, for that matter. But in her secret fantasies, she had allowed herself to imagine what making love with Matt might be like. And from there it had only been a short step to imagining him as the father of her child. She knew deep down that the game was ridiculous—and dangerous. She didn't need a man. She didn't want a man in her life. She wanted to be totally independent. So why couldn't she stop thinking about Matt Forester in such an intimate way? Probably because her hormones were so out of kilter, she told herself.

She was yanked from her secret reveries by a knock on the back door, and she felt a stab of guilt, like a kid caught snitching a piece of mom's apple pie.

"Miss Amanda?"

It was Ed Stanton, the foreman who had been with the family since she'd been a little girl. He'd taken her for rides on the front of his saddle when she could barely walk. And he knew as much about the operation of the ranch as her father had.

They'd always worked closely together, with the foreman making suggestions and Dad either accepting or rejecting them.

Then, as her father had lost his head for business matters and she'd taken over, she relied more and more on Ed's ranching experience. But she'd yet to cross the hurdle of letting him or anybody else know about her condition.

"Come in," she called, glancing toward the box of books beside the sofa. "I'll be right there."

Carefully closing the lid, she hurried into the hall. Ed was standing in the kitchen, and she saw that the lines of his weathered face were a little more deeply etched tonight.

"Is there a problem?" she asked.

"Just thought I ought to check in with you." He paused, cleared his throat. "I've been hoping not to bother you with this. But some of the ranchers have been talking about rustlers thinning their herds. So I've had the men checking the south range where we have most of our stock right now. We may have been on the hit list. There are tire tracks where it looks like a big truck pulled off our access road." He scuffed his foot. "Have you had some dealings with a trucking company or something that I don't know about?"

"I would have told you if I had, Ed," she answered quickly.

He nodded. "Well, I just thought I'd see if you knew anything about the truck."

"I appreciate that."

He stayed where he was, shifting his hat in his hands. "You want to come out with me tomorrow and see the spot I'm talkin' about?"

"Of course."

"I've got the men keeping an eye out tonight to make sure that truck doesn't come back. Tomorrow we may want to contact Dwayne."

Dwayne Thomas was the local sheriff.

"So, if you need me for anything tonight, you know where to find me."

"Sure. Thanks," Amanda answered.

He stood on the back porch for a moment as though there were more he wanted to say, then headed for the house about a hundred yards away that her father had built him. The rest of the hands lived in the bunkhouse. But Ed had rated a place of his own when he'd married twenty years ago. Unfortunately, Martha hadn't been content to be married to a man who was never going to be the owner of the property. So she'd left Ed and taken his son with her years ago.

Amanda stood watching until he'd disappeared from view, thankful that he was here to run the spread, but wishing he could be more direct in his recommendations tonight. His hesitation had increased the unsettled feeling she'd been struggling with all evening. Probably she should have asked more questions. But there would be plenty of time for that in the morning. Neither one of them was going anywhere. And maybe she'd even work up the gumption to tell him that there was going to be a baby on the ranch a little over five months from now.

THE SCREEN DOOR SLAMMED behind Matt as he charged through the living room of his guest cottage, hidden behind the grandiose structure of timber and stone Roy Logan called home.

Matt liked the modest three-room home a lot better than the mansion, where the ambience ran to enormous brass chandeliers, Remington table statues and leather upholstery. Probably Roy'd had it done up by some expensive decorator who had charged him double for every piece.

Grateful for the seclusion of the cottage, Matt crossed to the desk and quickly gathered up the notes he'd made on Logan's requested security evaluation. They belonged to the Randolph organization—until Logan paid for the extra work.

Carrying them and his notebook computer into the bedroom, he pulled down the duffel bag and the briefcase he'd stowed in the closet. The papers and the notebook went into the briefcase.

Then he started opening drawers and pulling out his clothing, figuring he had until morning before anybody was going to miss him. As he shoved shirts, pants and underwear into the bag, he thought about phoning Cam Randolph and warning headquarters that he was taking an unscheduled leave of absence. Or contacting the group informally called the Light Street Irregulars, who came to each other's aid in time of trouble.

But he canceled the thoughts even as they formed. He knew better than anyone else that all communications to and from the ranch were monitored. Besides, it was better that his boss and his friends back in Baltimore could honestly say that they'd had no knowledge of Matthew Forester's intentions, if Roy Logan asked.

He was in the bathroom tossing his razor and shaving cream

in his Dopp Kit bag, when he heard footsteps crossing the plank flooring in the front room.

"Forester?"

Coming back into the bedroom, Matt watched the Logan foreman poking through the contents of his duffel.

"What are you doing?" Matt asked, striving to keep the sudden flash of anger out of his voice.

"I could ask you the same question," Hewitt answered, his eyes narrowing as they flicked from the bag to the open dresser drawers.

Matt took several steps closer, deliberately crowding the smaller man as he scrambled for an explanation that would ring true with the likes of Roy Logan's foreman. "Okay, I'll give it to you straight. When I agreed to take this job, I thought it was strictly temporary. I didn't know I'd be without a woman in my bed for three weeks. There's only so much a man can take, so I've got a date with a hot babe in town."

Hewitt gestured toward the duffel bag. "You don't need to take most of your stuff on a date," he pointed out.

"That's true, if all you're expecting is a quickie. But I hit it lucky. The sweet thing asked me to move in with her."

"Yeah, well, Roy wants you available when he needs you. Did you get his permission to leave?"

"I'm not on call twenty-four hours a day." He looked at his watch, doing a good imitation of a man impatient to bed a woman. "I'll run it by him when I come back to work in the morning."

Hewitt's eyes narrowed. "Well, suppose we run it by him now."

"I don't think so." Matt tossed the bag of toiletries into the duffel and reached for the zipper.

"You heard me and Roy talking about the Barnwell girl."

From the corner of his eye, he saw Hewitt's hand go for the gun holstered at his right hip.

With well-honed reflexes, Matt whirled and brought his own

hand down in a quick, painful chop across the other man's wrist.

Before Hewitt's scream of pain faded, Matt pulled the man's gun from his holster and tossed it onto the bed, out of reach.

"Didn't anybody teach you manners?" he growled, assuming the matter was settled as Hewitt stood there rubbing his hand.

Apparently that wasn't the end of it. With more finesse than Matt would have given him credit for, his opponent reached left-handed into his boot and whipped out a knife, almost simultaneously springing forward.

Matt's counteroffensive was instinctive. As the blade flashed toward him, he dodged to the side, then brought his fist up, putting his considerable power and speed into the punch that connected with the other man's jaw. Then he landed another blow to his midsection.

Hewitt went down, landing in an inert heap on the floor.

Eyeing the foreman, Matt pondered his options. Unfortunately slitting his throat with his own knife wasn't one of them. Neither was leaving him here in the guest cottage.

Ripping the cord from the venetian blinds, he knelt and secured the hands and feet of the unconscious man. After testing the bonds, he pulled out one of his T-shirts and used it for a gag. Then he made a quick inspection of the foreman's limp body, finding another knife strapped to the guy's wrist. In the pockets were a large key ring, coins and a wallet with two hundred in cash and a few credit cards. After a moment's hesitation, Matt pocketed the cash, since it might come in handy.

Methodically he began to turn off the lights, except for the reading lamp in the bedroom. Then he walked silently to the front of the cottage and peered out the windows. In the silver radiance of the almost full moon, the ranch looked like an illustration from a Visit Wyoming ad. If Hewitt had come with reinforcements, they weren't in evidence.

When he returned to the bedroom, the foreman was awake and trying unsuccessfully to free his hands.

When he saw Matt, his eyes glittered with malice and his mouth worked, but he couldn't get any coherent words past the gag.

Matt stared at him, shifting his weight from one foot to the other, wishing that Hewitt hadn't jumped right on the assignment of dismissing him. Seeing the man awake and trussed like a Thanksgiving turkey on his bedroom floor brought home the consequences of his actions. Without a moment's hesitation, he had assaulted one of Roy Logan's most trusted employees. Never mind that it was technically self-defense. Hewitt could probably give a plausible explanation for his own actions. When he'd come to give the hired hand from Randolph Security his walking papers, the guy had gone berserk.

And now said hired hand was getting ready to compound his crime. Well, that certainly eliminated the possibility of changing his mind about his course of action, no matter how misguided it had been in the first place. Whether he liked it or not, he was already in deep trouble.

He'd overheard a conversation about Amanda Barnwell and decided to come to her rescue—based on feelings generated by a few brief meetings in town. Well, not just on those feelings. His chest tightened as he remembered a different decision he'd made years ago. That time the consequences had been disastrous.

He squeezed his eyes shut. Maybe his guilt over Bethany was his real motivation, he silently admitted. Or maybe he could plead insanity.

When he caught the foreman watching him, he forced his features to relax. "So where would be a good place to dump you?" he asked conversationally as he unstrapped the man's holster and restrapped it around his own waist. He'd thought it would be bad manners to arrive armed at the Logan Ranch. Now he wished he had his own Glock instead of Hewitt's more traditional Western piece.

After retrieving the gun from the bed, he tested it in his hand and holstered it. With a grunt, he lifted Hewitt onto his shoulder, fireman style, and strode toward the back door.

On the small patio, he waited for a few moments to make sure he wasn't being observed, then he struck out for one of the miscellaneous outbuildings. From his security inventory, he knew that many were storage sheds—some more likely to be used than others. He headed for one full of light gardening equipment that had belonged to Mrs. Logan. From what he'd gathered, tending flower gardens had been one of her hobbies, and nobody had kept them up since she'd passed away more than fifteen years earlier. Apparently she'd been a gentle soul who'd lacked the backbone to stand up to her husband.

Would Colin have turned out differently if his mother had lived? Matt wondered as he laid Hewitt not so gently on the floor, where he started to thrash around like a fish on a boat deck, making guttural sounds from behind the gag.

Matt dragged him to the middle of the room, where several two-by-fours helped support the roof. Using some of the excess rope, he secured the prisoner to the upright.

Puffing hard, the foreman tried to yank free. "Take it easy. You don't want to block off your air flow," Matt advised.

The bound man quieted, but his eyes gleamed with hatred.

"They'll likely find you in the morning," he said, hoping he was right, because he needed a few hours' head start. The distances around here were greater than back east, and it was at least a two-hour drive to Amanda's ranch, he knew from his survey of the surrounding area. Too bad he couldn't just appropriate Logan's helicopter, but that would be a bit conspicuous.

After securing the shed door, he returned to the guest cottage for his luggage, then snorted as he pictured a description of himself on a wanted poster: "Armed and dangerous with gun and briefcase."

Outside in the darkness once more, he surveyed the area again, then headed for the parking area.

He'd been met at the airport in Gillette by Hewitt, who was driving one of the ranch's pickups. There were several, along with a couple of SUVs and Jeeps. The keys were tagged and kept on a board inside a shed door. He took the ones to a green pickup, noted the gas level and started the engine. The noise sounded like a burst of gunfire in the stillness. But nobody challenged him as he backed up and headed for the ranch entrance road.

Twisting the radio dial, he found a classic country station and tuned into "Ride Me on Down," one of his favorite Bobby Bare songs, as he settled into the rhythm of driving, resisting the urge to go more than ten miles above the speed limit. Out here, the cops cut you some slack, but there were limits to official tolerance.

Two hours later he breathed a little sigh as he saw the entrance to the Double B Ranch. Barnwell and Barnwell—had that been the original name?

On the long drive he'd had plenty more time to seriously question his judgment. He'd even toyed with the idea of calling Amanda on the portable and warning her that he was on the way. But what he had to say was best said in person— partly, he admitted, because he wanted to see her reaction when he mentioned Colin Logan.

Pressing the button that illuminated his watch dial, he saw that it was after midnight. A bad time for a neighborly visit. But there was no question of waiting until morning.

He'd never been to the Barnwell place, and he wished he were seeing it by daylight so he could orient himself better. The scale of the house and the style were far more modest than Roy Logan's tasteless mansion, and the surrounding grounds appeared to be neat and orderly, but he couldn't tell much about the state of the ranch buildings in the dark.

Pulling to the edge of the driveway, he cut the engine and climbed from the truck, stretching his long legs in the cool night air.

He was heading for the front porch when he heard the sound of gravel crunching behind him. Before he could turn, something hard came down on the back of his head, and the world went pitch-black.

Chapter Two

Another sound—this time of voices—brought Matt back to groggy consciousness. Voices. He had no idea where he was or why his body felt like boiled spaghetti. But his hearing was functioning, and he glommed onto Amanda's warm honey tones. He wanted to drift with that sweet sound, to let the warm syrup drip over his skin. But another speaker kept getting in the way.

A guy. Who sounded a lot less sexy.

"I don't trust him," the man was saying, his voice raspy as if he had a sore throat or he'd been smoking a pack a day for the past forty years. "What the hell is he doing here— tonight of all nights?" he asked querulously.

"What's so special about tonight?" Amanda asked.

"I mean, with the rustlers and all."

"Rustlers don't come knocking at the door. I appreciate your protective instincts, Ed. But you didn't have to hit him over the head."

Hit him over the head? Was that why he felt like a concert group were performing the "Anvil Chorus" inside his skull? Cautiously Matt cracked his eyes. In the next second he wished fervently that he hadn't made the effort. Instead of seeing one image, he was blessed with two—and twice the pain.

Repressing a groan, he cautiously moved his hand, feeling

something soft under his touch. A bed or a sofa, maybe. At least he wasn't sprawled outside in the gravel.

He lay there for several moments, hearing the voices but unable to tune them in for the moment. Or maybe he drifted from consciousness again.

The word *concussion* wafted through his mind.

The next time he tried to get a look at his surroundings, he had the good sense to open only one eyelid.

Squinting, he saw Amanda and the other speaker, someone she'd called Ed, a short, compact man with a grizzled face and gray hair. The guy who'd hit him, judging from the conversation.

He should stay focused on the guy; instead he switched his attention to Amanda. She was much easier on the eye—in profile, barefoot with her golden hair tamed in a single braid down the back of her neck. Apparently she'd been in bed, because she was dressed in a baby-blue robe. It was made of some silk fabric completely at odds with the jeans and men's shirts she wore in town. The material clung to every feminine curve of her body, showing off the sexy fullness of her breasts and revealed the just budding swell of her abdomen. As he studied her burgeoning shape, Matt silently acknowledged the truth of Roy's information. She was pregnant.

His attention snapped back to the conversation when he heard his name mentioned.

"There's been talk in town about Forester," the man called Ed was saying.

"Right. All the women are plotting how to get him into bed."

"Maybe so. But the guys don't like him."

"I never heard that."

"Well, explain why he was sneaking up on the house," Ed demanded.

"It doesn't look to me like he was sneaking. He drove right into the yard and parked in full view," Amanda pointed out.

"For a midnight social call!"

"Maybe he had a good reason. When he comes to, we can ask him."

"I'm going to call Dwayne."

Dwayne. The name was familiar. Matt's fogged brain struggled to place it.

"You don't need to call the sheriff. You need to call a doctor," Amanda said, worry and exasperation mingling in her tone.

The cops. Great. Dwayne was the cops. And he was in Roy's pocket. Cursing silently, Matt moved his hand again, reaching for the holster he'd strapped on. It was still there, but the gun was missing.

He heard Ed's footsteps receding and tried to push himself up. But a stab of pain in his head sent him collapsing back onto the sofa.

Instantly Amanda knelt by the side of the sofa.

"Mr. Forester?"

Her hand soothed across his forehead, then his cheek, and he knew what it was like to feel an angel's touch.

"Can you hear me?"

If he just lay here without responding, would she keep touching him? It was tempting to test the theory. Instead he forced his eyes open, and found himself staring at two angels. Up close he could see the twin visions were wearing delicate white nightgowns showing through the V at the top of their celestial-blue robes.

"Mr. Forester?"

Much too formal, under the circumstances. "Call me Matt."

"Matt, I'm sorry. I don't know what got into Ed. I know your head must hurt, but we're getting you help."

"Mm-hmm." He closed his eyes, then realized he was passing up an opportunity to study her robe and gown up close. Cracking one eyelid, he drank his fill of the outfit. She probably thought it was demure. He thought it was sexy. "You sure dress pretty for bed. Much nicer than those work shirts you wear to town," he heard himself say in a thick voice as he raised a shaky hand and touched one of the delicate white bows that ran down the front of the gown. The front placket was right under the bow, and he slipped his finger underneath, feeling a shiver travel over his body as he touched her skin. It was warm and soft.

He saw a similar shiver ripple through her, saw rosy color creep into her face.

Somewhere in his logy mind he knew he was taking unacceptable liberties. But the conk on the head must have scrambled his brain, because he wasn't capable of stopping himself. Not when his vivid imagination had conjured up just such a scene as this.

His greedy finger moved, conquering more territory. His head was still throbbing—along with another part of his anatomy. In the back of his mind he wondered how a guy who couldn't see straight could still get aroused, but he wasn't complaining.

"Don't." Her beautiful blue eyes darkened, and she swayed toward him before catching herself. Reaching for her nightgown, she covered his hand and tried to tug it away. But he'd already cunningly slipped his thumb through the bow loop because holding his arm up was almost too much effort. Angling his hand down, he caressed the top of her breast. He wanted to slip his whole hand inside her gown, but that would mean undoing one of the bows, and he didn't think he could manage that.

"Don't," she said again, her honey voice thickening.

Even in his present befuddled condition, he knew he was pushing his luck. But the censor that usually governed his impulses had gone on vacation. "God, I loved your voice the first time I heard it," he said. "I don't know which I like more, the way you sound or the way you feel."

She drew in a quick, sharp little breath. When she tried to pull his hand away, the bow opened, revealing a tempting triangle of skin just below the hollow of her neck.

"Beautiful," he murmured, imagining what that warm skin

would feel like against his lips, his tongue. What her nipples would taste like. They had beaded beneath the thin fabric, and he could see them hard and tight, begging for his attention.

For several heartbeats she seemed frozen in place. Then disappointment coursed through him when she succeeded in untangling his hand and bringing it back to the couch.

"You have to stop this."

The rational part of his brain knew that she was right. Closing his eyes, he tried to pull himself together and focus on the reason he'd come here.

When he reached toward his head, she made a small sound. "I'm sorry about what happened. Ed hit you. With his gun butt."

"Nice way to greet company." He felt his lips quirk. The small movement hurt.

Before she could apologize again, he asked, "When?"

"Ten minutes ago."

That was good. At least he hadn't been out too long.

"Ed is very protective," she explained.

"So am I," he whispered.

"Why did you come here?"

"To save you from Roy Logan."

"What? You must be confused. I don't have any problems with Mr. Logan now."

"He wants the baby."

The effect of his words was instantaneous. He saw her face go stark white, her eyes flick downward toward her midsection, then back to him. "The baby?" she asked, her voice breaking.

"Did you have an affair with Colin?" he asked around the tight knot clogging his throat.

He hadn't thought it was possible for her complexion to go any paler, but he was wrong.

Then her eyes flashed, and her voice turned steely. "Colin. You can't be serious. Why would I get hooked up with a—a no good SOB like him?"

The knot loosened enough for him to breathe, even when he couldn't be sure she was telling the truth.

"We have to get out of here." He tried to push himself up, and pain lanced through his head. He raised his hand, pressing it against his throbbing temple as he blinked to clear his vision. "God. I can't even see straight."

"You can't talk straight, either," she said, her eyes several degrees colder than they had been a few moments ago. "Maybe you'd better explain the real reason you came here."

"I did."

The declaration failed to change the look in her eyes. He flopped back against the pillow, gathering his strength, because if he couldn't make her believe him, they were both in big trouble.

"Ed went to call the sheriff. He'll be here soon. Before I left the ranch, I heard Logan tell his good friend Hewitt that he's got the cops in his pocket. You can't stay here. They'll turn you over to Logan. That's what he wants."

And they've got good reason to arrest me, he silently added. But there was no point in damaging his credibility any further. Or in telling her that once they took him into custody, he'd probably be shot during an "escape attempt."

Instead he asked, "Have you told anybody about the pregnancy?"

She didn't speak, but he read the answer in her eyes.

"If you didn't confide in anybody...then how do I know?" he asked, fighting the whirring noise in his head.

She looked down at the soft fabric clinging to her body. "Dressed like this...maybe you can tell."

"Right. I figured it out on the spot—with a head injury. Then I concocted the story about Logan. Why the hell would I go to all that trouble?"

She was looking at him helplessly. "To cover a robbery attempt?"

He made a snorting sound. "Is that what you really think?"

The whirring noise was getting louder, and she shifted her gaze upward.

"You hear it, too?" He focused on the sound and realized it came from rotating blades. "That's a helicopter."

As Ed charged back through the doorway and crossed the room, Matt lay back against the cushions, feigning unconsciousness, but with slitted eyes as he watched the foreman approach.

The gray-haired man gave him a brief inspection, then turned to face Amanda. "They're here."

"When did the sheriff's department get a helicopter?" she asked.

"What does that matter?" Ed came around to face her, his back to the man he thought was unconscious, and Matt knew this was going to be his best—probably his only—chance. Before he could change his mind, he reached for Ed's gun, pulling it from the holster with more ease than he would have believed possible.

Ed whirled, and Matt made his voice hard. "Raise your hands and back up before I put a bullet in your guts."

To his surprise, the guy complied, with Amanda watching in shocked disbelief.

Teeth gritted, Matt forced himself off the sofa, forced himself to stand on braced legs. The world tipped and swayed, and he was sure he was going to pass out from the pain stabbing through his head. Somehow he managed to stay vertical.

The helicopter drone was like a steam engine pounding in his skull. His gaze switched from Ed to Amanda and back again. "Both of you, move toward the door," he growled. It made him physically sick to threaten the woman he'd come to rescue. But he couldn't see any other choice. Not with the cops about to land in her front yard.

"Move it!" he ordered.

Ed turned, and Matt lunged forward, bringing the gun down on the back of his head. The older man collapsed in a heap on the floor. Trembling from the sudden exertion, Matt braced his shoulders against the wall.

Amanda sucked in a sharp breath. "You hit him!"

"Poetic justice." He knelt, fighting a sudden wave of dizziness as he riffled the other man's pockets and pulled out a wallet and a key ring, both of which he slipped into his own pocket. "Come on. We have to get out of here," he growled, staggering to his feet again.

She folded her arms across her chest. "I'm not going anywhere with you."

"You are, if you don't want anything to happen to the baby."

"You'd hurt the baby?" Horror etched her features as her hands slid protectively downward to cover her abdomen.

"Not me! The other guys. Come on. We're wasting time." He clenched his teeth, praying he could stay on his feet for another few minutes.

Amanda hesitated. "Why should I believe you?"

He closed his eyes, then opened them and fixed her with a look he hoped conveyed his sincerity. "'Cause you know Dwayne doesn't have a helicopter."

"I don't know that for sure."

"Are you going to take a chance that I'm wrong?"

"Or crazy!" she retorted.

"We can argue that later. Come on!"

"Where are we going?"

"Your Jeep."

Maybe if he hadn't been holding the gun, she would have refused. He knew she wasn't entirely convinced. Still, she led him toward the front of the house. Stooping by the door, she grabbed a pair of tennis shoes and a purse from a shelf but didn't take the time to put the shoes on.

Outside, Matt could just see the copter blades disappearing behind the roofline of the house. Perfect timing. He and Amanda couldn't be seen from above, and the house blocked the Jeep from view.

The cool night air helped clear his head a little. By concentrating on putting one foot in front of the other, he made it to the Cherokee. "You have to drive," he muttered when she started to climb into the passenger seat.

"You're kidnapping me, and I have to drive the getaway car?"

"You'd rather have a man with double vision do it?" he inquired.

"No."

When he gestured with the gun, she climbed behind the wheel. Collapsing into the passenger seat, he leaned back, his breath coming in short pants. When he could talk again, he said, "Head for the pines. Any road into the trees. Now! Before they figure out what's happening."

He started to slump back against the seat, then jerked upright again when her hand went to the lights. "No," he barked, pulling her fingers away.

"You *are* crazy."

"Yeah. And stay off the brakes, if you can."

"Oh, sure." She started the engine, heading for the trees a hundred yards from the house. To his relief, a dirt track appeared. She slipped into the pine forest, driving slowly, feeling her way. Twisting around, he saw men converging on the house, unaware that their quarry had slipped away under cover of darkness.

How much head start did they have? Ten minutes? Fifteen? He hoped to hell nobody figured out they'd done something as insane as driving into the forest.

Amanda slowed to negotiate a turn, rounding a large rock outcropping that blocked his line of sight to the house. And blocked the bad guys' view of the escape vehicle. At least that was something.

"I need the lights," Amanda said, leaning forward as she peered through the windshield into the blackness that was relieved only by shafts of light from the full moon filtering through the tree branches.

"We can't risk letting them know where we are. Do the best you can."

"Tell me again why I should trust you," she said, her voice tight as she rounded another bend.

"What do I have to gain from this besides helping you?" he asked, wincing as the right front tire bounced over a rock, the subsequent shock wave reverberating inside his skull like a Chinese gong.

"I don't know. But you threatened me with a gun," she countered, her knuckles clenched on the wheel. "That doesn't exactly inspire trust."

"I had to—to get you out of the house before Logan's hired help scooped you up!" He'd made the mistake of saying the words with some force, and the sound stabbed into his brain tissue.

"You don't know that was Logan. Maybe it was the sheriff's department, like Ed told me."

"I know Logan has a helicopter. Why does a rancher need a chopper?"

"To survey his herd. To look for rustlers."

She turned her head toward him as if she expected some response. He didn't have the energy.

At least she kept on driving. He counted that as a good sign. With great effort, he turned his head toward her. The moonlight through the trees gave her a fairy-tale quality. Beauty in a blue bathrobe, escorting the Beast through the woods. Too bad he still didn't know whether she believed him. Probably she was just waiting for the right opportunity to dump him.

"Do us both a favor. Don't drive me straight to the sheriff's office," he said, his voice husky.

She didn't answer, only pressed her lips together and glanced at the gun in his hand and then at his perspiration-soaked face.

He knew she was sizing up the situation, waiting for the inevitable moment when he keeled over. Which meant he had only one choice. With a sigh, he snapped the safety on the weapon, turned the butt toward her and pressed it forward. "Here. Shoot me. Then all your troubles will be over."

"I can't believe this is happening," she muttered, and he hoped he was hearing exasperation rather than fear in her voice.

Removing one hand from the wheel, she accepted the gun and tucked it into the side pocket of her door. When she turned her attention back to the dark road, he studied her again from under half-lowered lashes. He could look at her all night, even in the semi-darkness. Maybe especially in that light. Bedroom light.

When he made a low sound in his throat, her eyes snapped toward him.

"Your head hurts."

He could feel himself sagging in the seat. If the jackhammer inside his skull was any quieter, he couldn't detect the difference. "I should have asked you to grab a bottle of aspirin before we left."

"In my purse."

He picked up the black leather bag from the console between the seats and opened the snap. With fingers that felt thick and clumsy, he pawed through a bewildering assortment of paraphernalia. A wallet, wadded pieces of tissue, a small penknife, a notebook, several small zipper bags, a half roll of mints, pens, a small plastic flower, a collection of loose change, a tampon that she wouldn't be needing any time soon.

"The pills are in the bag with the gold stripes."

Squinting, he retrieved that bag and fished among her lipstick, compact and other cosmetics he couldn't name until he located a small plastic bottle. Somehow he got the cap off and shook two aspirin tablets into his hand.

Apparently she had a sudden change of heart as she stared at the pills nestled in his palm. "I don't know if you should be taking that," she said.

"Too late." He slammed two pills into his mouth and somehow managed to swallow them with the saliva he had generated in his mouth while he looked for the medication.

"You should be in a hospital. You could have internal bleeding."

"If I die, I'll sue your friend Ed."

"Very funny."

"If you take me to the hospital, Logan will bag you. And Dwayne will make hash out of me."

"The last part's true. I'm still wondering about Logan."

"Then why don't you turn around and go back?" he asked as the wheels bounced over another rock.

She sighed. "The road's too narrow. And Logan has made a lot of trouble for folks around here, including my father. Maybe that's what this is all about. Getting even with the Barnwells."

"For what?"

"Boundary disputes. Unfortunately some of our land adjoins his."

He let her cling to that theory as he slumped down and closed his eyes, thinking it would just be for a moment.

AMANDA FLICKED HER GAZE from the darkened road. The man beside her was asleep. Unconscious. She could open the door and push him into the woods. Or she could do what he'd told her not to—drive straight to the law as soon as they reached the highway.

That would be the smart course of action. Yet something about Matt Forester kept her driving through the inky blackness.

Her gaze flicked to the gun in the door pocket. Maybe that was the deciding factor. Though the man was seriously injured, he'd hustled her out of the house at gunpoint, then turned over his weapon. He'd trusted her with his life. She could do him the same favor.

Unfortunately it wasn't that simple, because she wasn't just making decisions for herself. There was her child to consider, too. Was she putting the baby in jeopardy by staying with Matt Forester? Or was just the opposite true? Perhaps the man slumped unconscious in the seat beside her was the only hope she had of getting herself and the child in her womb to safety.

A whirring, chopping sound from above brought an abrupt halt to her thoughts. The helicopter was airborne again.

She held her breath, waiting for it to zip away toward town—or the Logan ranch. But it sounded as if it was in no hurry to leave the area. Then, through the windshield, she saw lights skimming the tops of the trees.

Without making a conscious decision, she eased her foot off the accelerator and brought the car to a gliding stop as close as she could get to the trunk of a tall pine.

Cutting the engine, she huddled in her seat and watched the light sweep across the treetops—coming closer and closer to the car as the sound of the blades increased, vibrating through every nerve ending of her body.

Her heart thumping wildly inside her chest, she imagined the beam of light stabbing into the hood of the Cherokee. Was there any place nearby that a helicopter could land? she wondered, picturing a squad of men jumping out to surround the car.

The lights swept closer, crisscrossing the forest, inching toward her hiding place under the pines, and her fingers closed around the butt of the gun as she waited.

Chapter Three

Amanda's whole body went rigid as the helicopter seemed to hover almost directly over the car.

When she thought she might crack from the tension, it moved off to the left, the sound fading away as the illumination receded.

She wanted desperately to believe the midnight searchers hadn't spotted the car. But there was another possibility she had to consider. What if they were waiting for her where the road met the highway?

She glanced at the man beside her. Despite the noise and the light, he hadn't moved a muscle, and she felt a ripple of fear slither down her spine.

"Matt?"

When he didn't respond, the fear exploded into her chest cavity. Closing her fingers around his arm, she gave him a little shake.

"Matt!"

His eyes snapped open, and his hand shot to the holster strapped around his waist. When he found the gun missing, he made a low, distressed sound.

"Matt, it's all right," she said, hoping she was right—on several counts.

His head swung toward the window, then back to her. "Where are we?"

"In the woods. The helicopter came right over us, searching. I pulled under a tree. I don't think they spotted us."

"You did good," he answered, his voice slurred. Before she could continue the conversation, he had slipped back into sleep.

She sighed, afraid to leave him in that state yet afraid to remain where she was. When Logan's men didn't find them, they'd come back to the forested area near the ranch house, since that was the most logical hiding place.

Matt made a strangled sound in his sleep as his face contorted.

"What?" she asked, laying her hand on his arm again.

"Bethany?" he muttered. "Is it too late?"

She stared at him, at a loss to answer the question. "It's Amanda," she told him, her name coming out on a quavery exhalation.

"Forgive me. I should have…" The sentence trailed off into something else that she couldn't catch.

When he didn't speak again, she felt her chest tighten. "Who is Bethany?" she asked, hearing the urgency in her own voice.

He didn't answer, and she sat there, staring at him, trying to read the expression on his face. Finally she gave up and started the engine, then eased out from under the tree and onto the dirt track again.

Leaning toward the windshield, she kept her eyes on the dark shapes of the pine trees her father had brought to the ranch as seedlings forty years before. But she couldn't keep her mind from circling back to the brief but revealing conversation she'd just had with Matt.

When she'd spun out fantasies about him, she'd assumed he was unattached. Now she realized just how much she didn't know about him. Was Bethany his wife? Or maybe his ex?

She glanced at his left hand, relieved to see that he wasn't wearing a wedding ring, although that proved nothing. Lots of men didn't wear rings. Then she brought herself up short.

She had no claim on Matt Forester. And more important, she'd decided long ago that she was better off on her own.

Still, she couldn't prevent the memory of his fingers slipping beneath the placket of her gown from stealing back into her head. His hand had been provocative, yet oh so gentle. He'd said she was beautiful. And she'd responded to his touch and his words like the loose woman he probably thought she was.

As she remembered those few intimate moments, she felt the thrum of her quickening pulse. Had he seen the way his hand on her breast had made her nipples harden? She hoped he'd missed that embarrassing detail.

Silently cursing her own foolish longings, she clenched her hands on the wheel and concentrated on negotiating the dangerous road as she considered her options. Every instinct urged her to get away from Matt Forester while she still could. Before she did something stupid, something she knew she would regret. Yet logic told her that survival might depend on sticking with him—at least until he gave her more information about Roy Logan. And Colin. She felt a shiver travel over her skin.

During the kidnapping, she'd deliberately kept herself from thinking about the murdered heir to the Logan Ranch. Now an image of his handsome, confident face flashed into her mind, and she squeezed her eyes shut to make it go away. The effort was wasted. Once she'd opened that door, she couldn't slam it shut.

She'd known Colin Logan since grade school; she'd been humiliated by him countless times. She'd always thought he was insufferable. The fifth-grade spelling bee, when he and she were the last remaining players, came to mind. He'd laughed when she'd messed up the spelling of *laboratory*. Everybody else had laughed, too.

She made a low sound, trying unsuccessfully to blot out the memory, like so many others from her supposedly carefree school days. Then sweet old Miss Benton had given *him* an easy one—*recommendation.* And he'd walked away with the grand prize—a gold bee. Which he'd waved in her face—and then crushed under his foot when they'd gone out onto the playground at recess.

That was Colin. As he'd gotten older, he'd grown even more malicious and arrogant. Even so, she'd been sorry when she heard he'd been murdered. But she hadn't really been surprised because it was easy to imagine him getting the wrong person riled. And he'd been far from home—in Denver—without the power of his father to protect him.

She shuddered as Matt's frightening words came back to her. He'd said Roy thought Colin was the father of her child—and he wanted the baby. Pressing her hand against her mouth, she struggled to hold back a wave of hysteria. Lord, what a mess she'd gotten herself into. And she'd thought she was being so clever!

THE RINGING OF THE PHONE jerked Tim Francetti from sleep. Opening one eye, he squinted at the clock. One in the morning. With a curse, he fumbled the receiver out of the cradle.

"Francetti here."

"The Barnwell girl's gotten away," a peremptory voice growled.

What the hell do you want me to do about it? The angry question formed in Tim's mind. *You didn't hire me to baby-sit her.* But he knew better than to get smart with Roy Logan.

Taking a moment to get his thoughts straight, he cleared his throat and switched on the light, blinking in the sudden brightness. "Give me the details," he said, pushing his straight blond hair out of his eyes before reaching for the notepad on the nightstand.

"The security guy I had working for me got wind of the situation. He showed up at her ranch a couple of hours after I talked to Hewitt. Then he bashed her foreman over the head and took off with her."

"What's in it for him?"

Logan made an angry sound in his throat. "Maybe he wants to sell her back to me. I don't know. But I want his dossier on my desk by tomorrow evening."

"Didn't you have him checked out before he came to the ranch?"

"The security company vouched for him, dammit! Now I want you to find out what the hell they weren't telling me."

"Twenty-four hours may not be enough time," Tim objected.

"Make sure it is."

Tim swallowed a shudder. "What's his name and social security number?"

Logan gave him the information.

"I'll get you what I can on him as fast as possible. Did the Barnwell woman go willingly?"

"How the hell should I know?"

"How did you find out Forester was hooking up with her?"

"I had some stuff to discuss with Hewitt. When I couldn't locate him, I sent some guys out looking. We found him in a storage shed, and as soon as he told us about Forester, we headed over to the Barnwell ranch in a chopper. The foreman was out cold, and Forester and the girl were gone."

"You're in ranch country. You have a helicopter. Why couldn't you spot them?"

It was the wrong question.

"How in thunder should I know?" Logan asked, the retort exploding out of him like a discharge from a double-barreled shotgun. In the next moment the phone slammed down on the other end of the line. With a grimace Tim replaced the receiver.

When Roy Logan had hired him to investigate the circumstances of his son Colin's death, he'd been bowled over by the fee. He'd soon found out that Logan demanded value for his money. And he'd also discovered that Colin had the morality of a barracuda. He was into a network of dirty deals and moneymaking schemes, and he'd stepped on enough tender toes to get himself killed several times over.

Now Tim was stuck with the task of sorting through the mess, trying to determine just who had rid the world of a real bastard.

He sighed again. He was damn good at digging up dirt on people, digging up stuff they thought was dead and buried. That was his bread and butter. But business had been slow for a couple of months, and he'd counted it a real piece of luck when Logan had come to him with a fat retainer.

That was before he'd found out that Roy Logan was going to make his life hell until he got results. So he'd scraped around for something that would knock Roy's socks off—and hit upon a choice piece of information about Amanda Barnwell.

Tim slammed his fist against his palm. Damn Forester. And damn Miss Amanda for flying the coop. If this didn't resolve the way Roy wanted, heads were going to roll. And Tim suspected that his would be one of them.

THE DIRT ROAD STRETCHED endlessly ahead of Amanda. As she drove, her mind kept turning in circles—circles that imitated the whir of the blades she'd heard above her. She kept expecting them to come back. But the helicopter did not return. Finally in the distance she could make out a break in the trees and knew she was coming to the highway. Peering over the wheel, she looked up and down the ribbon of blacktop. At this time of night, it was deserted.

Crowfoot lay in one direction. Cody in the other. And she figured the more populated area was the safer choice. There was a hospital in Cody, and, if need be, she could take Matt there. She could even go to the law, she supposed, although she silently admitted she'd given up that option for the moment. Until she got some more details from Matt, she was stuck with this harebrained scenario of his.

She was pulling out of the shadows when the wail of sirens

in the distance made her step on the brakes, then throw the vehicle into reverse. As she eased back into the cover of the trees, two police cars barreled around the bend in the road, lights flashing.

To her profound relief, neither of them spotted her. Maybe they were speeding to apprehend some of those rustlers Ed had told her about earlier in the evening. But she didn't think so. More than likely, they were looking for her and Matt.

She glanced over her shoulder but immediately discarded the idea of retracing her path. Returning to Double B land was only going to get her trapped. Yet it seemed the highway was a risk, too.

"Matt?" she tried, her fingers tightening around his upper arm. "Matt." She wanted to shake him, but knew that wouldn't do his head any good.

He roused himself enough to murmur, "Hmm?"

"There are patrol cars out on the highway. What should I do?"

He cracked an eyelid. "Stay away from them," he answered.

"I'm trying."

The conversation ended as abruptly as it had started, when he turned his head away. After giving him an exasperated look, she glanced up and down the road. The law could come back at any time. But in the end, there was only one choice. With a sigh she switched on her lights, then turned in the direction of Cody.

Four or five minutes later, headlights knifed toward her through the darkness. Hands fused to the wheel, she kept up a steady pace, praying that it was just a rancher on his way home from a late evening in town. When the car passed, she let out the breath she'd been holding.

The trees had given way to grazing land, and she divided her attention between the blacktop ahead and the far side of the highway.

About twenty miles down the road, she came to a large

outcropping of rock. Slowing, she crossed the center line and
drove onto another dirt road that wound into the hills.

After a moments' hesitation, she switched off the lights
again, navigating only by the moonlight. The car was completely exposed now. And if the helicopter came back, they
were sunk. But she couldn't see any better option at the moment. When she reached an area of low, sparse trees, she
breathed in a little sigh, glad she had some cover.

The road wound upward at an increasingly steep angle, and
the tires spun on loose gravel. When the engine began to labor,
she switched to a lower gear as she peered ahead into the
darkness.

Rounding another curve, she finally saw what she was looking for—a low, rough cabin. After pulling the car as close as
she could to the entrance, she retrieved her tennis shoes from
the back seat and pulled them on before lowering herself to
the hard-packed ground.

Outside it was silent except for a light wind rustling the
trees and the sound of a mountain stream bubbling over rocks.

Risking a brief inspection with a flashlight, she ascertained
that the door was secured with a padlock, but the jamb was
badly weathered. Using a large rock, she was able to break
off the hasp and open the door. Again she risked the light,
locating a bunk bed built into the wall, a table and chairs,
storage cabinets and a small kitchen area.

When she approached the bottom bunk, she found the mattresses gave off the rank odors of unwashed bodies. Apparently the hands who'd slept here last hadn't been much on
personal hygiene. The blankets folded at the end were simi-
larly ripe.

With a grimace she returned to the Jeep Cherokee, opened
the storage compartment where she kept her emergency kit
and got out several blankets. She was looking for a good spot
to lay them on the floor when she noticed something strange
about the rough wood. The direct beam of the flashlight re-

vealed where the boards looked sawed through, forming a rectangle about four feet by five feet.

Curious, she ran her hand along the crack and felt a slight draft. After rummaging in the cabinets, she found a crowbar, which she stuck into the crack. Using it as a lever, she pushed downward, and the rectangle came up several inches from the rest of the floor. Flipping it over, she peered down a ladder into a dug-out space below the floor. Was it just a cellar?

After a glance toward the door, she climbed onto the top rung and descended. There was nothing stored below the cabin. But she was surprised to find what she did discover— a tunnel, stretching away into the darkness.

An escape hatch. How interesting!

Amanda didn't know where the underground passage led, and she didn't have time to find out, but she filed the intriguing fact away before returning to the cabin floor.

She spread the blankets to the right of the trapdoor, then returned to the front seat of the Jeep and slipped behind the wheel.

Matt was leaning back in the passenger seat, breathing heavily. Reaching out, she stroked her hand against his cheek, relieved that his temperature appeared to be normal. When she let her fingers trail across the stubble of his beard, his eyes snapped open and his hand shot out, his fingers closing around her wrist in an iron grip.

Fear leaped in her throat as she tried to wrench away, but he held her fast. "Matt."

He seemed unaware that she was speaking as he pulled her toward him so that she half-sprawled against his body, her right breast pressed against his chest and her robe sliding halfway up her legs.

"Matt, don't. You're hurting me," she gasped, her voice catching as she wiggled against him, trying to wrench away. She might as well have been playing tug-of-war with a buffalo.

She got her free hand onto his shoulder and pushed, but he

only closed his fingers around her leg, his hand digging painfully into her flesh. "Matt, stop!"

Her voice rose in panic, and her hand formed into a fist as she started to pound against his rock-hard shoulder.

"Amanda?" His grip loosened on her leg and her wrist, his eyes flicking from her face to the thigh she'd exposed in their struggle.

Automatically she snatched at her robe, pulling it down to cover her legs before yanking at the V where the top had loosened.

All the while he watched her from under hooded eyes, and she heard his breath freeze in his lungs before he gulped in air. "Amanda. God, I'm sorry."

She was prepared to wrench away, but the anguish in his voice stopped her. Since he'd pulled that gun on her, she'd been holding herself together with putty and baling wire. Suddenly the events of the past few hours were too much. Unable to make her muscles work, she felt herself go slack against him. Then, to her utter mortification, she felt tears welling in her eyes.

"Amanda. Sweetheart." His hold tightened on her, but this time he was gentle, oh so gentle. "I'm sorry," he repeated, his head turning so that his lips could skim her cheek, the edge of her hair, as his hands soothed over her back and shoulders. "Did I hurt you?"

She tried to tell him he hadn't done any irreparable damage, but the words choked off in a sob. He rocked her in his arms, crooning low, tender words as his lips played along the side of her face, soothing her, offering comfort. Gradually she got control of her runaway emotions.

Raising her head, she swiped her hand across her eyes. When she looked up again, she saw that her face was a few inches from his.

She forgot to breathe when she realized he was staring at her lips, his expression hungry, his eyes dreamy. She could have jerked away. But the look on his face made her stay where she was, waiting to see what would happen next.

With a sound deep in his throat, he closed the distance between them, his mouth warm and possessive against hers.

"Oh." Her little exclamation was lost in the mingling of their breaths as he moved his lips softly against hers. When she didn't pull away, the pressure became more urgent.

His arm slid around her waist, holding her in place as his hand splayed against her ribs, his fingertips reaching the underside of her breast and sending darts of heat prickling across her skin. Somewhere in the back of her mind, she was astonished at what was happening, astonished that she was letting it happen.

Without conscious thought she leaned into the kiss, and for long moments, nothing existed in the universe besides the delicious teasing of his lips against hers and the feel of his big hands on her body.

It was a shock when he broke the contact, her name sighing out of him as his head fell back against the seat. He sat there, his breath coming in little gasps, his eyes closed.

"You shouldn't have done that," she accused, wondering if she were speaking to him or to herself.

"I know," he answered, his voice thick and raspy.

"You think I'm in the habit of letting strange men kiss me," she heard herself blurting.

"No."

"Well, you think I had an affair with Colin Logan. And you think it's okay to grab me like...some streetwalker or something."

"Streetwalkers don't kiss," he muttered.

"How do you know?"

He grimaced. "I read *From Here to Eternity* when I was a kid."

"Oh."

Clearing his throat, he made an attempt to sit up straighter.

The maneuver was only partially successful. "I'm sorry I hurt you when you woke me up."

She was profoundly grateful for the change of subject even though she was the one who had dragged them into the previous topic. "What the heck did you think—that I was attacking you?"

"Not you. I was dreaming about Al Hewitt. He was trying his damnedest to kill me."

"You and he didn't get along?"

"We got along okay until this evening, when he wanted to keep me from leaving the Logan Ranch." He paused and sucked in a breath, and she knew the conversation was using up his strength. "We had a little go-round, and I had to stash him in a storage shed."

"You've had a busy night," she observed dryly.

"Yeah. And now I need to lie down. Can you put the seat back or something?"

"I think it's safer if you come into the cabin and lie down."

He pushed himself up, looked around as if he'd just become aware of his surroundings. "Where are we?"

"Somewhere safe, I hope."

"Where exactly?"

She gave a little laugh. "One of Logan's line cabins. I figure it's the last place he'd look."

"One of Logan's line cabins," he repeated slowly. "Yeah, good thinking. But how do you know it's his?"

"He chased me and my brother away once when we were kids. Told us the next time he found us on his property, he'd shoot us."

"Sounds like him." Matt tipped his head to one side. "You have a brother?"

She closed her eyes for a moment, fighting the tight feeling in her chest that always came when she thought about Billy. "I did. He's dead."

"I'm sorry."

"It happened a long time ago. He joined the Marines and

had an overzealous drill instructor. They were training at night in a swamp—and he drowned.''

Before she let the pain get the better of her, she made another quick change of subject. "How's your head?"

He considered the question carefully, looked from her to the dials on the dashboard and back again. "A little better. It looks like the double vision's gone, anyway."

"Thank God," she said, praying that he wasn't in need of serious medical attention. Or maybe she was planning to kiss him and make him well.

Struggling to sound brisk, she added, "Ease away from the door, so I can open it."

Matt had already opened the door by the time she got around to the other side of the truck, but when he lowered himself to the ground, he had to reach out a hand against the vehicle to keep from falling on his face.

She moved in close, slipping her arm around his waist, taking part of his weight, feeling the warmth of his body in the cold night air. He was a big man. Heavy. And she knew she couldn't hold him up for long. Gritting her teeth, she helped him shuffle to the cabin door, then across the rough plank floor.

"The bunks smell like a family of bears slept there," she told him as she directed him to the blankets on the floor.

"This is fine," he answered, easing down to the less than comfortable surface. Covering him with the remaining blanket, she knelt beside him, staring down at him for a moment. Then she pushed herself to her feet and returned to the vehicle.

After pulling as far as she could into a small grove of trees, she climbed out and looked up into the star-filled sky, the twinkling points of light making her feel very small and very unprotected. In her nightgown the chill air raised goose bumps on her skin.

She wanted to get back to Matt, and the sudden feeling of dependence brought a flash of self-doubt. For years she prided herself on being able to handle anything that came along—

even her father's final illness. In the space of a few hours, she'd started to rely on Matt Forester.

Or maybe that wasn't what she was feeling, she told herself as she scrambled for a better explanation. Maybe she was reacting this way because she felt responsible for what had happened to him since he'd been injured by *her* foreman. In spite of that, a little while ago, he'd kissed her, and she'd tasted as much need in his kiss as passion.

If he'd been in better shape—or if she'd had more experience communicating with men—she might have marched back to the cabin and demanded to know exactly what that kiss had meant. But she didn't know how to ask the right questions. And she wasn't sure he would even know the answer—not when he was half out of his head, courtesy of her foreman.

So she worked off some of her frustration by scooping up several handfuls of fallen leaves and scattering them over the roof and the hood of the vehicle. Standing back, she swiped her hands together to dust away the bits of clinging leaf and surveyed her handiwork. Maybe the covering would disguise the shiny surface—if someone did decide to investigate this place from the air.

After retrieving the gun and her purse, she started back to the cabin. But one of the annoyances of pregnancy stopped her. Unfortunately these cabins out in the middle of nowhere didn't come equipped with bathroom facilities. So she checked the tissue supply in her pocketbook and made a strategic stop in a convenient thicket.

Back in the cabin, she laid the gun within reach, then knelt and touched Matt's shoulder, tensing as she imagined him lunging at her again. But this time he only opened his eyes and gave her a lazy smile.

"You're feeling better," she murmured.

"Mm-hmm."

"I should check your pupils with the flashlight. I should have done that before."

He winced. "Do you have to?"

"You know I do."

She reached for the light, switched it on and directed the beam toward his face. He sucked in a sharp breath as the brightness hit him, but both his pupils contracted the same amount.

"Do I pass?" he asked, rubbing his eyes as she switched off the light.

"Yes." *Thank the Lord*, she added silently.

"Then lie down and get some sleep. You're going to need it."

She looked around the cabin and back at the makeshift bed. "Lie down with you?"

"I'm in no shape to start anything."

"Aren't you?" she asked, remembering the potency of his kiss. What was he like when he *was* in shape?

"I won't do anything out of line. Promise." When she didn't move, he added, "You must be dead on your feet by now." Holding up the top blanket, he waited for her decision.

Perhaps the trembling of his hand was the deciding factor. Or maybe she was too tired to think straight, too tired to run any farther—from Roy Logan or from the man who'd kidnapped her and was now offering to share his bed.

Without understanding why she trusted Matthew Forester on such a basic level, when wariness was such an ingrained facet of her personality, she eased onto the blanket and rolled to her side, her face away from him.

Chapter Four

Matt awakened in the dark, disoriented until his bruised brain identified the soft female shape pressed against his body.

Amanda.

In the night he'd rolled toward her, until his front was pressed against her back and his hand had slipped across her body, to splay against the gentle swell of her abdomen.

He should move that hand away, he told himself sternly, knowing he had no right to clasp her so intimately. But he didn't have the power to shift away.

Holding her felt too good, too comforting—too sexually tempting. So he lay there, breathing in the flower scent of her hair, pressing his face into the golden strands as his mind worked through several urgent pieces of business.

First he evaluated his injury. His head still hurt, but the pain was manageable. The double vision was a distant, unpleasant memory. And he seemed to be thinking a lot more clearly than last night, when he'd abducted her at gunpoint, then kissed her without waiting for an invitation. He'd never been an impulsive man. It seemed that a lifetime of cautious habits had suddenly counted for nothing when he'd heard Roy Logan talking about kidnapping Amanda. And his impulse control had apparently gone AWOL when Ed had conked him on the head.

He grimaced, hoping he was in better physical and mental

shape now. At least he *knew* that he shouldn't be enjoying the sweet torture of wanting Amanda. At least he had the decency not to press his aroused body to hers.

Still, the memory of the kiss brought a stab of guilt that propelled him into another line of thought: how to keep her safe. There were still too many variables. He'd come on the scene too late to meet Colin Logan, but the things he knew made him sure he wouldn't have liked the man. A sudden unpleasant picture of the younger Logan and Amanda tangled together on a bed leaped into his mind, and he clenched his teeth to banish it. How had a woman who seemed as sweet and innocent as Amanda let herself get involved with someone like that?

Or had she? Had Colin forced himself on her? Was that it? The thought brought a surge of anger that must have communicated itself to her, because she made a low, frightened sound and stirred against him, increasing his physical discomfort.

"It's okay. I'm not going to hurt you," he murmured.

She said something he couldn't make out and seemed to sink deeper into slumber.

She was turned away from him, and he couldn't see her face, but he knew the exact moment when she awakened and became aware of the hand on her abdomen and the hard male appendage pressing against her soft flesh.

When she tried to pull away, he shifted his grip to her shoulder.

"It's going to be easier for you to talk to me about Colin if you stay this way," he said.

He felt her whole body go rigid. "Colin is none of your business!" The rejoinder sounded both automatic and self-protective.

"Maybe not. But if Roy Logan puts a bullet through my heart, I'd like to know why, exactly," he answered, keeping his tone level.

She sucked in a breath, then another, letting the last one out in a shuddering sigh. "I guess I know the picture of me you're carrying around in your head."

"I don't have any preconceptions," he lied.

"Preconceptions!" She gave a strangled little laugh that cut off as suddenly as it had begun.

"If I'm going to keep you safe from Roy, I have to know what's going on," he said in the same carefully rational tone he'd used before.

"I don't need your help!"

"I think you do. He's got the money and resources to get what he wants. And you have something he thinks belongs to him."

"The baby is mine!"

"I understand that, sweetheart," he answered in a low, reassuring voice, then waited for her to tell him what he needed to know.

He could feel her gathering her nerve before she whispered, "My pregnancy is none of your business."

"I concede the point."

Long seconds ticked by before she blurted, "I'm thirty years old, and I want to have a child. I went to a clinic in Cheyenne—" she swallowed, then rushed to clarify the point "—where they do artificial insemination."

"Artificial insemination," he repeated, wondering if he'd heard her right.

While he was still grappling with that, she turned to face him, her eyes flashing. "So I didn't get this baby in some cozy bed with Colin Logan. I was on an exam table, with a doctor in a white coat. And a nurse to help him with the procedure!"

He'd been mentally preparing himself for something he didn't want to hear, but her explanation left him at a complete loss for words.

"Do you think I made up that story to cover up a—a back-street affair?" she demanded.

"No."

"Thank you for that, anyway."

To hide his relief, he reached to brush his knuckle against her cheek, and he saw the wary expression that crept across her face. So he skipped the next logical question: why not get pregnant the old-fashioned way?

Instead he allowed his own features to turn thoughtful. "And somehow Tim Francetti got into the confidential clinic records."

"Who is Tim Francetti?" she asked.

"The scumbag P.I. Logan hired to find out who killed his son."

"How do you know?"

"It wasn't exactly a secret around the Logan Ranch. On the few occasions Roy invited me to dinner, he bragged that Francetti was the best—that he'd find out who murdered Colin. Last night when I heard Roy talking to Hewitt, I found out he wasn't planning to turn Francetti's information over to the sheriff. He's going to take care of it himself."

AMANDA SUCKED IN a little breath. "You mean—murder the person who killed Colin?"

"That's right. Roy thinks he's a law unto himself."

She nodded, remembering some of the nasty incidents between her father and Logan over water rights and land access. She'd been furious that he thought his money put him in the right. But maybe they'd actually been lucky that he hadn't poisoned their cattle or something. The thought sent her mind spinning from Roy to his son—who was hardly an improvement.

Matt must have seen her face contort. "What?" he asked.

"Are you sure?" she whispered.

"About what?"

"That—that Colin is the father of my baby," she managed to say, her voice thin as she struggled to get the sentence out.

"No. I'm not sure. I'm only going on what Roy thinks, based on the information he received from his detective."

She looked down toward the slight curve of her abdomen, toward the baby she'd been so happy to be carrying. "Then there's some chance he could be wrong?"

"When you have…" He cleared his throat. "When you have that kind of procedure, do they give you a choice about the father? Do they give you background information on several…prospective donors?"

All at once she wondered how she'd been carrying on this conversation lying in bed with Matt Forester. Scrambling to her feet, she stood and reached for the end of her braid, combing it through her fingers as she paced the few steps to the window and looked out.

Behind her she could hear Matt climbing to his feet, as well. When she angled herself enough to see his profile, she found him leaning his shoulder against the rough wall.

"The men fill out questionnaires. You can look at the information sheets on…various candidates." She stopped, wondering if the conversation was as embarrassing for him as it was for her. "The father I picked for my baby didn't sound anything like Colin Logan!"

"Do you have the information sheet?"

"It's back at the ranch. It said he was a college graduate," she recited one of the most important points. "It said—" She stopped.

"What?"

"That he was unmarried. That he was twenty-nine. I—I guess that fits Colin, now that I think about it, if he hedged a little about his age. But I wasn't thinking about him at the time! And why would someone like him go to the Highton clinic? It couldn't be because he needed the money."

Matt shrugged. "Anything else that fits?"

She frowned as she remembered the physical description. "Dark eyes and hair. Caucasian. That could be you!"

"It could," he said softly, folding his arms across his broad chest.

Color flamed her cheeks. "I didn't mean that. I don't know

what I mean!'' she shouted, then struggled to get back some measure of control. ''He was shorter than you. I remember that,'' she insisted, feeling the oxygen in her lungs thicken. Walking to the door, she opened it and took a deep breath of fresh air. It didn't help.

The silence between herself and Matt seemed to hum. If he crossed the space between them now and touched her, she would scream. She knew she would scream.

Maybe he read her mind, because he stayed where he was. ''Amanda, we're not going to prove anything this morning.''

She knew he was right, but she was too wound up to stop looking for reasons to deny it was Colin. ''It said he was in business for himself. That he enjoyed reading books, that he liked animals. Well, Colin hunted animals for sport. And he hated books.''

''He could have been in some kind of business.''

''I thought he worked for Roy,'' she insisted.

''Maybe he had some other interests on the side.''

''Stop making it sound like it's him!'' she almost shouted.

''I'm sorry,'' he answered, sounding sincere.

''Don't be sorry. Help me prove it's not Colin.'' She whirled to face him. ''If Roy got a hold of the records, why can't I?''

''I'm sure his guy obtained them illegally. I don't think you could just walk in there and request them. And if you did, you'd probably find Roy has somebody watching the place.'' He sighed. ''Didn't you sign some sort of release that you wouldn't seek out the father of the child?''

''Yes,'' she admitted. ''But if Tim whatever-his-name-was could steal the records, so could you! You're a security expert.''

''Maybe,'' he said, the tone of his voice making her realize she was asking something that she had no right to ask.

She turned her hands palm up. ''I'm sorry. Forget it, you've already gotten yourself into a heap of trouble because of me.''

He scuffed his foot against a floorboard. "If you want the records, I could try to get them."

"No." She raised her eyes to his, tried to probe their dark depths. She'd let herself get wound up thinking about Colin, and there was nothing she could do about him at the moment. The man standing a few feet away was another matter entirely. "Maybe you'd better tell me why you put your integrity on the line for me."

He folded his arms across his chest. "For starters I don't like Logan. He's meaner than a bear with a burr up his behind. And I couldn't stand the idea of his getting his clutches on you or your child."

"You hardly know me. Maybe I'm telling you a pack of lies," she answered.

"I don't think so. I'm a pretty good judge of character."

She shook her head as she stared at the man who had kidnapped her from her own ranch last night. "My baby's welfare is at stake here. I need to know why you risked your job, your reputation to come to my rescue," she pressed.

He looked around the cabin as if he were suddenly thinking about escape. A moment ago she'd felt the walls closing in on her. Now it seemed to be his turn.

Pressing her advantage, she planted her hands on her hips and demanded, "Give me a reason why I should trust you."

He swallowed hard, ran his hand through his hair, and the look on his face made her suddenly want to back off. But she stood her ground.

"Okay. I'll give you the best answer I can. Last time I had a chance to help a woman who was pregnant and single, I messed up," he choked out.

The strangled confession was the last thing she'd been expecting. Reaching out her hand, she steadied herself against the table. "You got somebody pregnant, then left her?" she whispered.

"No!"

"Then what?"

His face contorted and the hands at his sides squeezed into fists. "I'm talking about my sister. Bethany."

"Bethany," she breathed. "You called to her last night, when I was driving through the woods."

"Did I?"

She nodded, waited for him to go on.

The hands at his sides opened and closed. "She was in high school and she got pregnant. My father, good old Coach Forester, told her she was a disgrace to the family—that he'd lose his job if anybody found out his daughter had been messing around with one of the guys on the football team."

She could only stare at him, trying to take in the words. Now that he'd started, he rushed ahead.

"When he found out she was in trouble, my dad kicked her out of the house, and I stood there and let it happen," he said, self-accusation ringing in his voice.

"How old were you?" she managed to ask.

"Sixteen."

"It sounds like there was nothing you could do—not against a grown man, the head of your household."

"I should have—" He made a chopping motion with his hand, then turned abruptly away, his shoulders slumped.

The gesture of defeat from a man of such strength was more than she could stand. Acting on a deep, instinctive level, she closed the distance between them, opened her arms and pulled him to her. For long seconds he stood stiffly as she stroked her hands across his broad shoulders, feeling the tension shuddering through him. "You were just a boy," she reminded him, "and he was a big, tough man who liked to throw his weight around. Who used his fists to keep his family in line."

His head jerked up. "How the hell do you know that?"

"For starters you told me he was the football coach. But I didn't really need to know that. I've helped women who were married to guys like him. Grace Logan, Colin's mother, was married to a similar SOB."

The explanation didn't seem to matter to him. "I should

have helped Bethany. She didn't have anywhere else to go, so she ended up down by the railroad crossing when a freight train was coming through."

A cold shudder went through her as the implication sank in. "No!" she gasped, willing it not to be true.

"She made it look like an accident. Or the police wrote it up that way, so as not to embarrass good old Coach Forester."

"Oh, Lord, no," she managed to say, the shock and the pain almost too much as she took in the horror and imagined what it must have done to him.

"My mom never recovered from her death. I stayed home another year. But that was all I could take of being in my father's house. The summer before my senior year in high school, I took off—lied about my age and joined the army. I haven't been back to Tarenton, Georgia, since."

"Matt…" She didn't know what to say. All she could do was hold him, stroke him, wordlessly tell him that she knew none of it was his fault. He stayed in her arms for another few moments, then pulled away. She saw a fine sheen of moisture in his eyes and knew he was struggling to hold back tears— probably because Coach Forester had drummed into him that real men didn't cry. And they didn't air the family's dirty laundry in public, either.

She was sure of that when, without a word, he turned and fled the cabin, leaving the door ajar.

She saw him stomping off into the bushes and knew it would be a bad idea to follow. Instead she headed in the opposite direction, finding a thicket where she could take care of her own personal needs.

Then she found the mountain stream she'd heard the night before and bent to scoop up icy water to wash her hands and face.

She'd demanded that Matt tell her his motivation for hustling her away from her own ranch at gunpoint. Now she knew. The whole thing had nothing specifically to do with her. He'd heard Roy Logan talking, and he'd flashed back to the scene with his father.

An unmarried woman. Pregnant. Needing help. And this time he was going to do the right thing.

She dragged a breath and let it out. Well, it was better to know that from the beginning. Better to understand that his feelings regarding *her* were nothing personal.

She stood for a moment with her fist pressed against her mouth, sorry she'd gotten the answers she'd demanded. Then she went back to the Cherokee and pulled out some emergency supplies. Since the time she'd gotten stuck in a flash flood, she'd prided herself on being prepared for any eventuality. So she was able to pull out a knapsack with some food and a change of clothing.

She ate a handful of dried apples and nuts as she walked back to the cabin. Quickly closing the door, she exchanged her gown and robe for a plaid shirt and a pair of elastic-waist jeans.

Matt was still making himself scarce, and at the moment, she was grateful for that. She'd been spinning fantasies about the man who had kidnapped her. It was time to get back to reality.

Setting the gun within reach of the counter in the kitchen area, she checked the contents of the storage cabinets. The cabin was fairly well stocked. Using bottled water and powdered milk, she was able to make oatmeal on the propane stove. Then she stirred in some of the dried apples.

She heard footsteps coming toward the door just as she was finished boiling the hot cereal. Her hand was on the gun before she saw that it was Matt filling the doorway.

He stood watching her intently. "You would have been great on the frontier," he commented.

"My father taught me to be careful out in the back country."

"I'm glad," he answered, then sniffed in the direction of

the stove. Moving toward the pot, he looked in at the apple-flavored oatmeal. "How did you manage this?"

"There were some supplies in the cabinets. And I keep some stuff in the car."

"Including a change of clothes."

"Yes." Briskly she produced plastic spoons from her supplies. "Sorry. No coffee. Caffeine is bad for the baby."

"That's okay. It's probably bad for a concussion, too."

She winced. "I didn't ask you how you're feeling this morning."

"We got off onto other stuff."

"How's your headache?" she persisted.

"A lot better. I have a hard head. And an iron constitution."

She studied him as she poured bottled water into paper cups, deciding that his assessment was probably true. Most men would have ended up in the hospital after Ed's crack on the head.

They drank the bottled water and ate the oatmeal and apples, neither of them leaning toward idle conversation. Instead of remaining at the table after he finished, Matt got up, set his bowl in the sink and began poking through the cabinets, inventorying the contents.

"What are you doing?"

"Seeing if there's anything we can use. Maybe we'll take some of Logan's food when we leave."

She nodded.

"We should get out of here soon," he said. "I have to get to a bank. If it's not already too late."

"What do you mean?"

He made a wry face. "If I were Logan, I'd try to have my funds frozen."

She nodded tightly. "I have some money."

"I wasn't planning to sponge off you."

"What were you planning?" she asked.

"Getting you out of the state, for starters."

"Then what?" she pressed, leaning forward across the table.

"I'm considering a couple of options."

She gave him a direct look. "I'd appreciate it if you would share them with me," she said, hearing the sharp tone of her voice.

Instead of answering, he turned and started rolling up the blankets they'd used the night before.

Amanda got up and set her crockery bowl in the sink with a clunk.

Matt looked up questioningly.

"I'm not accustomed to just going along with a strange man's plans. I'd like to know what you have in mind. I don't think that's an unreasonable request."

"I get the feeling you're not accustomed to going along with *any* man's plans."

"What's that supposed to mean?" she demanded, aware that the tension zinging back and forth between them all morning was finally finding an outlet. The wrong outlet.

When he cocked his hip against the edge of the counter, she knew she wasn't going to like his next words. And she wasn't disappointed.

"Well, most women who want to get pregnant do it in bed—with a guy."

The rejoinder stung, but she wasn't going to let him see that he'd hurt her, not when hiding her hurt had become second nature. "I'm not most women," she shot back.

"That's what I heard in town. Apparently you can't get anywhere near a guy without getting into competition with him."

Her face burned. "Who said that?"

Before he could decide what to answer, a whirring, chopping sound from above made them both freeze where they stood. The helicopter was back.

Only now there were two helicopters swooping low over the cabin.

Chapter Five

Matt snapped his mouth shut. Moments ago he'd been lashing out at Amanda, acting defensive because she was asking him basic questions—questions that he was chagrined he couldn't answer. When he'd driven to her house last night, he'd only been thinking of whisking her out of harm's way. This morning he'd been embarrassed to admit that he still hadn't figured out what he was going to do from here on out.

In the space of a few heartbeats, everything changed.

Reaching for her, he pulled her close, feeling her body tremble as he wrapped her protectively in his arms.

"God, this is my fault," she wheezed. "They must have seen the Cherokee."

"More likely they got some help from your friend Ed. Maybe he was willing to speculate on how your mind works."

"He wouldn't sell me out," she answered, her voice sounding wounded.

Matt shrugged.

"I'm sorry," she whispered. "I'm sorry for getting you into my mess."

"I got myself into it."

Above the sound of the blades, an amplified voice rang from above. "Matthew Forester, come out with your hands up."

Even with the distortion of the loudspeaker, he knew the

voice. Cursing low and harshly under his breath, he clenched his arms more tightly around Amanda.

"Logan," she breathed.

"No. That's Hunter Kelley from Randolph Security, the outfit I work for. Logan must have been on the phone to them in the middle of the night to get them here from Baltimore already." A hollow laugh bubbled in his throat. "Apparently he's convinced them I've gone off the deep end."

"Matthew Forester, we have you surrounded. Come out with your hands up. You will not be harmed."

"Yeah," he muttered, the pounding in his head a thousand times worse than it had been a few minutes. "You'll just take me straight to the funny farm and throw the key away. Or maybe one of Logan's men will arrange for me to have an accident."

He looked at the gun on the counter, then around the cabin, knowing he was trapped—and Amanda with him. When his gaze came back to her, he saw the terror in her eyes. "Sweetheart, I'm sorry. I can fight Logan's goons with a clear conscience, but I can't take a chance on my friends getting caught in the cross fire because of me." He held her hands. "I'll draw Logan's guys away. Then you surrender to the Randolph men. Hunter Kelley. Maybe Jason Zacharias or Jed Prentiss is with him. They're all good guys. Honorable. Ask them for sanctuary. Tell them you don't want to go with Logan, under any circumstances. If you stick with them, you'll be okay," he told her, hoping his hands had the power to make it true.

"No!" When he started toward the door, she grabbed his arm and held him with an incredible fierceness. "Don't go outside. You could get shot. There's another way. Let me show you," she insisted, her voice taking on the tone of steely determination that he knew was etched into her soul.

Still, he wondered if she were the one who'd gone off the deep end as she whirled to the cabinet beside the sink and produced a crowbar. Kneeling, she started prying frantically at a crack he hadn't spotted in the floor. To his amazement a section of the rough planking came up, revealing a ladder that descended into a dark pit.

"A tunnel. There's a tunnel down there," she told him urgently as the loudspeaker blared again, this time directly overhead. "I found it last night before you came inside."

He stared into the yawning darkness. "Are you sure it's not just a cellar?"

"It's an escape hatch. I climbed down it to have a look. It goes off somewhere—I just don't know where it comes out." She looked at him pleadingly. "Please, we don't know what wild story Logan told Randolph Security." She waved her arm in exasperation. "And there's no guarantee that Logan won't whisk me away before your friends can do anything."

He gave a tight nod, acknowledging she was right even as his mind began recalculating their chances of escape. Logan undoubtedly knew about the tunnel. Which meant taking some precautions to make sure he couldn't follow them down there.

"Okay," he told her. "This is the way we'll do it. You climb down and start along the tunnel. I'll try to slow them down."

"How?"

"Just get going. I want you as far away as possible if they storm the cabin."

"Come with me now," she pleaded as she snatched up her purse and backpack where they lay on the floor. After shoving the purse inside the pack, she picked up the flashlight she'd used the night before.

"No. I've got to stop them from finding the trapdoor."

"How?"

"You go on. I'll catch up with you." He tightened the muscles of his face, wordlessly telling her they didn't have time for an extended explanation.

After a few seconds' hesitation, she started down the ladder.

He watched her, thinking how remarkable she was. The helicopter circling the cabin and the bullhorn would have reduced t̶ average woman to tears. But Amanda was too stubborn to give in to such weakness.

He waited tensely until she was out of sight, then crossed to the cabinet where he'd seen a gasoline can. Sloshing it, he found it partly full. It would have to do.

Next he found a box of old-fashioned kitchen matches above the stove and set them beside the can on the floor.

His preparations made, he strode toward the door. Before he could change his mind, he stepped into the morning sunlight and looked up. Even when he shaded his eyes, the glint of the sun off one of the helicopters sent a surge of pain through his skull.

The pain was a vivid reminder of his present vulnerability. Probably he was taking an unacceptable risk. But he couldn't put his plan into action if Hunter landed too soon. So he strode half a dozen yards from the small building, where he's be in plain sight, then waved both arms, attracting the attention of the helicopter pilots, who both swung back in his direction.

He didn't know which chopper Hunter was in. So he turned in a circle, using several of the Randolph hand signals that had been developed among the operatives for silent communication in just such a situation. First he held his right hand straight up, palm out, indicating that his message was urgent. Then he executed a chopping motion, right hand across the left, warning his friends of danger.

After giving the signal two times, he pivoted and started back to the cabin at a trot, increasing his speed when he heard one of the choppers swoop low.

Behind him, the ground where he'd been standing exploded in a cloud of dust as automatic-weapons fire plowed into the hard-packed soil.

God, he hoped the shooter was one of Logan's men. Or had the SOB somehow convinced Randolph Security that he had to be stopped at any cost?

Reaching the cabin, he slammed the door shut. The choppers were still in the air.

"Stay up there another couple of minutes, buddy," he muttered as he opened the valves under the stove's propane burners. Then, thinking it was too bad he couldn't leave a suicide note, he began sloshing gasoline around the cabin, the fumes and his headache an unfortunate combination.

After climbing halfway down the ladder, he grabbed the old-fashioned kitchen matches and struck one against the wood floor. Praying that the Randolph men didn't land within the next few minutes, he tossed the burning match into a pool of gasoline.

The liquid burst into flame immediately, tongues of fire spreading across the floor. As one arrowed toward him, he slammed the door shut and bolted down the ladder.

Ignoring the pounding in his head, he hit the ground running and took off down the tunnel toward what he hoped was the beam of Amanda's flashlight.

The tunnel ran in a straight line, and he judged he was several hundred feet from the cabin when the propane tank detonated with an unearthly boom. The whole tunnel seemed to heave and shake, and a shower of dirt started raining onto his head.

Amanda screamed and turned.

"Go on!" he gasped through panting breaths as he kept plowing forward. Before they could clear the shower of debris, it turned into a torrent. His forward progress slowed, then stopped. Helplessly he watched the ceiling rain down around him, until his vision and his air supply were choked off. Within seconds he was buried under a mound of dirt as the roof of the tunnel collapsed.

Though he wanted to scream, he kept his mouth clamped firmly shut as he tried to pull himself free. But the heavy earth held him fast.

Dimly in the distance, he heard someone calling his name. Not Hunter this time. It was Amanda, her voice high and frantic. He'd seen her right ahead of him. Now she sounded as if she were in the other end of a bad phone connection from Mars.

"Matt," she gasped. "Matt. Answer me, for God's sake."

It was impossible to respond, impossible to breathe as he clawed desperately with his fingers at the debris entombing him as surely as the mounded earth over a fresh grave. For endless moments he kept at the frantic digging. But finally his movements slowed. His lungs burned, and his head began to pound.

Not much time left.

Goodbye, Amanda, he silently called to her. *Goodbye. I'm sorry.* The syllables blurred in his head as his brain cells screamed for oxygen.

He could still hear her calling to him. But the voice was far in the distance now, a million miles from where he stood, trapped under the weight of the mountain above him.

His body felt like lead, and he would have sunk to his knees, but the earth pressing around him held him upright, even as the terrible pressure seemed to crush his lungs.

Then he felt the dirt moving, saw dancing specks of yellow light before his eyes.

Blinking, he stared at the illusion, entranced, as slender fingers brushed against the skin of his face and whisked away the dirt from his nose and mouth. He coughed, then sucked in a strangled breath, expelling it in a rush so that he could gasp in another.

"Matt, oh God, Matt," she cried out as she alternately clawed at the debris and pulled at his shoulders, trying to free him from the trap he'd made when he set off the propane.

He still felt like a mummy, but somehow he freed his hand, and began to dig. He suspected Amanda was doing most of the work. His movements were too slow and disorganized. But finally he pulled his legs free and tumbled from his prison, almost falling on top of Amanda.

He lay there panting for several seconds, icy shudders gripping his body. But he knew he couldn't afford the luxury of resting yet—not when the ceiling above them both might be just as unstable as the part that had come down on top of him. Gritting his teeth, he forced himself up.

"Come on," he gasped, taking her hand and tugging her away from the dirt fall.

"Wait," she insisted, snatching up her pack and the light before allowing him to pull her farther down the tunnel, stumbling through the debris that littered the floor. Finally the surface below his feet felt clear and the roof above him looked solid. But he staggered on for several dozen more yards before stopping to brace his shoulders against the wall and drag in great lungfuls of air.

"Matt, are you all right?" she asked, her breath coming in little gasps.

"Yeah. I don't know whether to thank you for getting me out of there or tell you you were a damn fool to get so close to the cave-in."

"Just thank me—politely."

He wasn't feeling polite when he reached for her and hugged her against his chest.

"I was so scared," she whispered as her hands moved over his cheekbones, his hair, his lips, brushing away the dirt.

"Sweetheart, you look like you've been in a mud fight," he muttered, studying her in the flashlight beam as he combed loose dirt from her golden hair.

"Do you think you'd win any prizes for looks?"

"No," he answered, although at that moment, he didn't give a damn about his appearance. All he knew was that he felt as if he had truly come back from the dead. And his resurrection was a miracle worked by Amanda's delicate hands.

His fingers skimmed her face. "Did anybody ever tell you you're too brave for your own good?"

"Nobody ever told me I was brave," she whispered.

"Did they tell you you were beautiful—even covered with dirt?"

Wordlessly she shook her head.

His body was still icy cold. Feeling the warmth radiating from her, he pulled her closer, holding her with all the strength he still possessed.

He'd thought he simply needed warmth. As soon as he had her in his arms, he realized he needed far more.

"God, you feel so good," he rasped, moving his hands over her, touching every place that he could reach.

His gaze dropped to her mouth. It was slightly parted, and maybe she intended to say something. But he took the trembling of her bottom lip as an invitation.

Without giving himself time to think, he lowered his head, the soft impact of his mouth on hers sending a jolt of sensation through his body. At that first wisp of contact, he was lost.

He'd been operating on some lawless plane of existence since he'd heard the conversation between Roy Logan and Al Hewitt. Ed Stanton's cracking him over the head had pushed him into a world where impulse control was forgotten behavior.

Greedily he angled his head so that he could plunder her sweetness, tasting her in great gulps that only drove him to seek more and yet more.

Ruled utterly by his own needs, he shifted their positions, pinning her against the wall, pressing his body against hers as he turned his head first one way and then the other, so that he could feast on her nectar from every angle.

Dimly, in some hidden recess of his mind, he knew that he had no right to stake a claim on her. Yet he was as helpless to stop himself as he'd been last night when he'd kissed her in the car. As helpless as he'd been when he'd lain in bed this morning holding her.

He felt driven by madness, by urgency that welled from some unexplored place within his soul. As his mouth plundered hers, his hands stroked up and down her arms, her back, before he shifted away so that he could cup the wonderful fullness of her breasts.

When his fingers brushed her nipples, she made a high sound of pleasure, arching into the caress and offering him more, offering him anything he wanted.

He wanted to feel her naked flesh against his, the length of her body pressed to his. Reaching behind her, under her shirt, he unhooked the catch of her bra, pushed it out of the way and caught her breasts in his hands, cupping their ripe weight as his long fingers stroked over the stiff peaks. The feel of her aroused body drove him almost to the point of madness.

When he cupped her bottom and lifted her against the throbbing shaft of his erection, he felt her twine her arms around his neck to hold herself in place.

He wanted her with a need that shook him to the very core. But as he pictured himself lowering her to the floor, some dim sense of reality returned. Lifting his head, he saw they were in a tunnel that had partially collapsed. The rest of it could come down on them at any minute.

Swearing, he set her onto her feet, then took a step back, his breath coming in ragged gasps and his hands clenched at his sides so that he wouldn't reach for her again.

"Matt?" she asked, swaying as she lifted her eyes toward him, her expression dazed.

"Amanda, sweetheart," he managed to say, dragging in a steadying breath of air. "We can't. Not here. Not like this."

She blinked, looked around at their grim surroundings, as if she'd just realized where they were.

The lost look on her face made him want to pull her back into his arms; instead he wedged his hands into his pockets. "We have to get out of here," he said, struggling to make his voice sound normal.

"Of course," she agreed, pivoting away from him as she lifted her arms to refasten her bra.

The sight of her standing there looking embarrassed and alone pierced his heart.

"I'm sorry," he apologized. "I think your friend Ed knocked the sense right out of my head."

"What are you trying to tell me?"

He raked a shaky hand through his hair. "I'm trying to say I'm sorry for taking liberties I had no right to take."

She made a sound that might have been meant as a laugh. "I guess this is the story of my life," she muttered under her breath.

Maybe he hadn't been meant to catch the words, but his hearing was excellent.

"What's that supposed to mean?"

Her face contorted. "Never mind. I should learn to keep my mouth shut."

Turning her back to him, she started down the tunnel. In two strides he closed the distance between them. When she kept moving away, his arm shot out and caught her. "Wait a minute. You can't say something like that and then drop it!"

"Let go of me!"

His hand fell away from her.

She faced him and squared her shoulder. "I can do anything I want. Just the way you can do anything you want—or don't want. You only kissed me like that because you got buried under a ton of dirt and you wanted to celebrate your escape from death. So you grabbed the first woman you encountered!"

"Dammit." Frustrated, he made another grab for her, but she danced out of his reach.

"If you're saying you think I don't want you, you're very mistaken."

"Not me. Any woman would do."

"Not any woman. You."

"And your reaction has nothing to do with my digging you out of that cave-in?"

He sighed, feeling as if they were playing a game of chess and she'd just said "Checkmate."

"I won't deny that."

When her face took on a look of mock satisfaction, he went

on quickly. "That doesn't change the rest of what I feel for you."

She snorted. "You don't even know me."

"I know you better than you think." He glared down at her. "But I'm not about to prove something to either one of us by making love to you covered with dirt on the floor of a tunnel when the roof could collapse on us or Logan's goons could come running in here with machine guns."

"Machine guns?" she gasped.

"Yeah," he answered, relieved that he'd gotten her off a subject he couldn't handle at the moment—and onto one he could. "When I went outside to stop the chopper from landing, somebody started shooting at me."

"Oh, God." Her hands had been hanging at her sides. They jerked upward. "Your friends?"

"I hope it was Logan's men. But whoever it was, we have to get away from here. Come on."

When she didn't move, he reached for her hand and started slowly down the tunnel, still unsteady on his feet.

TIM FRANCETTI SHUFFLED through his notes on Colin Logan.

This morning, while he was in the middle of collecting information on Matt Forester, Roy Logan had changed the assignment.

At least, he assumed it was Logan who had given the orders to switch his attention from Forester back to Colin and get the files in order. The message had been on his answering machine when he'd arrived at the office. But when he'd tried to call Logan to confirm the change in plans, he'd been told that the ranch owner was unavailable.

Scowling, he looked down at a paragraph that he hadn't yet typed, trying to decipher his hastily scribbled notes.

He'd already turned in some damn fine preliminary reports to Mr. Logan, some of it based on hard facts, some of it extrapolation from an assessment of various situations. But there were still parts of the report that he needed to type up—and names and dates he had to confirm.

Sighing, he went back to the material on Colin's business dealings that he'd obtained from a source in Los Angeles. The younger Logan had wanted to prove he was his father's equal. But money hadn't been his only goal. He'd been looking for excitement, for kicks, as well.

Shuffling through the folder, he pulled out the confidential information on Colin's extracurricular activities at the Highton Fertility Clinic. True to form, the young man had applied to be a sperm donor on a dare from one of his wild friends.

Tim opened another folder, detailing Colin's business dealings with Roy's brother Bud. Then he shifted to a different sheet of paper. There were five brothers in the Logan family. Three were strictly legitimate. One owned a hardware store in Boise. One had a dairy farm in Canada. And one sold sports equipment in L.A. The three of them had broken off relations long ago with Roy and Bud—who had even fewer scruples than Roy, if that were possible.

Which left Tim with a lot more digging to do before he could turn in a complete report.

He glanced at his watch and felt a trickle of sweat run down his armpit. Roy was waiting for whatever information he had, and he'd better start entering his notes in the computer.

BESIDE HIM MATT HEARD Amanda clear her throat. "Are you going to tell me what happened in the cabin? I mean, did Logan's men attack?"

"No. I opened the valves on the propane tank. Then I set the place on fire with the gasoline for the generator."

"Why? I mean, why start a fire? Why blow the cabin up?" Turning, she looked back down the tunnel where the pile of dirt blocked any chance of going back the way they'd come.

He gave a harsh laugh. "If they really think I'm crazy, maybe they'll figure I blew the cabin up and took you with me. And if they have their doubts, it's going to be a while before they can look for our escape hatch. Too bad I didn't figure on the explosion doing a number on the tunnel roof.'' He turned to her, his expression fierce. ''You saved my life, but—''

''You have some objection to that?'' she snapped.

''If more of the ceiling had come down, you would have been buried, too.''

''I make my own decisions. I wasn't going to leave you there.''

''I appreciate that. But you've got to remember you're making decisions for the baby, too,'' he said, hitting on an important point that he'd forgotten earlier.

She winced, and he pressed his fingers over hers. ''So next time when it's a choice between the baby or me, you have to pick the baby.''

She turned to face him, a raft of expressions crossing her features. She looked stunned and abashed, as if she'd forgotten in her panic to save him that she might be endangering her child.

''I wasn't thinking about that,'' she said in a low voice, then pulled her hand away and sped up, almost running down the tunnel.

When he saw a glimmer of daylight ahead of them, he caught up and grabbed her arm, holding her back. ''Wait,'' he whispered, switching off the light.

''We're almost there.''

''And Roy could be waiting for us.''

She turned her face toward him, gave her head a wry shake. ''I wasn't thinking about that, either.''

''He knows about the tunnel—unless somebody else dug it before he built this cabin. How long has he owned this land?''

''Forever,'' she answered.

''Let me slip ahead and have a look. You stay here.''

She didn't give him an argument as he made his way quietly down the passage toward the patch of sunlight at the end, keeping his shoulders near the wall and his footsteps light.

Near the entrance, he waited for his eyes to adjust to the brightness, then inched toward the opening, stopping when he saw the front end of a Jeep. Leaning against the passenger door was a hard-faced man smoking a cigarette and cradling a machine gun under his right arm. It was Al Hewitt.

Chapter Six

The moment Amanda saw Matt's face, she knew they were in trouble. Mouthing silent curses, he came toward her, his footsteps quiet and his shoulders tense.

"Hewitt's out there," he told her. "The good news is that it looks like he's alone. The bad news is that he's got a machine gun. And the pistol I took from him last night is buried under a pile of dirt."

She felt the blood drain from her face, drain from her brain. But she forced herself to keep some semblance of rationality. They'd escaped the cabin. They'd escaped the dirt slide. And now the way was blocked by one of Logan's goons. "What are we going to do?"

He looked at her, and she knew he was trying to see past the fear shadowing her face. "How good an actress are you?" he asked in a voice edged with steel.

"I get the feeling I'm about to find out."

Matt's eyes bored into hers. "Hewitt's mad as hell at me for getting away and tying him up. Probably he couldn't pass up the opportunity to go one-on-one with me, in case we found the escape hatch. But he won't hurt you." He clamped her by the shoulders, the pressure of his big hands making her feel both fragile and strong at the same time. "If I could think of some other way..."

"Just spit it out!"

"Okay." His fingers eased the painful pressure on her shoulders. "If you go out there screaming that I'm under a pile of dirt and beg him to help you, then run back this way before he can grab you, I can take him before he realizes what's happening," he said in one long exhalation of breath.

He looked as if he was hoping she would protest. But she wasn't about to let him see her fear. Instead she raised her chin, her gaze challenging his. "You think that will work? What if he doesn't realize it's me before he starts shooting?"

"I shouldn't have asked you to do it. I'm sorry. Not after I just gave you a lecture about protecting your baby," he said in a low voice.

He took a step back, but she grabbed his arm. "No. I can't think of any other way to keep Logan from getting his hands on my child." She closed her eyes, gathering her courage before turning to face the tunnel entrance. For a moment she stood poised on the balls of her feet. Then, like a madwoman, she started down the tunnel, picking up speed as she went. Waving her hands, she screamed, "Don't shoot. Don't shoot. It's Amanda. I need your help! Please, help me!"

When he spotted her, Hewitt jerked upright, pushed himself away from the vehicle and took a step forward, his weapon ready but pointed at the ground, she was glad to see. "Miss Amanda, what is it? What's happened?" he called out, taking several strides forward.

PRESSING INTO THE SHADOWS at a slight bend in the tunnel, Matt watched the spectacle, thinking that she surely deserved the Hitchcock Award for Best Actress in a Suspense Drama.

"Please! Help me." She gestured wildly into the darkness. "The roof fell in, and Matt is under all that dirt. I can't get him out!" she gasped, barely avoiding the foreman's hand as he snatched at her arm.

As she sped back into the tunnel, Hewitt leaped after her, stumbling as he entered the darkness. But Amanda moved quickly, sprinting back in the direction from which she'd come, forcing Hewitt to follow before his eyes had time to adjust to the dim light.

When the foreman reached the bend in the tunnel, Matt stepped into his path and brought his fist up—straight into the man's jutting chin. He went down like a wounded moose. Matt brought a rock down on Hewitt's skull—for extra insurance. Then he bent to search the man's pockets for the second time in less than twenty-four hours.

Hewitt's wallet yielded more cash, which Matt stuffed into his pocket, along with a set of car keys. He also took the foreman's portable phone.

"Come on," he said, steering Amanda toward the entrance again. He gave her extra points when she didn't spare Logan's henchman a backward glance.

They reached the vehicle, and Matt climbed into the driver's seat.

"Do you feel well enough to drive?" she asked.

"Yeah," he answered, making a quick evaluation and realizing to his relief that the headache had receded to a background roar.

As soon as Amanda was buckled up, he made a U-turn and started down the narrow road, picking up speed as he went. Beside him Amanda clutched the hand grip, but she didn't ask him to slow down.

Three miles later he braked at the highway and looked at her. "Which way?"

"Where do you want to go?"

"Where there are other people. Strangers."

"Left," she told him. "Toward Casper."

He nodded, stepped on the gas, taking a chance on exceeding the speed limit because he knew that they were sitting ducks in this vehicle.

"What do we do if the helicopter starts sweeping the area?" she asked.

"When they don't hear from Hewitt, they'll think we got blown up in the cabin," he said, as much to reassure himself as her. "They won't know we escaped until they can examine the wreckage. And it's still too hot to handle."

As he drove, though, he kept listening for the sound of rotary blades. Slowing, he tossed Hewitt's phone into the trees and he forced himself to stay within the legal limits. Now that he had the luxury, his thoughts turned back to the conversation with Amanda after he'd kissed her. He still wanted to know what the hell she'd meant, but he wasn't sure how to phrase the question. Finally, after he'd eaten up about twenty-five miles, he flat out asked, "Are you going to explain that crack back there—about the story of your life?"

"No."

There was a finality in her voice that grated on his nerve endings. But he knew that pressing her was the wrong thing to do. So he tightened his hands on the wheel and kept driving.

AMANDA WATCHED him drive, maintaining the silence until she couldn't stand it anymore. It was ten miles later by the odometer when she asked, "Are you going to tell me why you're not married?"

"I'm an ax murderer. I chopped up my wife and buried her in Druid Hill Park."

"Oh, please."

"It was a nosy question."

"So was yours."

Briefly he swung his head toward her. "You gave me some reason to ask."

"So did you."

"Mind explaining that?"

"I think it's fair for me to ask why you're not married." She swallowed. "Why you're fixated on me."

"I wouldn't call it fixated."

"What would you call it?"

"Attracted. And your predicament brought out my protective instincts," he growled.

When she didn't comment, he sighed. "Okay, if you really

want to know, I was married after I got out of the army and joined a private intelligence service. Janice didn't like the uncertainty of being hitched to a guy who was always away on assignments and couldn't talk about what he was doing. After a couple of years she asked me for a divorce. The marriage didn't seem worth fighting for, so I gave her what she wanted," he said in a weary voice.

"There must have been more to it than that," she probed.

"I picked her for the wrong reasons," he snapped.

"Such as what?"

"Looks. Sex. She was a damn sexy woman."

"You don't have to worry about that with me," she answered.

"You think you're not sexy?"

"I know I'm not."

When she snorted, he continued. "Not in a flashy way. You don't flaunt it, but it's there, wrapped up with a lot of other appealing qualities.

"Like what?"

"You're self-reliant. You've got more guts than most guys. You've got the courage of your convictions—or you wouldn't have gone to that clinic and gotten yourself a baby."

She thought about that, wondering if she dared believe him, dared let him get any closer to her than he already was. Before she could challenge him with another question, he turned off the highway into a rest area, and she watched him scan the parked vehicles. He seemed particularly interested in a battered minivan parked near a picnic table that sat in a field dotted with wild daisies. The man and woman sitting at the table drinking beer and eating from an ice chest looked as if they'd stepped out of the hippie era. The guy had long hair, a headband and a tie-dyed T-shirt. The woman's generous body was covered by a long flowing purple dress that set off her wild red curls.

Matt cut the engine and turned to her. "Wait here."

Unwilling to let her curiosity show, she answered, "I'm going to use the ladies' room, while I have the chance."

Exiting the Jeep, she marched off along the gravel path to the facility. As she turned into the doorway of the rest room, she could see Matt ambling toward the couple at the table. When she returned, he was deep in conversation with them. Not knowing whether to join in, she leaned against the bumper watching from a distance.

A few minutes later, Matt and the guy shook hands. To her amazement she watched as the man produced a key ring screwdriver and began to take the front license plate off the van. Matt stooped, doing the same to the Jeep. In five minutes they'd switched plates on the two vehicles. Then Matt unbolted the vinyl top from the Jeep, and he and his new friend carried it into the underbrush.

While they were busy, the woman approached Amanda. "Honey, I'm real sorry to hear about your troubles." From a distance she'd looked as if she was in her early forties. Up close Amanda could see the lines in her face and the gray in her hair.

"Name's Crystal Bell," she said, her voice as musical as her name, which was probably where she'd gotten it. "My man's Lee Walters, and I know you're Sally Mae Plunkett."

Sally Mae Plunkett? Give me a break, Amanda thought. Aloud she said, "What troubles?"

"I get why you don't want to talk about it. But Lee and I can dig it, and we're glad to help." She walked to the back of the van, pulled open the door and started searching through a large cardboard box, from which she pulled a dress similar to the one she was wearing—only in forest green and bright pink with voluminous sleeves. Along with it came a large, fringed shawl, which she handed to Amanda. "You put these on, honey, and Wayne won't be comin' after you no more."

Amanda nodded, not sure what to do as the men returned from ditching the Jeep's top. "You go on and change your clothes, precious," Matt said, giving her backside a little shove in the direction of the ladies' room. She stared at him for a minute, then hurried off.

When she returned, she was carrying her own clothing over her arm and wearing the pink-and-green dress, which luckily seemed to be of the one-size-fits-all variety.

The couple and Matt, who now sported a bright pink shirt, surveyed her with approval.

"Go on and cover that blond hair," Crystal said.

Still too stunned to protest, Amanda dutifully draped the shawl over her head.

"We'd best get goin'," Matt said, touching the bandanna headband he now wore. "Much obliged to you kind people for your help."

As he clasped Amanda's hand and led her to the Jeep, she gaped in amazement. Not only had she and Matt been transformed into refugees from a San Francisco flower-child convention, but the Jeep seats were now covered with a couple of bright throws that made it look like a commune living room—or at least what she imagined a commune living room might look like.

"What in the name of all that's holy did you tell them?" Amanda asked as they pulled out of the parking lot.

Matt waited until they were several hundred feet down the highway before replying. "I told them that your husband abused you. That you came to me for help and—" he turned his palm up "—one thing led to another, and you're carrying my child. Now we're escaping from Wayne, who is going to shoot us both if he catches us."

"Your child!"

"They bought it," he answered. "And for only two hundred dollars, they made the license-plate switch and gave you that sweet little outfit." He fingered the bright fabric of her left sleeve.

Amanda made a huffing sound and pulled the scarf more tightly around her head. "You paid them that much?"

"It was worth it. I think the Jeep is pretty well disguised. And so are we."

She tipped her head and looked at him. "You must have done some pretty fast talking. I would have liked to have heard it."

"Yeah, I'm a regular silver-tongued devil."

"Are you bragging?"

"Don't you think I'm entitled?" he asked, grinning.

Against her will she nodded, impressed in spite of herself. Then another thought struck her. "If you can tell such convincing stories, why should I believe anything you say to me?"

He turned his head toward her, his eyes dark and fathomless. "I guess you just have to trust me, sweetheart."

She swallowed, wishing she could give him the answer he wanted.

When she didn't speak, he turned back to the road, and they drove in silence until they reached the outskirts of Casper, where Matt slowed and began studying the motels.

As if the previous conversation had never happened, she asked, "Don't you want to put as much distance as you can between us and Logan?"

He followed her lead. "No. That's what they're expecting us to do. So I'll stop here, where we can mingle with the tourists."

"Won't your security company friends figure you'll do the unexpected?" she asked.

He laughed. "Yeah. But then they'll figure I'll switch tactics to throw them off," he added, turning off Route 20 onto a side road lined with motels and restaurants. He stopped at a slightly seedy motor court with individual log cabins set against a background of the Casper Mountains. The rustic theme was carried through by a stuffed grizzly bear holding a Vacancy sign.

"What name did you use to register?" she asked as Matt returned to the car from the office.

"I guess I could have tried out Al Hewitt. I decided it was safer to stick with Cal Flint."

"Who's Cal Flint? Someone else you knocked out cold?"

"No. I generally carry a spare ID, just in case."

"Oh, right. Of course." She thought for a moment. "Aren't your Randolph Security friends onto your alias?"

He shook his head. "I stopped in Denver on the way out here to test the underground-documents network. I was going to make a report when I got back."

"Whatever you say," she tossed out as he drove around to one of the units in the back. When he'd unlocked the door, she stepped inside. The cabin was plainly furnished but homey, with two narrow wooden beds, a dresser and a rag rug on the wood floor.

"At least I get my own bed," Amanda murmured as she surveyed the place.

Matt closed the door and propped his shoulder against the wall. "I'm trying to be accommodating." He cleared his throat. "We can play this any way you want, you know."

She stared at him, trying to read the expression on his face, but his features gave away nothing.

"So much has happened in a really short time that I'm not sure how to react," she answered, being as honest as she could.

"I know." He shifted his weight from one foot to the other, and she waited for whatever else he was going to say. It was only, "You get some rest. I'm going to go out to make a few arrangements."

She should just let him leave, she told herself. Instead she raised her chin slightly. "What arrangements?" she asked, making it a test. If he told her what he had planned, he passed.

After a brief pause, he answered. "I've decided our best bet is to have a talk with Tim Francetti, the guy who was researching Colin's background for Logan. We may be able to get some information that will give us leverage."

"By leverage, you mean blackmail?" she asked, folding her arms across her chest.

"Yeah."

"What makes you think Francetti will cooperate with you?" she challenged. "Logan's paying him."

"Remember, I can be very persuasive."

"Of course." She was pretty sure he was talking about his performance with Crystal and Lee. Probably he had other methods in mind.

"I'll bring back dinner," he said. "What do you want?"

"Milk," was her first answer. "Low fat. But not skim. I can't stand skim."

"And to eat?"

She thought for a moment. "Roasted chicken, if you can get it. And some side orders of vegetables. Mashed potatoes. Something green."

"Okay. I'll be back as soon as I can. Lock the door after me and don't open it again unless you know it's me."

"And if it's somebody else?"

"Use your discretion."

"Uh, don't you want to get the dirt out of your hair first?" she asked.

He ran a hand through his hair, dislodging the sweatband. "Forgot about that."

He crossed to the bathroom and closed the door, and she could hear him rustling around inside, hear him turn on the shower. As she listened to the sounds, it was impossible not to imagine him standing naked under the spray, not to picture lean hips and broad shoulders, and all the skin and muscles in between.

She felt her face heat, felt her body react. And she might have bolted outside to fill the ice bucket and rub the cubes over her cheeks if she'd thought it was safe.

Instead she sat down in the lumpy easy chair and picked up a booklet on the local attractions, because there was nothing else to distract her. She was reading about the Pioneer Memorial Museum and old Fort Casper when Matt emerged, his dark hair glistening with droplets of water. He gestured toward the bathroom with the wet shoes he was holding. "The tub's a little muddy. I'll clean it when I get back. But I need to talk to some people about transportation."

"Another car?"

"Maybe something more efficient." He paused by the door. "Are you going to be okay?"

"Yes" was the only answer she could give him, so she did. After she'd locked the door, she stood indecisively in the middle of the room. If she took a shower now, she'd be thinking about how he'd just been in there. But if she didn't do it now, then she'd run the risk of having *him* on the other side of the door, imagining her undressed the way she'd imagined him.

So she opted for cleaning the mud out of the tub and taking her own quick shower. Then she flopped on the bed and fell asleep almost instantly.

Matt knocked on the door several hours later, making her sit bolt upright.

They spent the evening being excruciatingly polite with each other, watching TV and denying the supercharged atmosphere in the little cabin.

HE NEXT MORNING, they were picked up by a man in a silver van who drove them to a small airport on the other side of town. Money exchanged hands, they climbed into a small two-engine plane, and a few hours later they were in Denver, where Matt left her again while he scouted out Tim Francetti's office.

"I watched the building for a couple of hours," he told her when he returned with more roast chicken and side dishes. "Either Francetti's holed up in there, or he's on vacation."

Amanda's brow wrinkled. "So what are we going to do?"

"Not we. Me. I'm going to do a little B and E, after it gets dark."

She set down her chicken leg hard enough to make her plastic plate bounce. "Like heck you are."

"You have a better idea?"

"I mean, like heck you are—without me."

"Staying here is safer."

"But you'll let me come because Colin is *my* problem."

He nodded tightly, and she picked up her chicken again, although her appetite had almost disappeared. When she'd demanded to go with Matt, her insistence had been automatic, because that was her usual pattern with the men around Crowfoot. She had to show them she was as good as they were. The longer she stayed with Matt, the more she found she needed to rely on that self-protective mechanism to ward off the fear that threatened to swamp her when she thought about letting herself be vulnerable to him.

She became aware that Matt was watching the play of expressions on her face.

"Changed your mind?" he asked.

"No. I'm just thinking about all the implications."

"I don't generally take pregnant women on illegal expeditions," he said quietly.

She knew he was reminding her that she was risking more than her own skin. Still, she never backed down when challenged. "Don't try to use the baby to talk me out of this. I'm doing it for the baby."

"If you say so."

She ignored his tone of voice and asked, "I suppose we wait until dark?"

He sighed. "Yeah."

The detective's office was in a run-down section of town he told her was called LoDo, where most of the buildings looked as if they were constructed around the turn of the past century.

"I thought Roy only hired the best," she commented as she eyed the seedy exterior and the dirty sidewalk.

"Maybe it will turn out to be a palace inside."

Amanda snorted.

Matt drove the battered Ford he'd acquired around the block

and pulled into a parking space behind a nearby building, then led her down a dark, trash-strewed alley to a back door with the lock taped open.

"Like the Watergate burglars," she commented as he led her into a musty-smelling back stairway.

"If it was good enough for Tricky Dick, it's good enough for me," he tossed over his shoulder as he started up the stairs.

Once she was inside the stairwell, she felt the back of her neck prickle. It was all she could do to keep from grabbing Matt's arm and telling him this was a mistake. Not just for her. For him, too.

Instead she silently berated herself for her jumpy nerves and followed him to the first-floor landing, then down a short, narrow corridor lit at each end by a low-watt bulb. He stopped at a battered wooden door, slipped on rubber gloves and handed her a pair. As she put hers on, he produced a set of instruments from the bag he was carrying, then went to work on the lock while she glanced nervously up and down the hall.

As soon as Matt opened the door, she sensed something was very wrong. It was too quiet. Too dark. Too much like a tomb.

Matt glanced at her, and she knew he felt it, too. Ushering her into the waiting room, he closed and locked the door behind them, then crossed the carpet to the inner office. When he opened that door, she knew from the awful smell what she was going to see inside.

Matt moved to the middle of the doorway, intent on blocking her view, but she couldn't stop herself from moving around him and looking inside—at the dead man sprawled across a broad wooden desk.

"Francetti?" she gasped, fighting the sickness that rose in her throat.

"That's my best guess." He took her by the shoulders and moved her toward a chair. "Stay here."

She lowered herself onto the slick plastic because her knees simply wouldn't hold her up. She'd seen dead animals. Large dead animals, like cattle and horses. She'd even been the one who had found her father dead in bed one morning. But this was different.

For long moments she sat in the waiting room trying to get a grip. She would not lose her chicken dinner, she told herself. And she would not simply sit here while Matt did all the work—not when she'd insisted that she come along. So she pushed herself up on wobbly legs and tottered to the inner office door.

Stepping inside, she saw what she hadn't noticed before because she'd been so focused on the dead man. The place was a mess with papers scattered all over the floor, some of them sticky with blood.

Matt looked up, saw her and cursed. "Get out of here."

"I...want to help you," she managed to say, forcing her features into set lines.

He gave her a considering look and must have realized she wasn't going to back down this time, either. "Okay, see if you can find anything in the filing cabinet."

"They already got what's in there," she pointed out.

"Don't make assumptions. See if they missed anything. See if there was some stuff on Colin in another file."

She slid into the room, staying as far away from the desk as possible. Reaching the filing cabinet, she grasped a cold metal drawer to steady herself. Then she began shuffling through folders. But she kept one eye on Matt, watching him coolly move around the dead man, avoiding the blood on the floor, checking desk drawers. Then he stood and looked around the room before starting to tap the baseboards. Next he lifted up the corners of the rug, took the pictures off the walls and inspected the backs.

There was a video recorder and a television in one corner. He checked under them, then began examining the stack of video cassettes on the shelf above.

"Bingo," he sang out, holding up one of the cardboard cases. Instead of a cassette inside, there were five three-and-a-half-inch floppy disks. "One of these is labeled Logan," he said.

"Colin Logan?" she managed to ask.

He shook his head. "Just Logan. I guess whoever killed Francetti and searched the place assumed he'd gotten what he came for."

He looked at the computer on the short arm of the L-shaped desk.

"Don't even think about reading that here!" she warned.

"What if it's the wrong one?"

"We have to leave." As she started toward the door, a noise in the outer hallway made her freeze.

Matt had heard it, too. After sprinting to close the inner office door, he dashed to the window and pushed at the sash. It wouldn't budge, and he banged on the frame, then gave a mighty heave. To her relief, it slid up and he motioned her over.

Sliding past the desk with eyes averted, she took in the view. There was a full story drop to the pavement below.

"I can't go out that way," she said.

He took her by the shoulders and turned her to face him. "You have to. There isn't any other way. I'll catch you."

As he spoke he was already stepping out the window. She watched him lower his body so that he was hanging by his hands. Then he dropped from view.

She stood there, her heart pounding, knowing she couldn't do what he'd just done—not unless she risked harming the baby. Then she heard the outer door open and voices in the waiting room.

Chapter Seven

Fighting sheer, blind panic, Amanda looked wildly around the office, almost gagging as her gaze collided with the top of the dead man's head.

"Come on!" Matt called from below.

No, she almost screamed. Yet she took a step closer to the window and peered out. He was standing right below her, his arms outstretched. "I'll catch you," he said.

"You can't. The baby—"

"I'll catch you," he said again, his voice so calm that it pierced her agony of fear. *God, I should have listened to him in the first place. I never should have come here. I never should have risked my child's welfare.*

Even as the thoughts were going through her head, she was putting one leg out the window, then the other, because she had no choice.

She was lowering herself from the window frame when the door to the office burst open, and she found herself face-to-face with a uniformed policeman.

"They're getting away!" he shouted, drawing his gun.

As she looked down the barrel of the weapon, her fingers let go their death grip on the windowsill.

Screaming, she dropped like a stone. But Matt's strong arms were there to catch her, cushioning her fall, holding her upright, even as the policeman's head appeared above her.

"Stop or I'll shoot," he ordered.

Matt grabbed her hand and pulled her around the corner of the building. A fraction of a second later, shots rang out in the alley where they'd just been standing. Still pulling her along, he reached the old Ford and threw open the back door. Shoving her inside, he climbed behind the wheel, started the engine and backed up so quickly that he almost smashed into the wall behind them.

As he careened down the street she huddled in the back seat, hardly able to think beyond the sound of sirens that sprang up behind them. Matt pulled into a narrow street lined with warehouses. Screeching to a stop behind a parked car, he opened the back door of the Ford and pulled her out. Hastily he swung her into his arms, carried her to the second vehicle and stuffed her into the back again.

Slamming the door, he climbed behind the wheel, backing out of the space, and was on his way again in moments. Only this time he drove at a normal pace.

Amanda stared at him in shock.

"You had two cars and two sets of keys?" she asked stupidly.

"Yeah," he answered matter-of-factly.

She was still struggling to take it all in when she spotted a police car speeding toward them, its lights flashing. Cringing, she slid low in her seat, but the cruiser flashed by without a second look. Breathing hard, she pushed herself up again, wrapped her hands around her shoulders and tried to stop the shaking that racked her body.

"Are you okay?" Matt asked, looking in the rearview mirror. "I mean…you and the baby," he said in a thick voice.

She leaned back, closed her eyes and pressed her hand against her abdomen. "I think so," she answered.

"Good."

"I was afraid to jump out the window," she whispered.

"I know. But I knew I could break your fall."

"That was…a miracle."

"No. That was muscle mass. You can thank your friend Roy Logan for letting me keep up my weight training—at the gym where his hired thugs worked out."

Leaning back, she closed her eyes and took a deep breath. "How did you think of a second car?" she asked.

"The way things are going lately, I wasn't taking any chances."

The way things were going. Not so good since he'd hooked up with her. And now she'd just made their situation a lot worse.

"That policeman saw me," she said, struggling to speak around the giant knot in her throat. "He came through the door into the inner office."

"He saw me, too."

She dragged in a breath and let it out before going on. "Not from twelve feet away. Not face-to-face." After another strangled breath, she added, "I'm sorry. I should have listened to you. I should have stayed at the motel. Then you would have gotten away with no problem."

"Don't worry about it," he snapped.

"But—"

"I said leave it alone. What's done is done."

She nodded, staring at his rigid shoulders as she huddled into herself. More words flowed in and out of her mind, but she left them unspoken. Words weren't going to change anything now that she'd gotten them caught at Francetti's office.

Neither of them spoke as he pulled into the motel parking lot or as they entered their less than luxurious room.

Amanda dropped into the chair by the window, wishing there was somewhere else she could go. But escape was impossible.

Matt was pacing back and forth across the dingy carpet. When she caught a glimpse of his face, she saw it was an angry mask.

"I'm sorry," she said again, spreading her hands helplessly.

He stopped pacing and stood towering over her. "You don't

have to take responsibility for this latest fiasco. This is *my* mess. I was trying to help you. Now you're on the run from Roy Logan. On the run from Randolph Security, and on the run from the law.''

Her eyes widened as she took in his words. He wasn't mad at her. He was mad at himself—with no good reason. ''Matt, you can't be serious. You're the one who just saved me.''

''Yeah, and I'm the one who's almost gotten you killed two or three times in the last few days.''

''No.''

''How would you describe it?'' he growled.

''I'd say the two of us have run into some bad luck,'' she answered.

He combed his hand through his hair, paced to the window and lifted a venetian-blind slat before letting it fall back into place with a metallic click. As if he hadn't heard her, he said, ''Maybe I should leave you.''

''What?'' she asked, feeling a cold shiver slither down her spine.

''Find a safe place for you and clear out of your life.''

She felt as if she were standing in an elevator that had just plummeted fifty feet. ''No!''

He raised his head and studied her. ''You've been uncomfortable with me since the beginning. And lately you've been acting like you couldn't wait to get away from me.''

''No,'' she managed to state around the giant fist clamped around her windpipe. Then more strongly, ''That's not true.''

''Then what?'' He stood with his hands on his hips, large and formidable and very male, challenging her to tell him the truth.

Ducking her head, she took refuge by casting her gaze toward the floor. ''It's not you. It's me. I mean, I'm afraid to…trust what I'm feeling.''

But he wouldn't allow her to hide from him. ''Which is…?'' he pressed, the force of his dark gaze piercing her like a laser beam.

Clasping her hands to keep them from shaking, she moistened her dry lips with her tongue. Here it was. She had to tell him about her miserable past and risk everything. Or keep silent and risk even more.

Closing her eyes, she tried to shut out the painful images flashing through her brain. She had promised herself she would never tell anyone about them. And now…

Her heart felt as if it were going to pound its way through her chest. When she tried to take a full breath, it was impossible to pull enough air into her lungs.

Unable to look at him, she said in a halting voice, "Matt, when you went to school—" She stopped short, sure she couldn't go on. But somehow she braced herself enough to say it. "When you went to school, there was probably some kid that everybody else teased, made fun of, played jokes on. And it was okay, because everybody did it. So that kid didn't have any friends. And…that made her afraid to trust anybody except her family." She dipped her head, then forced herself to raise it again and stare in the direction of his face, though her vision was too blurred to see him clearly. "In Crowfoot that kid was me."

He shook his head in denial. "That can't be true."

"You think I'm lying?" she whispered, swiping her sweaty palms against her hips.

His face had been angry before. The expression wasn't much different now. "No. I just don't want to believe it."

"Right, you can't believe you're mixed up with the class geek."

"That's not what I mean at all," he denied.

As if in a dream she saw him reach for her, felt those strong arms of his pull her up and into his embrace.

Her own arms hung at her sides like lead weights, but she let her head fall to his shoulder.

"Why? Why did they do it to you?" he asked in a low voice.

She sighed. "Maybe it was because I was real scared that

first day in kindergarten. Then a few days later, I got sick and threw up on the floor. When I tried to run away, I fell down and slipped in it. They all started laughing about it. About me. And they never stopped, until—''

Again the sentence choked off, and again she had to collect herself before she could continue. ''In high school things were different. Some of the boys started being nice to me. They took me out on dates—but we didn't go anywhere except maybe a fast-food restaurant, then to park in some deserted pasture.'' She sucked in a breath and let it out. ''They wanted me to do stuff with them. And I thought they'd like me if I did.'' She felt his hand tighten on her arm. Still with her face averted, she added, ''I didn't go all the way with any of them. But I was thinking about it—until one day I was behind a column in the cafeteria. And three boys were at a table where I could hear them laughing and talking about me, comparing notes on what they'd gotten me to do.''

Her face was hot. Her throat was thick. And she was glad she didn't have to look him in the eye, because now he knew why she was such a failure at things that were as easy as breathing for everyone else.

He made a strangled sound and shifted away from her, and she braced for the feel of his hands on her shoulders, pushing her away. Instead he lifted her into his arms and cradled her against his chest as he crossed to one of the double beds in the room and lowered himself so that he could cuddle her against him.

Overwhelmed, she pressed her forehead against his chest, her breath ragged as his hands stroked over her hair, across her back and shoulders. ''I thought things might be different if I could get out of Crowfoot. I thought I was going to go away to college,'' she told him. ''Meet some people who didn't know me. Then my father got MS, and he became more and more dependent on me. He was sick for a long time, and I couldn't leave him. When he died last year, I realized I was thirty and I was never going to figure out how to have a relationship with a man.

"But I wanted to have a baby to take care of and love. A baby who would love me for myself. A baby who wouldn't know all the stories about me. So I started doing research on the Web, and I found that clinic in Cheyenne. You said I had guts to get pregnant that way, but really it was the only way I could imagine doing it."

"God, Amanda, I didn't have any idea."

The way he said it made her eyes brim and at the same time sent a flood of relief rushing through her. She'd been terrified to share her shameful secrets with him. But he hadn't reacted the way she'd expected. Not at all. Struggling to keep her voice even, she said, "Of course you didn't know. I was ashamed to tell you. I'm only telling you now because I need you to understand why I have to keep proving I'm as good as you are."

MATT CONTINUED to stroke her. "Thank you for telling me. Thank you for letting me understand," he said, feeling humbled by her admission. God, no wonder she'd been nervous about the way he was coming on to her.

"So that's why I had to go with you to Francetti's office," she said. "Because that's the only way I can relate to men. I have to act like everything is a contest. Or a horse race, or something. Only Francetti was dead, and I thought I was going to throw up. Like that day in school," she added with a gulp. "And then the police came, and I knew I'd really screwed up." She ended with a hollow little sob.

"No. We've been over that before. I shouldn't have let you put yourself in danger," he said, hearing the self-accusation in his own voice.

"I didn't give you any choice."

"Let's not argue about it. Deal?" Putting his hand under her chin, he tipped her face up and brushed his lips against hers very gently before drawing back again. Then he touched the corner of her eye with his knuckles, brushing away the tear that hovered there.

"And you thought I was like those sorry jerks in high school? That I was out for what I could get with you? Is that it?" he asked softly.

"I didn't want to believe that. But I didn't know what to think." She gulped. "I don't know how to tell the difference between something real and something fake."

"So you thought I was feeding you a line when I said I was attracted to you."

She nodded.

"And now you need to be sure that you can trust me, before we can work things out," he pressed, wanting everything out on the table now that he knew why she'd been so skittish of him.

"How can we work things out?"

He brushed his lips back and forth against hers, touched his tongue to the seam, holding back from doing more. "I guess I have to let you know what kind of guy I am—now that my brain isn't bouncing around inside my head, and I've got a little better handle on my impulse control."

"But I'm four months' pregnant. And I haven't ever—"

"Let a man get close enough to hurt you—since those guys in high school," he finished for her, and saw heat creep into her cheeks.

Again she managed a little nod.

He stroked his knuckle against her cheek, then across her lips. "I'm very lucky you waited for me," he said in a husky voice, meaning it.

"But—"

"It's going to work out okay. I promise."

"You mean if the police don't come bursting in here and arrest us!" she blurted.

"Well, there is that," he answered easily, doing his best to appear unconcerned about their fugitive status. He settled her more comfortably in his arms.

"But they're looking for us! And it's my fault."

"Shh," he soothed. "They're not going to burst into every cheap motel room in Denver. They're not going to find us tonight. And even if they did, they couldn't prove anything. We had on gloves, so there are no fingerprints."

"But they saw us."

"One uniformed cop got a quick look at you when you were hanging outside a window in the dark. And he couldn't see much of me in that alley. Not with the low light."

"You're trying to stop me from worrying."

He allowed himself a small grin. "It's a reasonable strategy. But I'm also telling the truth."

"We have to figure out who killed Francetti and why," she insisted.

"But we can't do it now. We need a computer to read those disks, and my laptop was in the pickup I left at your ranch. You think I should go out and steal another one?" he teased.

"Of course not."

"Then what we're going to do is hole up here tonight. Tomorrow I'm going to get you out of town," he promised as he skimmed his lips along her jaw, then made a foray back to her lower lip for a quick nibble. "Four months?" he asked, changing the subject adroitly as he reached down to cup his hand over her abdomen, seeing how she reacted to the intimate touch. "I would have guessed three."

He felt a tiny shiver go through her, but her voice sounded steady. "The doctor says I'm carrying small."

"I always heard that good things come in small packages."

Before she could respond, he brought his lips back to hers, and this time he was more serious as he rubbed his mouth against hers, then used his tongue to nudge her open so that he could sweep along the sensitive tissue of her inner lips, tasting her, feeling her response.

The touch was gentle, but it kindled a fire in his veins.

"Matt, what are we doing?" she asked with a breathy little

gasp that told him the kisses were having a similar effect on her.

Taking our minds off the police out there looking for us, he thought. What he said was, "Fooling around a little." Finding her ear with his teeth, he took some delicious liberties.

"But you're not going to…" Her cheeks turned rosy. "I mean…"

"Naw, we're just doing some stuff I've been wanting to do since I saw you that first time at the post office." He ended by coming back to her mouth for a long, drugging kiss that left her breath coming in shallow pants.

"Matt, I'm not sure I can handle this." She looked down at their bodies—the noticeable shaft of rigid flesh at the front of his jeans and her legs meshed with his.

He held himself very still.

"I mean lying on a bed with you," she clarified. "Letting you do anything you want."

"Okay. I understand." He eased away from her, keeping a poker face as he saw her disappointment war with relief. "We should both get some sleep, because I want to be out of here early in the morning."

She nodded, watching him as he stood and stretched. He went into the bathroom, cooled off under a cold shower and emerged wearing his shorts and shirt. Casually he turned off the lamp on the nightstand, took off the shirt and climbed into the bed opposite Amanda, when what he wanted to do was crawl in with her and wrap her in his arms.

He could watch her in the shaft of light from the bathroom, watch her collect her knapsack and close the bathroom door behind her. When he heard the shower, he tried not to picture her under the running water, tried not to imagine the way her breasts and her belly would look with the water cascading down them. But he couldn't rid himself of the erotic image, or his erection.

The light creeping in around the shade was enough to let him see her emerge. Through slitted eyes he saw that she was wearing her gown and robe. Quickly she slipped off the latter and scooted under the covers.

Then they were both lying in the dark a few feet away from each other. He knew from her breathing that she wasn't asleep. Probably she knew he was awake, too.

He had a lot to think about, a lot of plans to make. But it was difficult to concentrate on them when he was so aware of the woman in the other bed.

"Matt?" she whispered.

"Yeah?"

"I…" Instead of finishing the sentence, she climbed out of her own bed and into his. Rolling toward him, she pressed her face against his naked shoulder. Within seconds he was hard as a rock again.

"Will you make love to me?" she asked in a strangled voice.

"No."

"What do you mean, no? I worked up my courage to come over here, and you tell me no."

"I thought you said you couldn't handle lying in bed with me."

"I changed my mind," she answered, her hand coming up to touch his cheek, his lips, then sliding down to lightly touch the hair that spread across his chest. It was only a tentative touch, but it drove him toward the point of no return.

Through gritted teeth he said, "Do you know that when you play with fire, you can get burned?"

"What's that supposed to mean?" she demanded.

"That I don't want you to have any reason to think I took advantage of you. And I don't want you to feel you have to prove anything to yourself. Or to me. Not tonight. Not when you're too vulnerable to know what you want."

She rolled away from him and started to rise from the bed. "I guess I made a mistake."

His hand whipped out and captured her wrist. Before she could protest, he pulled her back, pulled her hips tight against him, letting her feel his erection as he slanted his lips over hers, dizzy with hunger as he devoured her mouth, tasting his own need and hers and all the sweetness of a summer day in the high country.

"Matt, oh, Matt," she sighed when he lifted his mouth.

"I started things too fast with you, and this isn't an improvement," he said, hearing the strain in his own voice. He should turn her loose. But that was becoming more difficult by the moment.

His hands drifted to the front of her gown, drifted to her breasts. Through the cotton fabric, they were as firm and tantalizing as he remembered. And he couldn't stop himself from cupping them, squeezing gently, then brushing his fingers back and forth across the hardened tips.

She sucked in a strangled breath, pressed herself into his palms, and the thin cotton became more of a barrier than he could stand. Unable to deny himself the pleasure of touching her, he kissed her again, while his fingers undid the row of buttons at the top of the gown. Pushing the fabric aside, he cupped her, caressed her. Bending, he swirled his tongue around one distended nipple, then sucked it into his mouth.

The feel, the texture, the taste of her were heaven on earth. But once he'd tasted and touched, it wasn't nearly enough. Deep in his heart, he'd known it wouldn't be—which was why he'd tried to send her back to her own bed.

He wanted to strip off her gown, press the length of her naked body to his. But he thought that would be too much for her. So he found himself reaching under the hem of the gown, stroking the curve of her calf and then her thigh, working his way toward the juncture of her legs.

When his hand settled over the triangle of curly hair, he felt her jump. But now he was the one who had control. Distracting her with another passionate kiss, he slid his fingers against the wet, welcoming folds of her most intimate flesh, stroking and pressing before slipping a finger inside her.

Her tiny gasp made his hand still.

"Did I hurt you?"

"No."

"Good, that's good," he murmured, moving his finger, testing the resistance of the barrier.

Then keeping his own body under rigid control, he took a gliding stroke that made her quiver in his arms—then another, and another. He found the pressure and the pace and the angle that worked for her, pushing her higher and then higher still, until she was clutching his arms, pressing frantically against his hand.

He took her over the top, drank in her cries of release, wishing he could see her face as she came undone for him. As she settled back against the mattress, he kissed her cheek, her jaw, the tender curl of her ear.

She was silent for long seconds, then whispered, "Matt?"

"Mmm?" he tried to make his voice lazy, but there was no way to completely disguise the tension coursing through his body.

"Why did you do that?"

"I wanted to love you—without making any demands."

He heard her swallow in the darkness. "Every time you kissed me, you made me feel…wonderful. I came to bed with you because I wanted to feel more of what you were giving me. I just didn't know it could be that intense."

He brought her hand to his lips and kissed her palm. "There's going to be more. When we get to know each other a little better."

She gave a little laugh. "I can't imagine more."

"Trust me."

"I do," she said, her voice turning serious. "Or I wouldn't have come over here." She shifted against him, raised her head so that she was looking down at him, her face shadowed in the darkness. "The guys I was with…the ones I told you about—"

"You don't have to tell me any more about it."

Ignoring him, she went on. "They said that if I didn't…

uh…take care of them, they'd be in pain all night. Were they lying to me?"

He felt his face heat and was glad she couldn't see that in the darkness. "I'm not a randy teenager."

"No, you're a very generous and a very honorable man," She said, her hand sliding down his chest. Then lower, making the muscles of his abdomen jump. When she found his erection, she pressed him with her palm, rocking it back and forth against him, making the ache he felt a hundred times worse.

"Don't," he gasped, struggling not to thrust his hips against that tantalizing hand.

"I want to," she said, her voice warm with the honey quality he loved so much. Then she stopped any further protest with her mouth on his. Using the trick he'd just taught her, she kept kissing him as she eased down his briefs so that she could wrap her hand around his heated flesh.

"I never wanted to do this before. I want to do it now," she whispered against his mouth. "Please, let me."

He could only utter a strangled exclamation as she began to move her hand, doing what he had done for her, finding a rhythm that pleased him, that sent him blasting off into space like an out-of-control rocket ship.

When his breathing returned to normal, she snuggled against him.

"Thank you," she murmured.

He stroked his lips against her cheek, feeling peaceful and relaxed for the first time since he'd overheard Logan's conversation with Hewitt. "I think that's my line."

He felt her facial muscles work and knew she was smiling. "Well, yours, too." The smile faded again, and her voice turned serious. "Thank you for letting me do that with somebody I care about. Thank you for letting me feel like it was a good thing to do, not something I knew I was going to feel bad about later."

He felt his throat close, felt moisture sting his eyes. He slid his hand up and down her arm, the contact as much for himself as for her. She was one of the most remarkable women he'd ever met. Though it looked as if the town of Crowfoot had done its best to kill her spirit, she'd found her own way to survive.

Again he was glad of the darkness as he slipped his arm around her and held her close, knowing that she wasn't going to like what he had to tell her in the morning.

Chapter Eight

Amanda awoke to a feeling of panic—and knew immediately what was wrong. The bed was empty. Turning her head, she saw the impression of Matt's head on the other pillow. But he was gone. All the fears she'd dismissed last night came slamming back to her.

She pushed herself up, looked around the room, craned her head toward the bathroom. He wasn't in there. And she knew with a certainty that pierced her heart that last night he'd taken advantage of her. As soon as she'd gotten into bed with him, he'd known how it was going to end up—because he was a man and men made demands on women, whether they used pressure or more subtle techniques.

She was strung as tight as banjo wire, but she squeezed her eyes closed and willed herself to stop letting the past intrude on the here and now. She wasn't a teenager trying to get the boys in Crowfoot to like her. She was a woman—with excellent judgment. And she knew that what had happened between herself and Matt last night had been honest—and good. No matter what happened, she'd have that midnight encounter with him to remember.

Still, that didn't stop her from coming up with another very plausible reason why he'd left her. Maybe until this morning, he hadn't thought about the implications of her pregnancy. She was carrying another man's baby—Colin Logan's baby. And

Matt had finally realized the long-term consequences of getting tangled up with her. If he stayed with her, he'd be raising another man's child. A man who wasn't worth the spit to say his name.

That was something else she was going to have to deal with. But not now. She couldn't face that now.

Lowering her head, she cupped her face in her hands. Matt had done things in bed with her that she'd never enjoyed before—never thought she would enjoy until he'd started touching her and kissing her. But that didn't mean she was justified in thinking in terms of a lifetime commitment.

Sliding to the edge of the bed, she was about to push herself up when she heard a key in the lock. Swinging her legs back, she clutched at the cover as Matt stepped into the room.

"Where were you?" she demanded, then saw the white paper bags in his hand.

"Getting breakfast," he answered.

"I thought—" She cut off the sentence and began again. "I didn't know where you were!"

"I left you a note."

She cast her glance around the room, seeing nothing.

"Where I thought you'd find it. On the bathroom sink," he clarified.

"Oh." Throwing herself out of bed, she dashed into the bathroom and slammed the door. The note was where Matt said it would be.

It told her not to worry. He was getting something to eat, and he'd be back as soon as he could.

She folded it up and clutched it in her palm. Then she made a hurried attempt at getting herself in some kind of order.

When she emerged once more, Matt had set the food on the small table against the wall. He looked up as she came back, and she felt his eyes on her, burning through the thin fabric of her gown. Crossing to the bed she'd abandoned, she snatched up her robe and thrust her arms through the sleeves.

But she didn't tie the belt, since that would only emphasize the roundness of her tummy.

Matt had brought her orange juice, a container of herb tea and a country breakfast—two eggs over, ham and fluffy white biscuits.

She slid into the seat across the table and began spreading plum preserves on a biscuit, watching him take a sip of coffee, then cut a piece of ham and some egg, forking the two up in one bite.

When he'd chewed the mouthful, he raised his head. "Were you worried about where I'd gone?"

Lying was beyond her. "Yes."

"I'm sorry."

"It's not your fault. I told you—it's me."

His jaw tightened. "I keep thinking about the guys I've seen on the street in Crowfoot and wondering which ones I should beat the crap out of for hurting you like that."

"Matt, it was a long time ago."

"And you're still dealing with it."

"I—"

"You told me you have trouble relating to men. So I'll give you a hint about how to deal with me. Just be honest. And never do anything that feels wrong because you think it's what I want."

She swallowed and nodded, then concentrated on the biscuit. It was sinfully buttery.

They ate in silence for several minutes, but it wasn't really an uncomfortable silence, she decided. Then she saw the folded *Denver Post* he'd laid on the floor beside his chair.

"Did the murder make the paper?" she asked.

"Yeah."

"I want to read about it."

He gave her a pained look, then handed across the newspaper. The article about private detective Tim Francetti's murder was on page one. She winced when she saw the headline and the head shot that looked like an old publicity photo.

When she got to the part about a male and a female suspect escaping, she forgot to breathe. "We're right here in the paper!"

"That's stretching things a bit. They don't have any names."

Willing her hand not to shake, she went back to the story. "They say I'm blond. Midtwenties."

"You look young."

"But—"

"They don't have anything else. No fingerprints. Just that pretty blond hair of yours. You could dye it brown, and nobody would know."

"I'm not going to expose the baby to hair dye!"

His face contorted. "Sorry, I wasn't thinking about that."

She went back to the article and poked at a line of text with her index finger. "They have a description of the Ford."

"We're not driving it anymore," he said patiently.

"Where did you get it?"

"From a private sale. And I didn't use my real name."

"You carry enough money around to buy a car?"

"Yeah. I may not be able to get to my bank accounts, but I'm prepared for emergencies."

"What if—?" She stopped and swallowed. "What if somebody starts going back through the cases Francetti was investigating?"

"The pertinent files are missing, remember?"

She nodded.

Matt picked up his biscuit, took a bite and made an appreciative noise.

"How can you sit there calmly eating?" she asked.

"I'm hungry. I was engaged in a lot of strenuous activity last night."

She felt her heart thump, wondering which activity he was referring to, exactly. Burglary—or what they'd been doing in bed? She wanted to call it making love. At least it was as close as she'd come to making love. When she saw him watching her, she took a gulp of orange juice.

"Eat up," he said. "We've got a long day ahead of us."

"Do we?"

"Yeah," he allowed between mouthfuls.

"What are we going to be doing?"

He sighed, set down his plastic fork and reached across the table for her hand. She braced for the bad news she was certain he'd been holding back.

"There are a couple of factors I've been considering," he said. "The first one is that we need money. A lot of money."

"You're telling me you're going to rob a bank?" she asked, only half in jest.

He flashed a grin. "I'm not into stealing money—at least from banks. But you may have noticed, I have a pretty good poker face."

"Poker?"

"Yeah. I've got a talent for cards. So I'm going to get into some high-stakes games at various casinos around the west—not Las Vegas, where they'd pay too much attention to me the minute I started winning. Some of the casinos run by Native American tribes in California, Colorado, New Mexico, Montana, maybe Iowa." He shifted in his seat. "I can't stay in any one place too long because guys who lose to me are going to be angry. Some of them are going to think I'm cheating." He raised his eyes to hers. "And I can't have a pregnant woman with me, because that will draw more attention than a single guy." His fingers tightened on her hand. "So I need to leave you someplace safe while I spend a couple of weeks getting us enough cash to last through the winter."

"A couple of weeks!"

"I've been thinking about where to take you. It has to be someplace that I haven't been before, someplace that's not going to show up in my background check from Randolph Security. I remember a friend talking about a fishing camp he liked up on Lake La Platta. Henry's Camp, I think it's called.

"We can get you a cabin up there, somewhere you can walk to the grocery store, but where you don't have to interact with the neighbors. You can tell them you're a novelist working on a book and you came up there for peace and quiet."

"An artist."

"Okay, an artist. I'll register you as Mrs. Matthews, so nobody will think anything about your tummy."

He made it sound perfectly reasonable, yet she felt her stomach clench as he added details to the proposal that he'd obviously been thinking about for a while. She wanted to refuse. Then she reminded herself that she'd always been independent and that a couple of weeks away from him might help her sort out her tangled feelings.

So she gave her agreement, then tried to get down some more of her breakfast, because she knew she'd be hungry later if she didn't.

PARTLY AS A DELAYING TACTIC, she made Matt stop at a store where she could buy art supplies: watercolor paints, acrylics and plenty of paper.

Then they started for Lake La Platta, west into the mountains. They arrived at Henry's Camp in the middle of the afternoon, and Matt checked out the area, then made arrangements to rent a cabin with a spectacular view of the sparkling blue lake backed by towering mountains. Inside the cabin were a living room and bedroom with rustic furnishings and a small kitchen and bath.

"Are you going to leave right away?" Amanda asked Matt as he carried a box of groceries and set it on the counter in the small kitchen.

"I want to get in some travel time before it gets dark."

"You've already been driving most of the day," she objected. "You must be tired."

"I won't push too hard," he promised, then moved to capture her in his arms. "I've got something else to tell you," he said, the tone of his voice alerting her that she wasn't going to like what she heard any more than she'd liked the news that they were going to be separated for a few weeks. "I won't be able to contact you while I'm gone."

She felt her chest constrict. "Why not?"

"It's too dangerous. Logan may have hired someone with sophisticated satellite tracking equipment looking for us."

She gasped. "Can they do that?"

"A few months ago, it happened to a friend of mine," he answered, telling her something about Scott O'Donnell and Mariana Reyes, who had lived on the run while they tried to avoid an assassination squad as they'd desperately looked for their kidnapped daughter.

The story made her shudder.

"I don't want Logan or the police tracking you down," Matt said, pulling her close and nibbling at her cheek with his lips.

"You said the police don't know who I am!"

"They don't. But I'm not taking any chances."

"Don't leave tonight," she said, covering her fear by moving closer, letting him know that she wanted him in her bed.

He turned his head to capture her lips, and for long moments she thought she'd persuaded him to stay with her—at least for the night.

Then he drew back slightly. "You're making a real tempting offer," he murmured.

"Am I?"

"Oh, yeah."

She wound her arms around his neck and lifted her face. This time there was more desperation in her kiss.

Raising his head, he outlined the shape of her lips with his finger. "I'd be rushing things again," he said, his voice husky.

"You're not rushing anything. I'm trying my darnedest to seduce you. But I'm not very good at it."

"Oh, you're good at it, all right. And it's almost a crime not to give in. But how about giving me something to look forward to when I come back?'' That said, he kissed her very thoroughly, his hands roving over her until she was trembling.

When he eased away again, she struggled to catch her breath and to adjust to the reality that they weren't going to finish what they'd started last night—not now.

''I'm going to worry about you,'' she said. ''I mean, somebody who lost to you at poker could come after you.''

''They won't. And if they do, I can handle it.''

She wanted to protest again, but she knew that saying more was only going to make him edgy.

He eased away, separating them by mere inches. But it suddenly felt like miles. Gravely she watched as he took out his wallet and counted a thousand dollars. ''This should hold you till I get back in two weeks. Or maybe sooner.''

Her eyes widened. ''I guess you carry a lot of money.''

''Some of this is from Hewitt.''

She nodded, then asked the question she didn't want to ask. ''If you don't come back, what should I do?''

His answer was immediate. ''Call Randolph Security.''

''But we're running away from them!''

''I am. You're an innocent bystander.'' He thought for a moment. ''Try to speak to Hunter Kelley.''

''The man who was calling to you from the helicopter?''

''Yeah. He was just doing his job because nobody at Randolph had time to find out that Logan was lying to them before they arrived at the ranch. But if you tell him what Logan was planning to do to you, he'll be sympathetic.''

''Why?''

''Because he knows what it's like to be held in captivity by men who have no scruples.''

She waited for him to go on, but he shook his head.

''You'll have to ask Hunter about what happened to him. It's not something we publicize.''

''Oh,'' she answered, wondering what secret Hunter Kelley was hiding.

Matt squeezed her arm. ''I'd better go. I'll be back as soon as I get us a stake. I promise.'' He looked at the watch strapped to his wrist. "On or before July twentieth.''

She reached to touch his face, then gave him a quick kiss.

Without prolonging the moment of parting, he turned and walked out the door, leaving her feeling alone and scared.

She watched him drive away until he disappeared around a bend in the road. Then, with a hollow feeling in her chest, she walked down to the edge of the lake and stared at the blue water shimmering in the afternoon sunshine.

It was beautiful. Peaceful. But she didn't feel at peace. Before Matt had whisked her away from the Double B Ranch, she'd been content with the road she'd mapped out for herself. Now she was deviled by longings and uncertainties that were frightening in their intensity.

It's only two weeks, she told herself. *You can get through two weeks on your own.* But she knew that something fundamental had changed inside her when that helicopter had swooped down on the ranch house.

She'd been frightened and hurt in the past, but she'd trained herself to deal with it on her own. Then Roy Logan had threatened her child—and she didn't know how to deal with *that* by herself. She needed help. Specifically from Matt Forester, and the feeling of dependence was as frightening to her as anything she'd ever encountered in her life.

IN THE FIRST FEW DAYS after Matt's departure, Amanda was able to keep the gnawing worry under reasonable control— because she knew she was perfectly capable of managing on her own for the short term. She'd always wanted more time for her art, and kept busy with her paints and by searching through the woods and along the shore of the lake, bringing home pretty pebbles, bits of driftwood and other natural materials she arranged into collages.

She was pleased with the results, and eager to show them to Matt. But at the same time she couldn't help wondering if he was going to think they were a waste of time.

As the deadline for his return came nearer, though, she found herself spending more and more time staring down the road, looking for his car. Or listening for the sound of his footsteps on the gravel path or the wide boards of the porch.

The afternoon of July 20, she splurged on an expensive beef roast at Lingrand's grocery store a quarter mile down the road.

The roast was in the oven at six, and potatoes went in an hour and a half later. But by nine o'clock, Matt hadn't arrived, and Amanda ended up putting the food in the refrigerator.

He was delayed a little, she told herself, fighting the vise clamping her chest as she stood on the porch, watching the trail of light cast by the moon on the water.

But he didn't come the next day, or the next. And when the manager of the camp came to ask if she was intending to stay longer than the two weeks originally agreed on, she forked over another three hundred dollars from her supply of cash.

Lying in bed that night, her stomach in knots, she tried to send out a mental message to Matt, telling him how worried she was and how much she needed to talk to him. But there were no calls for ''Mrs. Matthews'' at the pay phone outside the grocery store.

Give him one more day, she told herself. So she forced herself to simply stay there and wait for him, until her nerves were as ragged as a wool coat full of moth holes.

On the fourth day after Matt's deadline, she seriously debated whether to call Randolph Security—writing down the pros and cons on a piece of paper, including the voice over the bullhorn booming down from the helicopter above Roy Logan's cabin. That had been Hunter Kelley urging Matt to turn himself in. Hunter Kelley—the same man Matt had told her to contact. Every time she started down the road to the pay phone, she remembered that threatening voice ringing down like the wrath of heaven—and she turned back.

Lying in bed the next night, unable to sleep, feeling the baby kicking inside her, feeling cut off from everything familiar, everything safe, she couldn't cope on her own any longer. In the morning she got up early, washed her face and walked down to the phone by the grocery. Needing to hear the voice of someone she trusted, she called the Double B Ranch.

Ed Stanton answered on the first ring, as though he'd been sitting by the phone since she'd left, waiting for her to call.

"Where are you?" were the first words out of his mouth.

Although she'd been eager to talk to Ed, something about the way he demanded the information set her nerves on edge.

"I can't tell you," she answered, her voice suddenly guarded.

He met the flat statement with silence.

"Ed, don't you want to know how I am?" she asked.

"Yeah. Right. I do."

"I'm fine," she lied. "How about you?"

"Your friend Forester gave me a concussion."

"Like you gave him," she countered.

"He was the one sneakin' up on the house. Then he set off that explosion and beat up Al Hewitt."

She sighed. "Let's not get into all that. Ed, I wanted to talk to you about the ranch."

"Sure," he answered.

"Can I count on you to keep things running? You can draw on the working account that Dad set up for your signature."

"You should come back," Ed answered.

"I can't. Probably not for a few months. Will you be there for me, Ed?"

"I'll do for you just like I've always done—but don't hang up. We have to talk about stuff."

"I know you can take care of anything that comes up," she answered, then replaced the receiver in the cradle.

It had been a stiff conversation, nothing like what she had anticipated, and as she went back in her mind over the things they'd said, she fought the gut feeling that she shouldn't have phoned him.

MATT'S FINGERS CLENCHED around the steering wheel of the used pickup truck he'd acquired in New Mexico. As he approached the rustic wooden sign that marked the turnoff to Henry's Camp, he could feel his heart rate accelerate. He was six days late, and he knew that Amanda was probably frantic. Probably angry, too. Because that was the way she would react, given her previous experience with men.

God, what if she'd panicked and left? What if she'd decided that he'd ditched her? What the hell was he going to do then?

More than once he'd longed to take a chance and reach for the phone on the bedside table in his motel room to tell her he was going to be delayed. But he'd known he'd have to give a reason why. And he wasn't prepared to lie—or to tell her about the knife fight in Albuquerque.

He'd imagined that conversation.

"A guy tried to take my leg off with a knife. And the wound got infected. But everything's okay now, because I got a greedy pharmacist to give me antibiotics. So the infection's under control. Don't worry about me. I'll be there as soon as I can stand up without toppling over."

He'd spared her the long-distance worry. But when his temperature had climbed to 104, he'd started to hallucinate, imagining her on the bed with him, holding his shaking body. God, he'd never needed anyone more than he needed her then. But he'd gritted his teeth and pulled himself through—because she was waiting here for him.

He'd gotten a couple of hours' sleep last night, and he'd driven since early in the morning to get back to her today. Fatigue dragged at him, but his nerves were humming as he took the turnoff to Henry's Camp.

He was so focused on getting to her cabin that he almost missed the knot of men congregated around the phone at the grocery store. Then something about the way they huddled together like football players getting a play caught his attention. Something was up—and he suddenly had the bad feeling that it might involve Amanda.

He warned himself not to jump to conclusions even as he jammed a Broncos cap onto his head, parked on a side road, then made his way back on foot toward the small commercial center that served Henry's Camp.

Cursing his weak right leg, he concealed himself behind a screen of pine trees as he approached the store.

The first man he recognized was Ed Stanton, Amanda's ranch manager—the grizzled little man who'd bashed him over the head first and asked questions later. Stanton was talking to Al Hewitt and several other guys that Matt knew worked for Logan.

Well, wasn't that interesting? Stanton and Hewitt.

The hairs on the back of his neck rose as he edged closer, trying to hear the conversation. But it was hopeless. They were speaking in low tones, and he couldn't get close enough without being seen.

Matt considered his options, then ducked around the side of the grocery. Just before he reached the soft-drink cooler, two boys who looked to be about ten years old burst through the door, chattering excitedly.

Figuring he had nothing to lose, he pointed toward the front of the building. "Say, do you know what's going on out there?" he asked, striving for innocent curiosity.

"Sure," the taller one allowed. "I heard a couple of them asking Mr. Lingrand questions about that woman, Mrs. Matthews, who's been living in the cabin up the road. One of them said she's his wife and she ran away."

"He says she can do whatever she wants—after she has the baby," the other one chimed in.

Matt's mouth went dry, but he fought to keep his voice even. "So why are they standing around the phone?" he asked. "Why don't they just go get her?"

"They will. But I think they want…uh…this guy, Ed, to go up there first and talk to her. Get her to go quietly. At least, that's what I heard," the first boy clarified, looking embarrassed, and Matt knew they'd probably been avidly eavesdropping on the fascinating adult conversation.

Matt swallowed. "Pretty big stuff for Henry's Camp," he allowed.

"Yeah."

The boys scuffed their feet. "Gotta go," the first one said.

"See you around," Matt answered, turning back the way he'd come. Ed was still getting instructions from Hewitt, so Matt had a little time, he hoped.

Keeping a lid on his raw emotions, he retraced his steps and stared at the truck. He'd been planning on driving Amanda out of here. That didn't look like an option anymore, not with Logan's guys able to give hot pursuit.

The only way out was the lake. But where was that going to leave them when they got to the other side?

Exasperated, he looked around and spotted a gas station down the street. As he eyed the place, a more elaborate plan began to form in his mind. Pulling his cap down low to conceal his features and jamming on his sunglasses, he drove past the group of men, who were too intent on their conversation to pay him any mind. At the station, he stopped near one of the repair bays where three teenagers hovered around an SUV with the hood up.

One was working, while the other two were shooting the breeze.

"Anybody interested in making some money?" he called out in a friendly tone.

"How?" the taller of the spectators asked.

"Driving this truck to the other side of the lake."

The kid definitely looked interested.

Matt swung easily into the story he'd thought up only moments ago. "I'm planning to take my wife fishing. Then we're heading west. It'll be quicker if we leave from over there."

"If I take your truck over, how do I get back?"

"You can take the boat back to the rental dock."

As the kid thought it over, Matt added, "I'll give you fifty dollars now. And another hundred when we pick up the truck.''

"A hundred and fifty!''

"I need you to start over there now, 'cause we're ready to move out,'' Matt answered.

"Okay. You've got a deal.''

Matt climbed out of the truck, taking his pack. "I'm Mark Waverly,'' he said, holding out his hand.

"Jerry Tucker,'' the teen answered, shaking hands.

"Park at the Yuma campground,'' Matt directed, glad that he'd studied the geography of the lake and knew where there were other pockets of civilization.

Tucker nodded, and Matt extracted a fifty from his wallet, and handed it over.

"You get there before we do, you get a bonus,'' he said, handing over his keys.

"You bet!''

As Tucker slid behind the wheel, Matt wondered if he could trust the guy. But he really had no other option.

Before the truck was out of sight, he headed for the boat dock, cursing the bum leg that kept his speed down. He hadn't walked much since the knifing, and his thigh was beginning to throb. Ignoring the pain, he climbed down a short flight of steps to a weathered shack.

"Anybody home?'' he called.

No one answered, and the attendant who took care of the rentals was nowhere in sight—which was good. No explanations. No conversations. No lies about when he'd be back. Matt peeled off another hundred dollars and left it on the desk. Then he selected a sweet little speedboat and topped off the gas tank. After casting off the ropes, he pulled away from the pier and headed toward Amanda's cabin.

The short ride along the rocky shoreline gave him time for unwelcome thoughts. About Ed and Logan's men. And how they'd found Amanda. He cut off the speculation as he reached her private dock and cut the engine.

The gravel path to the cabin was uphill—another grueling workout for his damn leg. When he reached the porch, he was disgusted to realize he was sweating. He gave himself thirty seconds to cool down, then clenched his fists as he put his full weight on the leg. It would hold, he decided. Long enough for him to sit down in the boat again.

Realizing he was stalling and that he couldn't afford the luxury, he pushed open the door, calling out Amanda's name as he entered.

She was sitting in the rocking chair in the living room, her arms wrapped around her shoulders. As he stepped through the doorway, her head jerked up. When she saw it was him, she sprang to her feet, hands on her hips, the action pulling the fabric of her shirt tight across her prominent middle.

"Matt! Where the hell have you been?" Anger and relief mingled in her voice. It was the reaction he'd been dreading— the reaction he'd been expecting.

"I know you're riled."

"Riled! That's an interesting way to put it."

"Honey, believe me, I got here as soon as I could. But I don't have time to explain now."

Her eyes flashed. "You've got a nerve calling me honey. You leave me here for three weeks and you don't have time to tell me why."

"Two weeks and six days. But I'm here now. And we have to leave—before it's too late."

"Right. Distract the woman by making up an emergency."

He laughed sharply. "Believe me, I'm not making anything up."

"How long did you expect me to stay here waiting for you? Groceries here are outrageous. Next week I would have been down to five hundred dollars. Was I supposed to ask Mr. Lingrand if I could get a job scrubbing the floor in the grocery store?"

"Of course not!"

"Then what?"

"I would have thought of something."

She came back with some answer he didn't hear, because all his attention suddenly focused on the path. Ed Stanton was about fifty yards away, bearing down on the cabin with a nervous look in his lying eyes. How far behind was the wolf pack?

Chapter Nine

"Damn!"

"What's wrong?"

"Your friend Stanton is outside. That's going to mean a change in plans," he muttered.

"Ed? Here?" she asked, her voice suddenly guilty.

"In the flesh. And he's come with a bunch of Logan's men."

Amanda pressed her hand to her mouth. "No! He wouldn't. He said—"

"Don't tell me you were dumb enough to talk to him," he snapped, immediately regretting the choice of words.

She gave him a defiant look. "When you didn't come back, I had to talk to someone I trusted."

"You picked the wrong guy! He's here to scoop you up."

"No!"

A knock on the door cut off the argument.

Matt lowered his voice. "Either you trust me, or you trust him. And if you trust me, get him to come in." Stepping behind the door, he shifted the pack off his shoulder and set it on the floor. From under his shirt, he drew the gun tucked in the waistband of his pants. "And whatever you do, don't let him get you outside."

Amanda shot him a look he couldn't read. Then her hand

was on the doorknob, and there was nothing he could do but trust her.

"Ed, what are you doing here?" she asked, her voice ringing with surprise as she opened the door.

"I came to persuade you to do the right thing and come back." Through the crack between the door and the frame, Matt could see the ranch foreman take a step forward, but he stopped before he reached the threshold.

Come in, you bastard, Matt silently urged.

Amanda echoed the invitation, trying to draw him nearer with her body language.

Stanton stayed planted where he was, his hands in his back pockets as he took in Amanda's appearance. "You didn't tell anyone you were pregnant," he accused. "You could have told me."

"I was going to."

The man's head bobbed.

"How did you know where to find me?" she asked.

"Well…"

Before he could finish, she stepped back. "Let's not talk out here."

To Matt's vast relief, Stanton followed her inside. As the door closed, Matt stepped forward, pressing the barrel of the gun into the foreman's back. "Don't move. And don't do anything that's going to alert your friends down the road."

"You!" Stanton spat.

"Surprise." Matt kept his gaze on the man as he spoke to Amanda. "Is there anything we can use to tie his hands?"

"Rope, in the pantry."

"Get it." God, the last thing they needed was a hostage— unless he could turn it to his advantage.

"Can you keep him covered while I tie him up?" he asked when she returned.

"Yes," she said, her voice firmer than he'd expected.

Giving her the gun, he tied the intruder's hands, then took back the weapon and explained what they were going to do.

"There's a boat at the dock. We're going out the back door. Stanton first. Then me. Then Amanda. Don't try anything funny," he warned the foreman, "or you'll end up with a bullet in the kneecap. I promise."

Stanton gave him a deadly look, but he followed orders. When they reached the boat, Matt directed Amanda to the bow, then helped Stanton into the middle where he could keep an eye on him.

Casting off, he jumped in, grimacing as his bad leg came down too hard on the metal seat.

"You won't get away," Stanton spit out.

"How long have you been working for Roy Logan?" Matt asked as he steered the boat.

Stanton clamped his mouth shut.

"How much is he paying you?"

When the foreman didn't answer, Matt raised his head, throwing Amanda an inquiring glance. "Can he swim?"

"Not with my hands tied," Ed yelped.

"Well, you're going to give it a try—unless you start talking," Matt told him calmly. "How long have you been working for Roy Logan?" he asked again as he cut the engine speed.

He saw Stanton swallow. "Don't throw me in. I'll tell you! Logan called when he found out about the baby. He told me he'd pay good to keep Miss Amanda at the ranch."

"And now your duties have somewhat expanded," Matt pointed out as he speeded up again.

Stanton's eyes flashed. "It ain't right to deprive a man of his grandchild."

"What a touching sentiment," Matt growled. "Is that why you let Logan tap the phone at the ranch?"

Stanton looked daggers at him. "That's right."

Behind Stanton, Amanda gasped.

"And you kept her on the phone long enough so Logan could locate her. Then you led his men here."

Amanda gave her foreman a piercing look. "Ed, you were

like family to me. Why did you do it?'' she asked, her tone stricken.

His face registered defiance—and apology. ''Do you know what it's like to work hard all your life and watch somebody else get the benefit? Your pa owed me. You owed me. I figured I'd never collect from you. But Logan came through with cash.''

''How much did you sell me for?'' Amanda breathed.

''That's between me and Logan.''

Matt might have thrown him into the water for that smart remark, but he figured it wasn't worth a murder rap—since they had a witness. The teenager he'd paid to drive the truck around the lake, Jerry Tucker, was standing on the rocks at the edge of the campground, waving his arms.

Matt waved back, then brought the boat in close and cut the engine. ''We've got a complication,'' he told the kid. ''This guy's after my wife—which was why I wanted to get her out of town so fast. What I'd like is for you to take him about halfway around the shore, and leave him to walk back to Henry's.''

''No!'' Stanton objected. ''That'll take all day.''

''Exactly.'' Matt tossed the kid the rope, which he caught and wrapped around a tree trunk. When the boat was secure, Matt picked up his pack from the seat and helped Amanda out, then made it to dry land with a distinct lack of grace.

''You need a gun to keep him out of trouble?'' Matt asked Tucker.

The boy grinned. ''Naw. I figure if he tries something, I can toss him overboard.''

''You and I are on the same wavelength,'' Matt said, peeling off an extra hundred. ''If anyone asks about me and Mrs. Waverly, I'd appreciate it if you'd tell them you don't know anything.''

''That's not his name,'' Stanton shouted. ''He's Matthew Forester, and he's wanted for murder.''

Matt winked at Tucker. ''Sure. In fact, he'll probably tell

you a bunch of strange stories before you drop him off. But don't pay him no mind. He's only been out of the state mental hospital for a few weeks. And it looks like he's going back real soon.''

''That's a lie!'' Stanton shouted, ending the accusation with a string of curses.

Tucker wagged his finger. ''Watch your language in front of Mrs. Waverly.'' Still, he didn't look entirely comfortable with the idea of taking a madman for a ride in a small boat.

Matt clapped the young man on the shoulder. ''He only goes after women and children, so you're safe.'' Then he addressed the foreman directly. ''I assume you have enough sense not to show up at the ranch again. Send them a letter so one of the hands can ship you your things.''

''That place will fall apart without me,'' Stanton growled.

''We'll take the chance. Now get going.''

Stanton started to curse again, then fixed his angry gaze on Matt. ''You're going to regret doing this. I promise.''

''I guess you'll have to catch me first,'' Matt answered as Tucker climbed into the boat. When the young man was settled at the tiller, Matt cast off.

As the craft headed into open water, he took Amanda's arm. ''Come on. We'd better make tracks.''

She let him lead her toward the truck, which was parked about fifty yards from the lake. ''I shouldn't have gotten angry at you,'' she murmured.

''You were entitled.''

''I was worried about you.'' She gulped. ''And—and then you came running in, and I had to leave everything. The paintings I wanted to show you. The collages. Maybe you would have thought they were dumb, but—'' She stopped, her lip quivering. ''I guess none of that's important.''

''No. I would have loved to see them. I'm so sorry.''

He put his hand on her shoulder and turned her toward him. When he saw her eyes were moist, he felt his throat close and all he could do was pull her close.

"Oh, sweetheart," he said, "I know you've had a rough time." One hand combed through her lush hair; the other stroked up and down her back. For almost three weeks he'd been longing to hold her body against his, and the relief was as great as the sexual pull.

"If you'd just called me, it would have been all right," she answered, the words ending in a little sob.

He kissed the side of her face, her hair, knowing that if he brought his lips to hers, his body would start to shake.

"I couldn't. Believe me, I couldn't," he whispered.

"Matt, you've got to tell me what happened."

"Later."

When he felt her stiffen against him and try to pull away, he didn't turn her loose.

"Trust me, it's better if we wait on that."

"Are you trying to drive me crazy?"

"I'm trying to get us out of here before the hounds pick up our trail."

She sighed. "Okay."

Then he heard her take a hitching breath. "What is it?"

"Ed's right. The ranch will fall apart without him."

He thought for a moment. "It's common knowledge right now that we're at Lake La Platta. That's no secret. So I'll make a quick call to Randolph Security and ask them to help you out, then we'll get the hell out of here."

"Why should they?"

"I think they will," he answered, hoping it was true, because he didn't have any other solution to the problem. Climbing behind the wheel, he gritted his teeth so that he didn't wince.

About a quarter mile down the road, he spotted the camp office. There was a pay phone outside. Feeling Amanda's eyes on him, he pulled out his wallet and found the phone credit card that was still in his name. As long as he was giving himself away, he might as well go all out.

The call was picked up on the first ring. Jed Prentiss, one

of the agents he'd worked with on several assignments, answered. "We're glad to hear from you, Matt."

"Yeah, I'll bet. I'll make this really brief, so just listen and don't interrupt." Knowing the message was being recorded, he talked fast, figuring that Jed could play it back later.

"Whatever Roy Logan told you about me and Amanda is a lie. He's after her because he thinks his son, Colin, fathered her child. He wants to take the baby away from her. You can check out her record at the Highton clinic in Cheyenne, if you want. Hell, check out Colin's record for all I care. But that's not the immediate problem. Logan paid off Amanda's ranch foreman to double-cross her. He was going to scoop her up and deliver her to Logan today. I'm betting nobody informed you about that little operation, or I wouldn't be taking the chance of making this call. Anyway, she's in the lurch for someone to run the ranch while we're hiding out. I'd appreciate it if Randolph Security found someone to do the job. You can send the bill to me. I'll pay it when I get the mess with Logan cleared up."

"Matt, don't hang up."

"You know I've got to. If you hire the foreman, put a classified ad in the *New York Times* under Automotive. Tell me you're selling a—" He stopped and thought for a moment. "A 1931 Pierce Arrow in mint condition." Without waiting for an answer, he replaced the receiver.

He looked up to see Amanda watching intently. "Did they say they'd do it?"

"I didn't stay on long enough to find out. I asked them to put an ad in the *New York Times* to let me know."

"Oh."

He stopped beside her window, torn between vanity and expediency. Expediency won. "Do you mind driving?" he asked.

She raised questioning eyes to his, and he didn't know which was worse, her uncertainty or the truth. Well, he wasn't going to tell her that every time he stepped on the clutch, his leg throbbed. Instead he said, "I've been up most of the night. I need some sleep."

She gave him a considering look, and he was glad the sunglasses hid the smudges under his eyes.

Without a word, she climbed out and opened the driver's door, then slid behind the wheel. He collapsed into the passenger seat, hoping she hadn't noticed how much he needed to get off the damn leg before it gave way under him.

"Where are we going?"

"Durango. There should be plenty of motels there."

"You have a route in mind?"

"Not from this side of the lake. I was figuring we were leaving straight from Henry's," he answered, glad they'd switched topics as he dug into his pack and brought out a map of Colorado and the surrounding states.

He'd known plenty of women who refused to read a map and was glad Amanda wasn't one of them. Folding it to the pertinent section, she found a route, then started the engine.

AMANDA KEPT HER EYES on the uphill dirt track that led out of the campground, then turned right onto a two-lane mountain road, all the time wondering how long she could keep from quizzing Matt about his activities while they'd been separated. The man had a nerve stonewalling her, after he'd practically driven her out of her mind with worry.

When she finally couldn't stand it any longer and turned to him, she found him sleeping. From the slump of his shoulders, it looked as if he needed the rest.

Thinking this was where she'd come in, she kept herself from shaking him awake and drove toward the western edge of the state, pleased with the truck's ability to handle the steep climbs and the long sweeps down the other side of each mountain.

The ups and downs made her think about her own emotions over the past few months. Pregnancy had played havoc with her equanimity, of course. But her mood swings had accelerated to roller-coaster proportions with the arrival of Matt Forester in her life.

She slid him another look. Even in sleep he was an impressive man. Big. Powerful. Thoroughly masculine, with a half day's growth of beard darkening his cheeks. Awake, he was devastating—and not just to her.

He had an ability to handle people that she'd never encountered before. Like the way he'd suckered that kid from town into dropping Ed off in the middle of nowhere. Or the way he'd gotten those refugees from the hippie era to switch license plates.

He'd laughed and called himself a silver-tongued devil. But it was no joke. He had a line for every situation and she couldn't quite get over the fear that he had a line for her, too. Was he just stringing her along until he left her flat?

But why would he do it? Certainly not for amusement. He was in a heap of trouble because of her. More trouble than she knew about, judging from the way he'd put off her questions about his recent activities.

THE SUN HAD DISAPPEARED behind a distant mountain peek when she reached the outskirts of Durango. As she pulled into a gas station, Matt's eyes blinked open, and he pushed himself up straighter. Looking at his watch, he swore. "I missed a pill."

"What pill?"

"An antibiotic." The way he said it was designed to end the conversation, but she wasn't about to let him get away with it.

"What for?"

"We'll talk about it over dinner."

She could feel her facial muscles tightening. "We'll talk about it now!"

"I got knifed," he said, his voice grudging.

A gasp escaped her lips. "Knifed? Where?"

"In the leg. It was no big deal."

"It kept you from getting back to me when you said you would."

"Yeah. It got infected. But I'm okay now."

"Matt—"

"I'll fill the tank. Then I'll tell you my adventures."

"I'll do it," she said, looking around for the gas-tank lock.

Letting her win that round, he handed her a twenty-dollar bill, and she climbed out, glad she had something to do while she absorbed the shock. He'd been wounded. He said it was no big deal, but she knew darn well he was lying.

When she paid for the gas, she bought him a can of orange soda, which he used to swallow a pill. Then they were on their way again.

"Let's find a nice place to stay," he said gruffly.

"Why?"

"Because we can afford it."

"You made a lot of money?"

"A hundred thousand." He laughed. "Tax free!"

She stared at him, dumbfounded. "You made all that playing poker?"

"I told you I was good at it." He tipped back his head and drank more of the soda. "Well, I did take a couple of turns at the craps table, too. Doubled my stake once."

"And lost it the next time?"

"Part of it," he allowed.

"Let's get back to your poker playing. I suppose some guy who lost to you wanted his money back," she said.

He nodded. "He came at me from behind, in a parking lot. The cut wasn't all that deep, but it got infected. I had to find a druggist who would give me the antibiotics."

"And you didn't think that was worth telling me about, instead of just leaving me in the Colorado wilds for an extra week?"

"Six days," he corrected. "And it was the lesser of two evils—having you worry about me when there was nothing you could do, or having you angry because I was coming home late.''

''I was more scared than angry,'' she admitted in a low voice, keeping her eyes straight ahead on the road.

''I know.'' He reached over to gently stroke his knuckles against her cheek. ''So it's not so surprising that you called Stanton. I'm sorry I yelled at you.''

She still felt compelled to explain. ''I've known him all my life.''

''And he never let on that he held a grudge against your father?''

''They used to argue. I thought it was because they disagreed about ranch stuff—and my father always had the final say.''

''Yeah. I understand.''

She let out a long breath. ''I should have guessed. He was acting funny the night you came to the house.''

''You trusted him. But it's over now.''

Well, she'd escaped getting hauled back to the Logan Ranch, but she and Matt hadn't settled anything. They'd just agreed not to argue for the moment.

They passed a motel on the other side of the road with a carved wooden sign reading Little Switzerland suspended over a blacktop driveway. The main building looked like a Swiss chalet with decorative boxes of colorful flowers under the windows. Behind it, spread across an upward-sloping meadow, were smaller replicas, each with fancy woodwork and peaked roofs.

''Make a U-turn and let's stop there,'' Matt said.

Amanda waited for a break in traffic, then swung around in the opposite direction. When she pulled up beside a bed of pink-and-purple petunias, Matt put his hand on her arm. ''I don't want us seen together. So you wait here.''

She glanced around at the quaint buildings and the flowers waving gently in the breeze. The place looked like a set for *The Sound of Music,* but that didn't mean they weren't in danger. "You're sure it's safe to stay here—so close to Lake La Platta?"

"Like I said the last time we made a break for it, they're expecting us to drive farther."

"Okay," she agreed, accepting his judgment.

But she noticed that he reached for his baseball cap and pulled it down to partially hide his features before approaching the office. He was gone longer than she'd expected, but he returned looking smug. "I got a suite with a living room and fireplace. And I ordered dinner. They'll bring it over in an hour." He pointed up the hill to the small chalets. "It's the last one on the right."

The mention of dinner made her stomach rumble.

He must have heard, because he reached into his pack and brought out a bag of apples, which he handed to her. "Munch on one of these."

The apple was tart, juicy and just what she needed. Pulling into the parking place in front of their unit, she followed Matt past the flower boxes that flanked the door. The inside was just as appealing as the exterior. They stepped into a large living room with two comfortable couches. Beyond were two separate bathrooms—one as big as the ranch kitchen back home—and a bedroom with a king-size bed.

When Matt had left, he'd kissed her and told her he wanted something to look forward to when he saw her again. And she'd been thinking about their reunion quite a bit—until she'd gotten so upset about his failure to return. Now she didn't exactly feel easy with him.

Nervously she glanced at the bed, then back at Matt. But he was busy getting something out of his pack.

"You've been driving for a long time. Go on, take a shower and unwind," he said.

"Okay," she agreed too quickly, then made her escape into the larger of the bathrooms, debating about whether to lock the door. Even after she'd decided he wouldn't come barging in, she glanced at the door a couple of times as she took off her man's shirt and elastic-waist jeans. She was unsnapping her bra as her reflection in the two wall mirrors captured her attention. She hadn't gotten a good look at her naked body since before Henry's Camp. Now she inspected herself from the front, then the side, seeing how large and dark her nipples had become, seeing that she'd definitely grown rounder since she and Matt had parted.

Did he really want to make love to a totally inexperienced woman who happened to be close to five months' pregnant? Did he really know what he was letting himself in for?

When they'd spent the night in bed last time, he hadn't taken off her clothes. If she let him make love to her, he'd want her naked. She was pretty sure about that.

The prospect was embarrassing. But exciting, too, judging from the way her breasts had suddenly become heavy and tight, and her sex had begun to throb. Silently she acknowledged that she wanted to feel what he'd made her feel before. And more. If he was telling the truth about that.

But in the bedroom, with the lights off, so he wouldn't see how big she was.

Quickly she turned on the shower, adjusted the water and stepped under the spray. As she lathered her hair, she thought she felt a draft. Peeking through the shower curtain, she spotted Matt and drew in a sharp breath. "What are you doing?"

"Leaving you the clothes I bought you. Unless you want to come out of there and climb back into the jeans and shirt you've been wearing all day."

Before she could tell him that buying her maternity outfits wasn't in his job description, he withdrew from the bathroom, leaving her wondering what she was going to do with the man. She'd worked out a method for dealing with guys that had carried her through the bad times and into a self-reliant maturity. Matt Forester kept making it impossible to follow her own rules.

She toweled off and dried her hair with the hairdryer that

the motel provided, before letting herself open the bags he'd laid on the counter.

There were two pairs of stretchy slacks, two pretty flowered tops, and a navy blue nightgown and robe that made her heart lurch. The gown was full and flowing, but the neckline plunged into a deep V that looked indecent. When she tried it on, she found it practically exposed the inside curves of her breasts. But the robe would cover that, she decided as she slipped it on and turned first one way and then the other, inspecting herself in the mirror, liking the way the dark color set off her hair and eyes.

She could put on slacks and a top instead. But she'd be going to sleep anyway soon, she reasoned. And this would give her a chance to wash and dry her underwear.

Still, she had to urge herself to step out of the bathroom dressed in the gown and robe. Padding down the hall, she found Matt sitting on one of the sofas. He must have taken a shower, too because his hair was wet. The dark shadow was gone from his cheeks. And he'd changed into black jeans and a black T-shirt that emphasized his dark good looks.

He had a notebook-size computer on his lap and his feet up on the coffee table, the casual intimacy of his bared toes starting her pulse pounding.

He looked up, saw her and swept his gaze over her, his eyes brightening, so that she wondered if she'd been wrong about the modesty of the outfit. Maybe he really could see her breasts through the robe. Somehow she stopped herself from looking down to see.

But all he said before turning back to the computer was, "I see I got the right size. And the color is good on you."

"What are you doing?" she asked.

"Nothing. Playing Minesweeper," he said, moving his hand to touch the keyboard. "I'll put it away."

Crossing to his side, she peered at the screen and saw the game.

Still, something about the look on his face made her think

that he wasn't being straight with her. After thinking for a moment, she asked, "Before you changed the window, were you looking at the disk you got from Francetti's office?"

He pulled a guilty face like a kid who'd been caught sneaking out of school early. "What if I was?"

"Were you planning to share the information with me?" she asked, struggling to keep her voice even.

"Yes, but I didn't want to get into it right now."

She crossed her arms over her chest. "Why do I detect a pattern here?"

"Meaning?"

"Meaning every time you think you have some information that's going to upset me, you try to hide it."

He set the computer on the coffee table with a thump. "I was hoping to stay off the subject of Colin Logan for the evening."

"Why?"

"Because you need to relax."

"I need—"

Before she could finish, there was a knock at the door, and every muscle in her body went rigid as she pictured Ed or one of Logan's men breaking down the door.

Matt saw her expression. "It's okay, that's just dinner," he said, although she saw him reach for the gun in the waistband of his slacks, saw him check the spy hole carefully before opening the door.

He kept the gun out of sight as a waiter brought in a rolling cart with covered dishes. Before the man could get a good look at her, Amanda moved to the shadows of the hall, watching as he cleared the table under the window and set it with a white cloth, then gleaming china and cutlery, before withdrawing.

She stared at the elegantly set table, impressed with the sophistication of the Little Switzerland operation.

"I would have ordered wine," Matt said, "but I figured you wouldn't want to drink it because of the baby."

"That's right."

"Well, sit down, and I'll serve you."

She followed orders, then saw that he was limping. "Your leg still hurts."

"I'll get off it in a minute," he answered, removing the silver dome from a plate and setting it in front of her.

Immediately a heavenly aroma wafted toward her.

"It's hunter stew," he told her. "I hope you like it."

"It smells delicious."

Matt brought an identical plate to his place. Then two salads with spinach, mandarin-orange slices and slivered almonds.

She forked up some of the stew. It was as good as she'd expected. And she knew she shouldn't spoil the occasion, but she couldn't keep her mind off the computer disk—or the question that had been tearing at her since Matt had showed up at the Double B Ranch almost a month ago.

"Did you find out if Colin really…uh…donated to the Highton clinic?" she asked.

Matt's fork stopped in midair. "I'd like to enjoy my dinner. Can't you think of another topic of conversation?"

"I'm sorry. The answer is important to me. If you don't know that then…"

"Then what?"

"Then you're only pretending to be sensitive to my feelings."

He sighed, leaned back in his chair and stared at her. "If I'd found out that Colin couldn't be the father of your baby, then I would have told you the good news as soon as we got rid of your friend Stanton."

"So you found out Logan's information is correct?"

"I found out the clinic used an elaborate coded system to protect the privacy of their donors. So far I can't crack the code. I don't know if Francetti is a better cryptographer than I am, or if he got some inside information, or if he was lying to Roy Logan because he knew he wouldn't get caught. So I don't know any more about Colin's role in your pregnancy than I did a month ago. Does that answer satisfy you? Or would you like to check the disk?''

''I'll take your word for it,'' she answered in a small voice.

''Thank you. Now eat your dinner,'' he said, attacking his stew as if he were afraid somebody was going to whisk the plate away in the next few seconds.

She bent her head and managed a few more bites of the meal. Moments ago it had smelled wonderful. Now she might as well have been eating a bowl of wheat bran.

Matt gave her a long look, but she refused to lift her head.

''Amanda, don't do this,'' he said.

''Do what?'' she managed to say.

''Put distance between us.''

''I'm not the one who's doing anything.''

He sighed. ''Okay. Whatever you say.'' Pushing his salad away, he stood up and went back to the couch, picked up the computer and touched the keyboard, all his concentration focused on the screen.

Unable to stay where she was, she scraped her chair back, turned and rushed down the hall to the bedroom. Closing the door, she stood with her shoulders pressed to the wood, her body trembling.

Chapter Ten

Amanda squeezed her hand into a fist and pressed it against her mouth.

You will not stand here and start to bawl, she told herself. *You will not.* It took several repetitions of the order, but finally she managed to hold back the tears that brimmed her eyes.

Damn him. Damn the man for acting as if she didn't have a right to know about the father of her child. She sniffed, then went rigid as she heard him get up. *He'd better not be coming in here!*

But he only crossed to the kitchen and opened a cabinet. Then she heard a glass clank against the counter before he walked back into the living room. This time there were two clanks. The glass and something else.

She focused all her attention on the living room, but she could hear no more sounds from where she stood.

Still angry, she started toward the king-size bed, thinking that she might as well lie down. In the dim light coming from the bathroom, one of the pillows looked wrinkled or lumpy. As she moved closer, the wrinkle took on shape and form—the shape and form of a long-stem red rose.

She stared at the elegant flower, pretty sure it hadn't been provided by the management of Little Switzerland.

It must have been Matt who had put that rose there, because

he had been planning to bring her in here and make love to her.

She squeezed her eyes shut, trying to hold back fresh tears, but they gathered in her eyes and spilled down her cheeks. Sinking to the edge of the mattress, she cradled her head in her hands.

Lord, she'd accused him of not considering her feelings. But he'd been considering them all evening. He'd brought her to this place because he could see it was charming. He'd given her a sexy gown, he'd ordered a dinner he thought she'd like, he'd put a rose on her pillow and he'd tried to keep the conversation away from Colin Logan. Because he hadn't wanted any talk of Colin to interfere with what he had planned for the two of them. The realization brought more tears.

She'd told him he was being insensitive. She should have leveled the accusation at herself, since she'd plowed ahead with a subject he'd wanted to avoid this evening at all cost, then run away when he'd reacted to her bullheaded insistence.

She sucked in several breaths, letting them out in little gasps. What was wrong with her? Why did she always have to push—to challenge—to use her sharp tongue, when deep down she wasn't as hard and tough as she pretended? Why did she always have to prove to herself and everyone else that she could hold her own?

Now that she understood what she'd done, it was tempting to stay hidden in the bedroom where she wouldn't have to face Matt again. Instead she pushed herself up, crossed to the small bathroom and washed her face.

Trying to keep her hands from trembling, she retraced her steps down the hall. Matt was sitting where she'd left him. Only now there was a bottle of bourbon on the table and a half-full glass of amber liquid beside it.

He glanced up, noted her presence, then flicked his gaze back to the computer screen.

Without looking at her again, he asked, ''Did you come out for the full report? Well, I have a lot more interesting information on Colin. I may not be able to prove that he donated sperm to the Highton clinic and that the donation was used to impregnate you. But I do have some juicy information on his activities in Los Angeles and Las Vegas. In L.A. he helped finance a lab that was making a potent designer drug. And in Las Vegas, he—''

"Stop!"

He looked up inquiringly. "If you don't like my executive summary, you can read it in the privacy of the bedroom. You can take the computer back there and scroll through Francetti's report.''

The man she'd bullied and insulted a few minutes ago was only twelve feet away, but it felt as if the whole continental United States was separating them. Putting one foot in front of the other, she crossed the distance, then sank onto the couch—close enough to touch him if she stretched out her arm. Instead she pressed her hands against the sofa cushions to keep them from shaking. "I didn't come out here to talk about Colin,'' she answered.

"Funny, that's all you wanted to talk about a little while ago.''

She felt as if a giant weight were crushing her chest, but she managed to say, "Yes, well, I warned you that I don't know much about…about how to get along with…people.''

When he said nothing, she felt the weight grow heavier. "I'm sorry. I shouldn't have insisted,'' she whispered, unable to manage more volume.

"I understand why it's been on your mind,'' he answered, his voice neutral as he set the computer on the coffee table.

"You've been on my mind, too.'' She wanted to raise her eyes to his, but she knew her tears would start to flow again if she did. So she kept her gaze focused on her knees. "I missed you so much. Then when I got you back, I went right into my old behavior patterns—making sure you couldn't get close to me.''

She saw his Adam's apple bob.

"See, you're unlucky enough to have gotten hooked up with a woman who's afraid of intimacy. I don't mean the sex part." She stopped. "Well, I'm kind of worried about that, too. But the main problem is letting somebody I care about get a chance to hurt me. So I make sure he backs off first. Even when that's not really what I want." Her voice went high and quavery as she twisted toward him, risking the rejection she feared by slinging her arms around him and pulling herself against him. Pressing her face against the side of his neck, she waited with the breath frozen in her lungs.

When his arms came up to cradle her, she breathed out a little sigh.

"Matt, I'm sorry. I'm the one who should have been more sensitive." She ended the apology by raising her head and finding his mouth with hers. There was a moment of resistance, then his lips softened against hers. His response was both tender and hungry. He tasted of whiskey and warmth and of all the things she craved—all the things she feared. She damped down the fear and concentrated on the warmth and the need—his and hers.

When he lifted his head, she could hear his rapid breathing, feel the pounding of her own heart.

His eyes were fierce as they gazed down into hers. "I told you the last time we had breakfast together that you don't have to do stuff because you figure it's what I want."

"Is that why you think I left the safety of the bedroom?" she managed to ask.

"I don't honestly know."

The words stung. But she understood why he'd spoken them, and she knew what kind of answer she had to give him. "Let's be logical here," she murmured. "I'm almost five months' pregnant. I've never made love with a guy, and I'm nervous about starting now. I'm embarrassed about how fat I look. I know you're…upset about my spoiling the dinner you planned for us." She heaved a sigh. "But I came out here because I missed you like crazy when you were away. And instead of us fighting, I want to get as close to you as I can. That's about as direct as I can be.''

''That's pretty direct, all right,'' he conceded. His voice was grave, but the harsh lines of his features had softened considerably.

''Can you deal with all that?'' she whispered.

''Yeah. I can deal with it,'' he answered, bending to her, his mouth playing with hers, stirring hot currents within her. She wanted more, so she pressed her lips more tightly against his, a needy sound rising in her throat.

He gave her exactly what she craved, his lips moving on hers, changing the pressure, changing the texture, changing the level of heat. And when his tongue began to play with hers, she felt the flames licking at the core of her.

She tried the same thing with him, gratified by the sound he made deep in his chest.

''I want you,'' he breathed when the kiss finally broke.

''Good,'' she answered with more boldness than she felt.

''But—''

''No *buts*.''

''It doesn't have to be tonight,'' he finished. ''I mean, if things start going too fast for you, we can slow down.''

He was offering her a safety net. And she was touched by the chivalry, but she wasn't planning to bail out.

She wanted to tell him as much. She wanted to tell him that she'd fallen in love with him. But she was afraid to make the declaration.

So instead of answering with words, she drew back a little and unbuttoned the robe, pulling her arms out of the sleeves and lifting her hips so she could toss the garment onto the arm of the couch.

She was wearing only the gown he'd bought her now. And she heard his breath catch in his throat, felt his eyes go to the deep V of the bodice. ''I knew that would look fantastic on you,'' he said in a thick voice. ''I didn't know just how fantastic.'' With one finger he traced the edge of the V, starting at one top edge, following the fabric down to the point a few inches from her navel, skimming the roundness of her abdomen, the sides of her breasts, then tracing up the other side, scorching her flesh as he went.

His touch was light, but it was enough to tighten her nipples, to make them bead against the thin fabric. She knew he saw the reaction because his eyes were riveted to her front.

"Almost as fantastic looking as the woman who's wearing it," he added huskily, bending to press his face into the V, turning first one way and then the other, his mouth and tongue playing with the sides of her breasts, making her feel as if she were going to melt under his scorching touch.

He nudged the fabric aside far enough to swirl his tongue around one aching nipple, then sucked it gently into his mouth, and she felt an answering response deep inside her body.

"I think maybe it's time to retire to the bedroom," he said, his voice a shade more raspy.

When he saw her eyes flick to the glass of bourbon on the table, he gave her a questioning look.

"How much of that did you drink?" she asked.

"Why do you want to know?"

She looked down into her lap. "Because I've heard that…uh…that guys who drink too much want to make love, but then…they can't."

He laughed. "Oh, is that what you're worried about?" Reaching for her hand, he pressed it against the erection straining at the front of his jeans. "I think we have the essential ingredient here."

"Oh." Her hand jerked, and he let her pull away.

"You caught me before I had more than two sips," He said. "So I'm operating on full power."

Before she had time to worry about anything else, he led her down the hall and into the bedroom where the light from the bathroom was enough for her to see him, but still dark enough to make her feel comfortable.

Turning her toward him, he held her captive in his arms, but not tightly. He was still giving her time to slip away.

"I've had fantasies about this ever since I left you," he said. "And when I saw the gown, I wanted to see you wearing it. Thank you for putting it on tonight."

"You didn't act like it was any big deal when you first saw me," she answered, and mentally kicked herself.

"Well, I didn't want you ducking back into the bathroom and grabbing a pair of slacks and a top. No, I wanted you just like this." He stepped away from her and picked up the rose from the pillow, holding it toward her, tracing the V that barely covered her breasts.

She wasn't sure which was more erotic, the velvety touch of the petals or the very idea of being stroked that way.

"Was this part of the fantasy, too?" she managed to ask.

"Not until I went into the restaurant to order dinner. They give the flowers to their female guests at the end of the meal. So I asked for one," he answered, pushing the shoulders of the gown onto her arms, baring a little more of her flesh and stroking the newly exposed skin with the flower. When she felt the soft rose petals circle one nipple, she drew in a whimpering breath.

"Lord, that's beautiful. The red rose against your skin," Matt whispered, pushing the fabric farther off her shoulders, trapping her arms while he played the flower over her breasts, alternating the touch with his mouth, making her dizzy with desire.

Her eyes drifted closed so that she didn't see him pull off his shirt. But she opened her eyes as she felt the gown being swept over her head. Before she had time to worry about being naked, he pulled her into his arms, rubbing her breasts against his chest, drawing a gasp as the crisp hairs on his chest abraded her sensitized nipples.

"You like that?"

"Mmm."

As she twisted against him, his hands moved up and down her back, over her hips.

His mouth nuzzled her ear. "Sweetheart, I've got a little problem here. These jeans are killing me, but I don't want to turn you loose to get out of them. So could you give me a hand?"

She nodded, then fumbled for the snap at his waistband. The zipper was more difficult because she could feel his erection on the other side of the fabric. But she managed that, too, then slipped her hands inside—under his shorts as well as the jeans. Without giving herself time to be embarrassed, she pushed the fabric down, her fingers sliding over his narrow hips.

When she reached his right thigh, she gasped, and her eyes flew open. "Matt!"

"It's okay. Just help me get these pants off."

Instead she looked at the long, cruel scar that her fingers had exposed. Somebody had done a pretty rough job of stitching it closed. "Matt, you said he cut you. You didn't say he damn near butchered your leg."

When she started to bend to give herself a better look, he put his hands on her elbows and held her in place. "You can inspect it later, because we've got better things to do now."

She felt the words of protest bubbling in her throat, but she held them back. Because that was what he wanted, what *she* wanted too, if she just had enough sense not to argue with him.

Still, she couldn't help looking at the angry, half-healed flesh as he kicked off his pants. Then he took her mind off the scar by pulling her naked body against his, as his hands cupped her buttocks and his mouth devoured hers.

The impact of his naked flesh pressed to hers made her knees wobble.

"I think it's about time to get you off your feet," he murmured.

She thought he was going to bring her to the bed, but instead she saw him swing around and pull out the desk chair before seating himself and pulling her gently down so that she was straddling his lap, facing him, her feet on either side of the chair and her sex pressed intimately to his.

"Oh!"

He nibbled his lips along the side of her cheek, nipped at her ear before starting to speak. "You know, I gave considerable thought to how we should do this the first time. I decided that this might be the best way."

As he spoke, he grasped her hips and tilted them back and forth so that her most sensitive flesh slid against his erection, sending tongues of fire licking through her.

"Oh," she said again, "oh, that feels—"

"Better than my fantasies, and they were pretty vivid," he admitted as he tipped her back a little so that he could find her nipples with his mouth while his fingers stroked over her belly and then lower. She clung to his shoulders, almost lost in the pleasure he was giving her.

He was bringing her to the point of climax, and she was drowning in the sensations. Then he lifted his hand away from her, and she made a pleading sound of protest.

When she slid frantically against him, he stilled her hips with his hands. "Sweetheart, this is the time to take me inside you, if you want," he said, his voice gritty. "And if you want to stop, you're the one in charge. You can do this however you like."

He'd known how much she needed to be in control, and she was grateful for that. But she wasn't planning to disappoint either one of them.

"I'm not going to stop," she told him, standing and then bringing herself down again to meet the tip of his shaft. A tiny wave of fear stilled her for a moment, but she had never turned away from a challenge, so she continued the downward plunge. As he slid into her, there was pressure and a quick stab of pain that made her gasp.

"Sweetheart, it's okay. You don't have to—"

She felt her lips curve into a grin, felt an inward surge of triumph as she shifted to accommodate him more fully. "I think I already have."

"Are you all right?" he asked, strain roughening his voice.

"Yes," she whispered. "But I suspect I'll be even better if you do the things you were doing to me before."

"You mean this?" he asked, as his hands caressed her breasts and bottom. "And this?" he inquired as he shifted one hand to the place where their bodies joined.

She could only gasp out her pleasure as she rocked against him while he bent to suck one dark nipple with his mouth.

She shattered then, feeling herself contract around him, the exquisite pleasure of it spiraling through her, bringing a cry of joy to her lips—a cry that was echoed by his shout of release as he joined her.

She sank against him, boneless, her damp body plastered to his. For long moments neither of them moved. Then his lips skimmed the side of her face.

"Well?" he murmured.

"Well, you were right. It was…sensational."

She felt his lips curve into a smile. "Next time I'll do more of the work."

"You knew I had to feel like I could escape if I needed to."

"Yeah," he answered lazily.

"Thank you."

"Thank you for trusting me," he answered. Before she could reply, he added, "I think we're going to be a little more comfortable in bed."

"Mmm."

She let him lift her, let him carry her to the bed, where he bent to sweep the spread and blanket aside. Scooting onto the cool surface, she pulled the sheet and blanket over her.

"Sometime we've got to work on the modesty thing," he murmured as he slipped into bed beside her.

She'd been half-asleep, but her eyes snapped open. "I'll let you look at my bulging middle, if you let me look at that scar.''

"Uh…maybe you're right. We both need to get some sleep.''

A few hours ago she would have pressed the issue. Now she allowed herself to settle against him.

ROY LOGAN LOOKED at the hole in the plasterboard where he'd put his fist through the wall eight hours ago. Then he flexed the fingers of his right hand. The knuckles still smarted, but the physical pain was nothing compared to the pain of defeat.

Temporary defeat.

Roy had been in his office waiting for the phone to ring, anticipating victory. Then Al had called from outside the grocery store at Henry's Camp to say that Ed Stanton had bungled the job. Amanda Barnwell was on the loose again.

Apparently the monkey wrench in the works had been that bastard Matthew Forester, who kept sticking his nose in where he wasn't wanted. When Roy's phone tap at the Double B Ranch had pinpointed Amanda's location, he'd sent out men to investigate and found her hiding out at a run-down fishing camp on Lake La Platta. Then, when they'd been about to scoop her up, Forester had showed up again. Just in time to take care of Stanton and hornswoggle a local kid into driving his truck around the lake before ditching Ed in the woods.

Al had finally gotten the straight story out of the kid, after he'd gone up to two thousand dollars in bribe money. But by that time it was too late. Forester and the woman could have been anywhere.

"I hear you had a little mishap this afternoon," a voice interrupted his thought.

Roy whirled to face his brother Bud—the last person he wanted to see at the moment. "What mishap?" he growled.

"You're chasing the Barnwell woman, and she got away."

"How do you know so much?" Roy demanded.

"Oh, I hear things," Bud said, slipping his hands into his

pockets, exaggerating the disgusting paunch that pulled the fabric of his shirtfront tight, so that the bottom button looked as if it was going to pop open.

Roy looked at his older brother with distaste. Bud ate and drank too much and he didn't work out. Worse, he didn't have sense enough to keep his nose out of other people's business. Probably Bud had a guy or two at the ranch he was paying for information. And whoever it was had better clear out before Roy discovered him.

"What are you doing here?" he snapped, walking around and sitting down at the desk. It always made him feel more secure to have the polished mahogany desktop between himself and a visitor. Particularly his brother.

"What a way to greet your own flesh and blood," Bud remarked, seating himself in one of the leather chairs across from the desk as though he owned the place.

Roy snorted. He and Bud had been rivals since childhood. When they'd been young, his older brother had had the advantage. But Roy had made up for that in spades. He was the one who had taken this ranch away from their grandfather. He was the one who had turned it into a profitable operation—before he'd started branching out into even more lucrative avenues.

He'd planned to leave it all to Colin. Now it would go to his grandson, as soon as he wrested the boy away from that crazy Barnwell gal. Because in his mind he was sure she was carrying a boy—a replacement for Colin. What kind of woman went to a clinic and had some doctor stick a test tube full of semen up inside her instead of doin' it the regular way? A crazy woman, that's who. And if a judge didn't think she was crazy now, he would by the time Roy and his men got finished with her. Because she wasn't going to raise the child. He was going to do that. He was going to do it right—give the kid his values. And not spoil him rotten the way he'd done with Colin.

"I can help you out on those detective records," Bud said.

Roy's head snapped up. "What the hell? You have them?"

His brother shook his head, raised a hand, palm outward. "Didn't mean to give that impression. But I know how much you want that information, so I've got a guy I know who can go over the same ground. I can give you a report pretty soon."

"Why would you want to do that for me?"

"I figure it's time we mend our fences. Neither one of us is getting any younger. We should start workin' together instead of against each other."

Roy laughed. "Yeah, we just got to figure out how to trust each other."

"So let me take the first step. Let me help you with the investigation."

"If you really want to." He didn't trust Bud any further than he could throw him in a windstorm, but he figured it was better to know what he was doing than not—so he could take appropriate action.

"So, did you have a preliminary report I could start with?" Bud asked, his eyes hooded.

"Yeah, I got some stuff for you," Roy allowed.

AMANDA AWOKE once in the night, made a trip to the bathroom, then raided the minibar for cheese and crackers because she was starving. The next time she woke, just after dawn, she felt Matt's hands on her, bringing her body to life again.

This time he didn't let her hide by pressing close to him. Instead he stripped away the covers, watching her body as he aroused her. He teased her breasts with his hands and his mouth, gently stroked the roundness of her belly, then dipped into the moist flesh at the juncture of her legs, making her move restlessly against his clever fingers.

"You're so beautiful," he breathed.

"You must have bad eyesight," she managed to reply.

"Have you ever seen a statue of an ancient fertility goddess? This is the general body type. So you're programed to turn guys on."

"Am I?"

"In this case, I think you can tell."

There was no denying the hard shaft that pressed against her thigh.

"How about if we try it the traditional way?" he whispered as he nudged her legs apart with his knee.

"Are you sure that's okay?"

He gave a low laugh. "I'm a trained covert agent. I never venture into new territory without doing my homework. The pregnancy books say this is fine—until you get quite a bit bigger."

"You were reading pregnancy books?" she gasped as he gently rolled one nipple between his finger and thumb, then bent to swirl his tongue around the tightened flesh.

"Uh-huh," he answered thickly. "I figured you didn't have any reason to study up on sexual intercourse for expectant mothers so I'd better do it." He ended the sentence with a series of kisses as he covered her body with his and eased inside her, keeping his weight on his elbows. "Does that feel okay?"

"It feels...oh, that's wonderful," she breathed as he began to move inside her.

She gave herself over to the sensations he was building climbing upward through layers of sky until she broke through a meteor shower of sensation.

She knew he had followed her there when she heard his groan of pleasure, felt his body convulse above her. He stayed where he was for only a few moments longer, then shifted to the bed beside her and pulled her close.

"This could be habit-forming," she whispered, her lips against his ear.

"That's one of my intentions."

He'd given her an opportunity she would be a fool to turn down. Yet it was hard to get the words past her suddenly clogged throat. "What are the rest of your intentions?" she asked in a small voice.

"Keeping you safe. Keeping you with me."

There was a long pause. The next question was, "For how long?" Since she couldn't go that far, she only nodded and snuggled closer to him.

"I mean, for as long as it takes," he said. "I mean, I'm not going off on any more trips. Well, unless I've got something to do, and it's too dangerous for you to come along."

"Gee, thanks, I think," she murmured, not daring to push her luck any further.

THE NEXT TIME SHE WOKE, it was to the aroma of bacon and eggs. Blinking her eyes open, she saw Matt, dressed in another of his dark T-shirts and faded jeans, pushing a cart into the bedroom.

"What time is it?" she asked.

"Ten."

Her eyes shot to the window, where the heavy drapes still blocked the sun. "You should have opened the curtain. I've never slept that late in my life!"

"You needed the rest, after all that driving yesterday—and all that other unaccustomed activity."

Looking amused by the flush that spread across her skin, he pushed the cart to the side of the bed. Reaching behind her, he fluffed up the pillows. "And now you need to eat. Although I saw you raided the refrigerator in the middle of the night."

She nodded, suddenly remembering why she hadn't had much dinner. But she didn't spoil the mood by mentioning it. Matt brought his plate to the desk, and as he moved the chair, their eyes met.

He grinned at her. "I guess you won't be able to look at another desk chair without thinking about last night."

"I guess not."

He grinned again, then attacked his breakfast with gusto.

"How's your leg?" she asked.

"Better."

He said it quickly enough so that she wasn't sure how accurate he was being. But she elected not to press him.

He ate several more bites of breakfast before remarking, "Last night I didn't want to talk about business. This morning we need to discuss Francetti's research—and what I've come up with on my own."

She felt her shoulders tense. "You mean about Colin?"

"Most of the information is on him. But my main aim is in getting Roy off your back. Is the discussion going to spoil your breakfast?"

"No."

"Good." Matt stood, kicked off his shoes and picked up his coffee mug. Circling the bed, he climbed onto the other side, then slid over so that he was sitting next to Amanda.

"How bad is the report on Colin?" she asked.

He knit his fingers with hers. "I'd say Logan must have raised him to feel like he could never measure up. So he worked out various ways to prove he was better than his father."

"That's bull! He was one of the most arrogant boys, then one of the most arrogant men, I've ever met."

"Yeah, well, apparently he had to prove his worth over and over. Unfortunately he had a lot of help from his uncle Bud. Heard of him?"

She shook her head.

"There are five brothers in the Logan family. Three of them are upstanding citizens. Bud is another matter. He's a couple of years older than Roy, but he never did as well. Of course, he keeps trying, and part of his aim was to get some influence over Colin."

"Why?"

"Maybe to get back at Roy for treating him like he treats everyone else. Maybe to get his hands on some of the money Roy gave to Colin when he was twenty-five." He paused. "I told you about the drug lab in L.A."

She nodded.

"Colin was one of the backers. Bud's not connected to that. But he's an investor in a Las Vegas syndicate of legitimate businessmen who are building a casino. Apparently he tried to get Colin in on that deal, but he was killed before the papers were signed."

"Oh."

"So our next stop is Las Vegas."

"You think legitimate businessmen had him killed? Why?"

"They're not the likely candidates, unless they have mob backing. But I want to poke around in their operation a little bit and find out what's what. See if they might have had anything they wanted to hide from Francetti. If there's anything criminal regarding their relationship with Colin, it'll be easier to prove than the L.A. drug connection."

"Why?"

"Because all Colin provided to the drug guy Dexter Perkins was cash. And Roy could argue he didn't know what he was financing. But there are very strict laws in Nevada governing gambling casinos."

He took a swallow of coffee, then set the cup down again. "And I thought that while we were there, we could get married."

Chapter Eleven

Matt sat there, waiting for her response, feeling the line of his jaw tighten from the tension.

"Did I hear that right? We could get married?" she asked carefully.

"Yeah."

"Why?"

Because of his own blind, selfish need. Deep down he must have known he was going to fall in love with her from the first time he'd laid eyes on her. But he didn't think Amanda was ready to accept the simple answer, not from a guy she'd barely met a month ago. Not when she didn't believe that *anyone* would want to marry her.

"To protect you and the baby," he answered, making it sound convincing. "If we're married, then the baby will be legally mine."

He felt his breath turn shallow as he watched her think that over. "You'd marry me to protect Colin Logan's child?" she clarified.

"We don't know the baby's Colin's."

"Roy sure thinks it's true," she answered.

"He's taking the word of a two-bit detective who was more anxious to collect his fee than get his facts straight." Matt paused for breath, then continued. "I don't think Francetti had enough time to decode the records. Which means either he had inside information that Colin fathered your child, or he was simply telling his client what he wanted to hear—that a piece of Colin still remained. That way Logan could snatch some kind of victory from the ashes of his son's death. It was safe enough to make the claim, since as things stand, it can't be proved or disproved one way or the other.''

She digested all of that. ''You're giving me some hope that Francetti was wrong about the baby's paternity,'' she whispered.

He really didn't know the answer, but he could honestly tell her, ''I hope so, too. Meanwhile, we've only got a couple of options. We can figure out how to get the devil off our backs or we can hide for the rest of our lives. Since we haven't had much luck with the former, I want to give you the legal protection of my name. So stop making a big deal out of it and say yes to my proposal.''

''It *is* a big deal. It's my life we're talking about.'' She swallowed. ''My life and the baby's. I mean, marriage is a big step,'' she said, her voice quavering.

He clenched the fist she couldn't see, his nails digging into his palm. ''I know that, and I had time to think about it while I was lying in that motel room wondering if I was going to pull through.''

''You told me it was nothing to worry about,'' she answered.

Deliberately he kept his voice mild. ''That's how it turned out. At the time, it wasn't much fun. But we're not going to get off on that now. The point I was making was that while I was evaluating my life, I realized it didn't have a lot of depth. And I wanted something more meaningful than going to work every day. The more I thought about it, the more I knew that something was you.''

Her expression told him she still wasn't convinced. ''Whoever the father is, I'm carrying another man's child,'' she said. Her face solemn, she reached for his hand and dragged it to the rounded swell of her tummy. When she pressed his palm against her, he could feel the kick of a tiny foot or the flailing of a hand against his skin. The sensation awed him.

Smiling, he smoothed his fingers over her abdomen, pressed his palm as close as he could get to the life within. "I had time to think about the baby, too. And I figured that if I'm there while you're carrying her, and I'm there when she's born, and I help you raise her, then I'm the one who has a claim to her."

"Why do you think it's a girl?" she asked.

"I guess I keep picturing her looking like her mom."

"Rather than a boy who looks like his father."

"I told you, as far as I'm concerned, I'm going to be the father. You already told me there's a good chance the baby will look like me, anyway."

"Matt, I…" Her voice hitched and she started again. "I'm having trouble taking all this in."

"I know sweetheart. And I understand," he added as he continued to caress her, establishing his connection with the unborn child—yet at the same time starting to feel the sensuality of the intimate touch. He made a little throat-clearing sound to hide the thickness in his voice. "I'm having trouble myself because I thought I'd never ask another woman to marry me. When you asked me about my first marriage, I didn't tell you that I felt like a failure when we broke up. That I felt like Coach Forester had raised a son who couldn't make a marriage work."

"That's not true! You're the complete opposite of him."

"Oh, yeah? Are you switching sides?"

"No, I'm arguing—the way I usually do. Because I'm independent and stubborn," she added for good measure.

"Yeah. Those are two of the things I like about you."

"Oh, come on. We disagree all the time."

"Because you're strong enough to stand up to me. And you make your point. You don't sulk."

"Maybe I do."

"Maybe it's time to stop talking. If I can't persuade you

with logic, I guess I'll have to try another approach," he muttered as he took away the breakfast plate she'd forgotten about and set it on the floor.

Then he lowered his mouth to hers, his lips persuasive and urgent as he strove to convince her that the two of them belonged together. He had her flat on her back before she could protest. He had her aroused before she could take ten shaky breaths. And he had his way with her before motel-checkout time.

Unfortunately that wasn't the end of it. After the mind-blowing sex, he had to further prove his good faith by letting her look at the scar on his leg and make clicking sounds over the job he'd done of sewing the damn thing closed.

But after he'd endured that, she agreed to the marriage plan. And he'd felt some of the awful tension seep out of him.

While Amanda got ready to leave, he paid their bill, then returned to the chalet. She was in the living room, dressed in one of the outfits he'd bought her, and his mind emptied of everything else when he saw her. He'd always had a good eye for color, and he'd guessed right when he'd picked a soft blue top with little yellow flowers over navy maternity pants. It took away the hard edge that her own clothes gave her and substituted a softly feminine image.

"I like the way that looks on you," he told her.

The pink of her cheeks deepened. "Thank you," she answered, and he knew that they had made some major progress, since she didn't feel compelled to tell him what she didn't like about the outfit.

He was in a good mood as they hit U.S. 160 heading southwest. His future wife was sitting beside him, and the pain in his leg was down to manageable proportions.

"It's an easy drive to Las Vegas," he told her, handing over the highway map. "We cut across Arizona."

She studied the map, then cocked her head in the way she did when she was about to ask a hard question.

"I suppose I'm still a murder suspect," she said, her voice casual but laced with underlying strain.

He made a face. "You would have to bring that up."

"Tell me how we're going to get married and use our real names."

"One cop may have caught a glimpse of you, but the Denver police department doesn't have anything to tie Amanda Barnwell and Matthew Forester to Francetti. The only person who'd have a reason to suspect us is Roy. And he doesn't want you apprehended. He wants you at the Logan Ranch. So we'll make a quick trip to a wedding chapel, then disappear back into anonymity."

"With the fake ID you've been using?"

"I bought a couple of new sets. When we get to Vegas, I'm going to pick up something for you."

"Just like that?"

"You can buy anything in Vegas, drugs, ID, white slaves, if you know where to look."

Her eyes widened. "White slaves?

"Well, women who will act any part you want—for a fee."

She was silent for a few minutes, then said, "There's something else I need to do. I haven't been to a doctor for over a month. And I should have a regular prenatal checkup. Really, I should be seeing the same doctor the whole time, but I guess we can't manage that."

"No. We don't want to establish a pattern. But we'll get you an appointment before we leave Vegas."

She apparently considered the answer satisfactory and went to another topic. "Can I see the material from the Highton clinic?"

He repressed a sigh. "The computer is in the pack on the floor by your feet. There's enough battery power for you to use the machine for a while."

She pulled the compact machine out of the pack and set it on her lap. To his amusement, her belly got in the way of the keyboard, but she managed anyway. He could tell at once that she knew her way around a hard drive.

"The file name's Highton?" she asked.

"Right."

She scanned the coded entries, then looked at him when she reached the detailed information on donor Colin Logan.

"I thought you said there was no way to tell it was him. But here's his record," she said, pointing to the screen.

"Well, the two issues are separate. Francetti could pull the record for Colin Logan. But there's no way, specifically, to link this record to your donor without breaking the code."

She moved the cursor through the file. "There's a lot of personal stuff here. They think his IQ was 135!"

"Was it?" he asked, although he had no problem remembering that detail—or anything else he'd read about the bastard.

"Maybe. He was smart. Cunning, I guess. He knew how to make people like him—teachers, coaches. Of course, his daddy's money didn't hurt. One year Roy donated all the equipment for the high-school football team."

"A real humanitarian," Matt muttered.

She scanned through the report. "Here's the medical information. Colin's blood type is A positive. He had his wisdom teeth extracted when he was seventeen. He said he never had any major illnesses. That's a lie. He had pneumonia when he was in third grade."

The computer started to beep, and she switched off the machine. As she returned it to the backpack, he asked, "What else can you tell me about Colin that might help me understand who murdered him?"

She shrugged. "You want to hear about the girl he raped our senior year in high school?"

"Rape?"

"Well, forced sex. The way I heard it, they were both drinking. When he tried to do it to her, she said no. And he didn't take no for an answer. His father gave the family enough money to send her to a very nice college and that was the last we heard of that.''

"Convenient.''

She was silent for a moment, then told him about the dead frog Colin had put in her lunch box when she was in third grade.

"How do you know it was him?''

"I don't for sure, but he was the one who laughed the loudest.''

"He sounds like a real nice guy.''

"Which is why I wouldn't have picked him for my child's father.''

"Maybe he isn't. And even if he is, we'll make sure the kid turns out differently.''

"I hope,'' she said in a shaky voice.

"I know!'' he answered with all the conviction he could put into the affirmation. "And I can guarantee she'll like country music,'' he added, turning on the radio to lighten the atmosphere in the truck.

For lunch they stopped in a little town in Arizona where he coaxed her into the guilty pleasure of joining him for a root-beer float at a fast-food drive-in.

In the afternoon she slept, and he took his eyes off the road every few minutes to watch the peaceful expression on her face. He wanted to guard that serenity, to keep the anxious look out of her eyes. But he knew he couldn't do it until he got Roy Logan off their backs.

AMANDA WOKE WITH A GASP as her eyes focused on what looked like Mt. Kilauea spewing lava into a lagoon.

Blinking, she struggled to orient herself in time and space.

"That's the fake volcano at the Mirage Hotel,''. Matt told her, obviously amused by her reaction. "It goes off every half hour or so,'' he added as he pulled up along the curb to give her a better view. "But in this case, it's all done with underground gas jets.''

Next to the hotel with the volcano was another sprawling edifice—this one a transplant from Imperial Rome. Beyond that was the Eiffel Tour, which vied for attention with a miniature version of New York City.

Wide-eyed, Amanda tried to take it in. She'd never been more than three hundred miles from Crowfoot, Wyoming, and she'd never felt more like a country girl as she stared around her at this fantasy land.

"You look like you're in shock," Matt commented.

"I guess I've seen movies filmed in Las Vegas. I didn't think it was going to look so..." She struggled for the right word and came up with "outrageous" just as a man wearing six-foot stilts and a clown suit crossed the road.

The whole place was a circus, she supposed. And under other circumstances, she might have wanted to join the fun. Instead she found the atmosphere set her nerves on edge.

When she couldn't repress a little shiver, Matt put his hand on her arm.

"You okay?"

"Yes," she answered automatically as he turned off the main road. "Where are we going to stay?"

"Away from the action, to the extent that it's possible. There's an elegant little hotel I've been meaning to try for the past few years. They only have a small casino and a couple of high-stakes poker tables."

"You come here often?"

"A card shark has to keep up with the latest in the field," he answered as he turned in at a short driveway flanked by beds of exotic flowers.

"Right," she murmured under her breath. Apparently he felt right at home in this fake city in the desert. And suddenly all she could think of was the silver-tongued con man whom she'd seen in action on several occasions. The same man who'd asked her to marry him this morning.

Even before he cut the engine, a uniformed doorman hurried to the side of the car. But Matt waved him away. Following his usual cautious routine, he went in alone to register, and she felt some of the anxiety ease out of her. But her stomach knotted again the moment he reappeared.

He hustled her quickly through a plush lobby, where wild ducks with bright plumage swam in an artificial stream.

Upstairs, she waited with her arms stiffly at her sides while the bellman showed them the features of their luxury suite, including the controls of the hot tub.

When they were alone again, Matt gave her an assessing look. "Why don't you rest while I see what I can find out about some of the men involved in the gambling consortium?"

"Okay," she answered quickly.

"You're not going to insist on going along?"

"I learned my lesson in Denver," she answered, hoping that her voice conveyed sincerity. "Just tell me what name we registered under, in case I need to know."

"We're Mr. and Mrs. Fred Marvin."

"Classy!"

When Matt finally left her alone, she sank into a puffy white chair and threw her head back against the cushion, struggling to catch her breath as she remembered how casually he'd introduced the topic of marriage—then maneuvered her into saying yes.

Now she wondered if she'd been out of her mind to go along with his plans. She'd known Matt Forester only a few weeks—and under totally unreal circumstances. What was going to happen when the immediate danger was over? When the excitement of running and hiding was behind them?

And what about her own motives? Matt had snatched her and her unborn child out of Roy Logan's clutches. Now she felt more dependent on him than on anyone else who had ever been in her life—including her parents.

Was that why she had agreed to the marriage? Because she knew she couldn't protect the baby on her own? Was that why she'd convinced herself she was in love with him?

Struggling to hold on to her sanity, she wrapped her arms

around her shoulders. Heart racing, she sat there, her mind circling and circling around the painful questions she'd posed. She had resolved nothing when Matt returned. To her vast relief, he suggested going out to dinner at a little Italian restaurant he'd found, and she accepted at once, figuring that it was probably better to be in a crowd than alone. But Matt requested a booth in a quiet corner.

"Do you want me to tell you about the results of my research?" he asked as he stretched out his legs under the table and buttered a piece of bread.

"Yes," she answered, grateful that he was providing the topic of conversation.

"First I checked out the chamber of commerce for any black marks against Colin's would-be partners. They're squeaky-clean in that department. Then I drove over to the real-estate offices of Chet Houston."

Aware that she should be vitally interested in the information, Amanda dredged up a question. "Does he sell houses?"

"Commercial property. I told one of his agents I was looking for a suite of offices in a well-maintained, upscale building. That gave me a chance to ask a lot of questions."

Amanda cut off a piece of chicken cacciatore, chewed and swallowed. Normally she would have enjoyed the rich tomato sauce. Tonight it had no taste, but she kept eating because pregnancy had made her hungry.

Matt had launched into a description of his next stop—a condo management company owned by Chris Tallwood. "I had a similar scenario ready. But I didn't get to use it," he said.

Something about the tone of his voice raised goose bumps on the skin of her arms. "Why not?"

"Tallwood was killed this morning in a hit-and-run accident on the way to the office."

The news blasted through her own dark mood. "Do you think that's just a wild coincidence?"

"I don't know," he answered quietly.

Leaning toward him, she asked. "What about the rest of them? Have any others had accidents?"

"Not as far as I know." He chewed and swallowed another bite of rosemary-grilled veal chop. "There are three more guys I want to investigate. But I decided to leave that for tomorrow."

They ate in silence for a few more minutes.

"Sorry I spoiled your dinner," he finally said.

"It's not you," she answered quickly. "It's been a long day."

"Want to go back to the hotel?"

"Yes."

He signaled for the bill and had her back in their room almost before she could blink.

"You go on to bed," he told her. "I'm going to review the computer files again—see if I can put anything else together on Houston and his friends."

She escaped into the bedroom. But as she lay in the king-size bed, she knew she was in for a long, sleepless night.

At one-thirty Matt finally turned off the living-room light.

She listened to him undress, felt the mattress shift, then lay with her eyes closed, vividly aware of his big body only a couple of feet away.

"Are you going to tell me what's bothering you?" he finally asked in a low voice.

"Nothing."

"Sweetheart, you've been acting like a possum who's stepped on an anthill ever since we got to town."

"That's a great image," she muttered, her arms stiffening at her sides.

"Is it the news I gave you at dinner?"

"No. Let me go to sleep."

"You've been in here for four hours. If you didn't fall asleep when I was out in the living room, what makes you think it's going to be any easier now?"

"Matt, please."

She heard him shift so that he was facing her. Her own body going rigid, she stared into the darkness.

"Maybe it will help if you get it off your chest."

"Help you? Or help me?"

"Both."

"I'm not used to telling people what's bothering me."

"I know," he answered, reaching for her. Before she could scoot away, he moved behind her, holding her the way he had the first morning in the cabin. "But you told me about Colin. You told me about what it was like for you growing up in Crowfoot. You can tell me what's bothering you now."

She moved her lips, but no words escaped from her constricted throat.

"Amanda, when two people are going to get married, they confide in each other."

She felt hysterical laughter bubbling in her throat and struggled to hold it back. "That's the problem. Don't you understand? That's the problem!" she almost shouted, hearing her voice fill the darkness of the bedroom.

Matt's hands gripped her shoulders. "For God's sake, what is it?"

"I can't marry you," she gasped out the words that had been building inside her for painful hours.

His fingers tightened on her flesh, but he didn't speak.

"I mean, I'm not sure it's the best thing for me…or the baby. I've got to think about my child." When she tried to pull away, he held her fast. Desperate to make him understand, she rushed on. "Nothing that happens to us is like real life. We're on the run, and you're protecting me. But what happens when the danger is over?"

"You want an escape clause? You want me to tell you I'll turn you loose as soon as we figure out how to thwart Logan?"

"No!" she answered quickly, surprised by the vehemence of the denial.

"What do you want?"

"I don't know," she answered honestly. "It's just that the idea of standing up in front of a justice of the peace—"

"A minister," he corrected her.

She felt a shiver travel over her skin. "A minister. That's worse! We're going to be exchanging solemn vows."

"I know."

"But how can anything be solemn and serious in a fantasy town where volcanos go off like Old Faithful and pirate ships are down the street from the Statue of Liberty?"

Gently he turned her toward him. "Because we're taking it seriously," he answered, tipping her face toward him. When he felt her tremble again, he rubbed his hand up and down her arm. "You're still afraid to trust me, aren't you?" he asked. "Because so many people let you down."

"I don't know," she whispered, pressing her face against his chest.

When she heard him curse under his breath, she raised her questioning gaze to his.

"Dammit, I was trying to avoid this," he growled.

"Avoid what?" she asked, every muscle in her body tensing.

"If you think about it, you'll realize there's only one logical reason why I'd be pushing to marry you!"

"What?"

She heard him suck in a breath, then let the air out on a rush. "Because you've crawled into my soul. Into my heart. Because I love you."

She stared at him in dumb-eyed astonishment. "How can you? I mean, you don't even know me."

He answered with a bark of a laugh. "I knew you'd say that." She felt his chest heave. "If you want to call it chemistry, you can. If you want to call me crazy, you can do that, too. I prefer to think I've found the woman who's perfect for me. I gave you the reasons before. Do you need to hear them again?"

Stunned, she could only continue to stare at him, trying to read his expression in the dim light.

"Dinner this evening with you was torture, because I kept thinking you were going to tell me you'd changed your mind. And then I didn't have the guts to come in here to bed until I figured you were asleep. If you have an ounce of compassion in your body, you'll put me out of my misery and tell me the wedding is still on."

"Oh, Matt." A sob escaped from her throat, and he gathered her close.

"Honey, don't let the things that happened to you before you met me keep you from trusting my motives."

Another sob racked her. "How can you stand being hooked up with a woman who can't…who can't…?"

"Shush," he murmured, rocking her in his arms. "I know you're scared. I know how hard it is for you to believe in what we have. But it's real. I promise. Trust your instincts."

"What do you mean?"

"Does our being together feel right?"

She thought about that for a few moments. "Yes."

He brushed his lips against the side of her cheek. "Good. Because getting married is the right thing to do. For all three of us. You, me and the baby."

"I want to believe that," she breathed.

"Then let me take care of you. For the rest of your life."

"I don't want someone to take care of me. I want to be your partner!"

"I guess I said that wrong. You are my partner. My other half."

She laid her head on his shoulder, breathing in his scent, absorbing his warmth, feeling a calm come over her.

He held her for long moments, then murmured, "Better?"

"Yes."

"Don't do that to me again. Don't shut me out."

She nestled in his arms, feeling warm and safe at last. And

as his hands stroked over her back and shoulders, the feeling of comfort transmuted into something more sensual.

"Matt, I want to make love with you," she whispered.

"Tomorrow night."

She raised her head, looked down at him. "You're not in the mood?"

"Oh, I'm in the mood, all right," he answered, pulling her hips against his so that she could feel the truth of the statement. "But we're going to wait."

"Why?"

"Because I arranged to have our wedding ceremony tomorrow. And if we both practice a little self-denial until after it's over, the wedding night is going to be a lot more memorable."

"Why didn't you tell me the ceremony is tomorrow?"

"Because I didn't want to hear you say you'd changed your mind." He nuzzled her cheek, then eased away from her. "You think you can sleep now?"

"Yes," she answered, the syllable ending on a yawn as she snuggled into her pillow.

WHEN SHE WOKE the next morning, she found him in the living room, sitting at a breakfast table reading the *New York Times* and looking pleased.

"It's here," he said.

"What?" she asked, sitting down and taking a sip of fresh-squeezed orange juice.

He pointed to a classified ad for a 1931 Pierce Arrow.

"They did it? Your friends are going to make sure someone takes care of the ranch?"

"It looks that way."

"Is it a trick?"

He shook his head. "If Randolph Security says they'll do something, they will."

"But it's still not safe to surrender to them?"

He shook his head. "Not until I have some proof that will

get them out of their legal obligation to Roy Logan. Otherwise he can make life hell for them—since I was on their payroll when I went berserk.''

"You're not berserk."

"Tell it to the judge."

MATT JANGLED THE CAR KEYS in his hand. "The wedding is at six this evening," he informed Amanda, watching her eyes.

"Okay."

"Until then, I'll continue with the investigation of the syndicate members—and do some shopping."

"For what?"

"Wedding outfits."

She seemed to take the news without panicking, but he wasn't going to kid himself. He could walk in here this evening, and she could still say the deal was off again.

He wanted to sweep her into his arms and cling to her. Instead he kissed her on the cheek, then made a hasty exit before she said something else he didn't want to hear.

The only way he could get through the endless day was by staying busy every minute. First he asked around about Tallwood, the man who had been killed, and found out that the guy had been a pillar of the community. Then he checked on two more of his associates, Will Marbella and Harry Hill. Again, there was nothing out of the ordinary about their backgrounds. They were all macho guys who liked to hunt and fish—when they weren't busy making money.

By the afternoon, he was jumpy as a bullfrog on a hot rock. So he knocked off and double-checked the arrangements at the wedding chapel, then went shopping. Instead of a tuxedo, he bought himself a Brett Maverick outfit—old-fashioned black suit, ruffled shirt, string tie and black broad-brimmed hat—to fit his gambler image. Then he picked out a dress he knew would be a knockout on Amanda.

He stopped in his tracks when he got back to their room and caught sight of her. Apparently she'd been busy, too. But her time had been spent in the hotel beauty salon. Her golden hair was tamed into a sophisticated, unswept hairdo. Her eyes were accented with subtle liner and shadow, and her skin glowed with a hint of blusher.

"You look like a movie star," he breathed.

"Oh, go on!"

"I mean it."

"I've never spent a day indulging myself like this. It was expensive."

"Feel free to do it any time you want," he said, then held out the dress box that had been tucked under his arm. "Let's see how you look in this."

"I hope it's big enough."

"It's a size fifty tent."

She made a face as she took the box, then disappeared into the bathroom.

He went to the bar and poured a shot of bourbon, downed it and thought about another. But he only allowed himself the one.

An eternity later Amanda emerged wearing a peach-colored Victorian gown trimmed with lace and ribbons that made her look as if she'd stepped out of an old photograph.

"Matt, it's beautiful," she breathed.

"Very beautiful," he agreed, crossing to her and folding her close. "I think you're the most beautiful bride this town has ever seen."

"Maybe the roundest," she murmured.

"Naw. They probably have weddings in the delivery room here."

Later he didn't remember the drive to the wedding chapel. He just remembered stepping into the reception area, which was furnished like an old-fashioned parlor with brocade couches, globe lamps and crystal chandeliers. It was the perfect setting for the outfits he'd bought.

He was aware of Amanda standing beside him, looking as dazed as he felt. Then the Reverend Mr. and Mrs. Philips stepped forward to greet them, followed by two assistants, a man and a woman who would act as witnesses.

"My, but don't you look fancy," the minister's plump wife chirped. "We'll get started with the ceremony in a minute. But first you have to fill out some forms," she advised, her gray taffeta skirt rustling as she led the way to an antique mahogany desk.

Matt held his breath as he watched Amanda write in the basic information required. When she signed her name, he felt as though he'd leaped another major hurdle. And when she accepted the spray of white orchids he'd ordered and cradled them in her arm, he relaxed another notch.

"This way." Mrs. Philips gestured toward tall oak doors set in a stone archway. They stepped into a chapel that looked to have been transported from an English estate. The ceiling featured Gothic arches that could have been a hundred years old, and there was a stunning rose window at the front with a light behind it to set off the colors of the glass.

It seemed almost anachronistic when Mrs. Philips asked them to stop so she could snap several photographs.

"I didn't think we were going to have pictures," Amanda whispered.

"We're having all the trimmings," Matt corrected, his hand tightening on hers. "And later we're going to do it all over again, in front of our friends."

She nodded gravely, and they posed for the photo. He led her to the altar, his heart drumming so hard inside his chest that he could hardly breathe.

"This place is beautiful," she whispered, looking around at the stone walls and the three rows of dark wood benches.

"I was hoping you'd like it," he managed to reply, amazed that he could make his voice sound normal.

The Reverend Mr. Philips, who had slipped on a traditional black robe over his suit, cleared his throat. "Are we ready to begin?"

Every muscle in Matt's body tensed as he waited to hear

Amanda's answer. When she said yes, he almost allowed himself to relax. But it wasn't until they'd said the ancient vows and exchanged the gold rings he'd bought that he felt a profound surge of relief.

Then the minister pronounced them man and wife and told Matt he could kiss the bride.

He looked into her face, seeing that she still couldn't believe what had just happened.

"It's all real. We're husband and wife. For keeps," he whispered as he gathered her close and touched his lips to hers. He'd meant it to be a light, short kiss, but the moment her mouth softened under his, he was lost. Pulling her into a fierce embrace, he melded his mouth to hers, tasting her, then greedily deepened the kiss, thinking of how lucky he was to have made her his bride.

The sound of the Reverend Mr. Philips clearing his throat reminded him that he and Amanda were not alone. Blinking, he brought the chapel back into focus.

"Come out in the parlor and cut the cake," Mrs. Philips said brightly. "And let's have a toast to your happiness."

Back in the reception area, a small wedding cake waited along with champagne glasses. Amanda elected to have ginger ale; Matt sipped champagne, wondering how long he had to stay here before he could whisk Amanda back to their hotel room and into bed for what he knew was going to be a very memorable wedding night.

The cake cutting took another fifteen minutes with Mrs. Philips fussing around, posing them for more photos. They were Polaroids, as it turned out, so Amanda was able to take them in a large envelope, which the minister's wife tucked inside a white album along with the marriage certificate.

They made their escape then, and Matt left Amanda by the door while he walked around the side of the building to the parking lot.

He was inserting the key in the car door lock when a loud voice stopped him in his tracks.

"You son of a bitch. I swore if I ever saw you again, I'd kill you."

Chapter Twelve

Amanda rounded the building in time to see a tall blond man leap toward Matt. She'd never laid eyes on him before in her life, but she knew that he was intent on mayhem.

"Watch out!" she screamed.

Matt was already whirling to protect his back, already ducking fast enough to avoid the large, solid fist aimed at his jaw. But the keys in his hand went flying.

All his attention was centered on the attacker. His own fist came up and connected with the man's shoulder. Then he spotted her from the corner of his eye and shouted, "Amanda, get out of here."

To her dismay, the distraction cost him a fist in the gut. He ducked the next blow, then initiated an assault of his own.

The Reverend Mr. Philips and his wife must have had a surveillance camera aimed at the parking lot, because they came charging out the side door of the chapel, stopping short several yards from the brawling men.

"Oh, no. Your husband! I'll call the police," the minister gasped.

"No!" Fear shot through Amanda as she imagined the two of them being hauled off to jail. Then present reality slammed back into focus as she saw Matt take another blow, then deliver one in return.

Scurrying around the brawling men, she bent to snatch up

the keys. As she knelt there, a leg came down near her hand, missing her fingers by millimeters. It wasn't Matt's leg. Instinctively she turned, twisted her finger in the brown trousers, and sank her teeth through the fabric into a calf muscle.

As she clamped on to his flesh, the man yelped, tried to wrench away and yelped again as he succeeded in pulling free of her teeth.

"You bitch," he screamed, drawing back his foot to kick her in the abdomen.

Matt's howl of rage was accompanied by a burst of strength as he grabbed the man by the shoulders before his foot could connect with Amanda, and flung him against the wall of the wedding chapel, where he slid down into a heap.

Panting, Matt pulled Amanda to her feet.

In the distance she could hear a siren wailing. Handing over the keys, she let Matt steer her toward the truck. They were in the vehicle and out of the parking lot almost before she could blink again.

"Who was that guy?" she asked between panting breaths.

"That was one of the jerks I cleaned out in a poker game two weeks ago."

"He came after you here?" she asked, fighting confusion.

"No. It's just damn bad luck he came to Vegas to lose some more money and spotted me."

"He hurt you!"

"I'm okay," he insisted, but she watched his hands clamp around the wheel.

"What are we going to do now?" Amanda asked.

"Get out of town."

"Can we stop at the hotel?"

He thought about it for a moment. "That's probably okay, since we registered under a different name. Anyway, we should get out of these clothes. They're too conspicuous, even for Vegas."

BUD LOGAN WOULD HAVE BEEN gratified to witness the altercation in the wedding-chapel parking lot. Instead he was several miles away in the office of Chet Houston, one of the Las Vegas businessmen he'd introduced to Colin.

Bud had called the meeting and he was conscious of holding the undivided attention of Houston and his partners, Dave Trafalgar, Harry Hill and Will Marbella—even as he kept his own fear firmly in check.

Marbella's eyes narrowed. "You're telling us Chris Tallwood's death wasn't an accident?" he asked.

Bud gave him his best salesman's look. "Yeah, that's what I'm telling you. And I know who ordered the hit. It was my brother Roy."

He waited for the inevitable babble of reaction to subside, then continued, "I've got an informant at his ranch, and I know what he's up to. He thinks you were responsible for his son Colin's death."

"We weren't," Trafalgar growled.

"I know that," Bud answered without missing a beat, not caring whether it was true. "But once he gets an idea in his head, it's like trying to make a cur drop a bone. He's going to take you out, one by one."

The circle of eyes around him was hard, nervous. Nobody spoke, so Bud filled the silence with more information.

"But you've got something you can use to stop him. See, he's convinced that Colin fathered a child before he died and he wants to get his hands on that baby. Which is how you're going to get him off your backs."

"Okay, we're listening," Trafalgar said. "But what do you get out of it?"

"A nice-size finder's fee."

MATT AND AMANDA PARKED in the garage under the hotel and took the elevator to the second floor. Somehow, closing the door behind them triggered the reaction she'd managed to repress until then.

Starting to shake, she folded her arms across her chest and

struggled with the sudden, sick feeling that she and Matt would spend the rest of their lives like hunted animals. When she made a moaning sound in her throat, Matt was at her side.

"Sweetheart?"

She tried to speak, but her teeth were chattering too badly. Turning her, he pulled her into his arms, and she linked her trembling fingers behind him, his solid body a shelter against the storm raging around them.

His hands soothed up and down her back until she was able to stop her jaw from trembling.

"Oh, God, Matt, when I saw him coming after you, I didn't know what to do," she gasped.

"*I* was afraid *you* were going to get hurt. Or the baby!"

"All I want is a normal life. Is that too much to ask?" She hated the pleading note she heard in her own voice.

"No. It's not asking too much. It's what you deserve. And I'm going to make sure you get it.'

She clung to him, marveling at the strength of his commitment. Never in her most secret dreams had she dared to imagine a man who knew all the things she'd tried to hide, who understood her to the depths of her soul—yet still wanted her. And she'd almost been foolish enough to let him go. Her arms tightened around him, binding him to her.

She heard him swallow. "This was supposed to be our wedding night. I'm sorry I messed it up."

"No. Don't think that! It wasn't your fault." Tipping her face up, she met his dark, brooding gaze. "You had no idea this was going to happen. Neither did I. It was just bad luck, like you said. And now that we're married, our luck is going to change."

The intensity of the look that passed between them almost shattered her. Sharing that much naked emotion with someone else was still hard for her. Shifting her gaze away, she inspected the places on his face that were going to be bruised in another few hours. "You need some ice on your jaw," she said in a shaky voice.

His eyes turned warm. "Maybe you can kiss it and make it well."

Obligingly she reached to gently touch her lips to an emerging bruise.

"A little higher up, and to the right," he said, his voice husky.

That would put her lips on his, she realized as she complied with the request, making the kiss gentle so as not to hurt him.

Within seconds she discovered he didn't want gentle. He wanted hot and passionate. One hand slid to her bottom, stroking her through the soft fabric of her gown as he pressed her against his erection. Suddenly her whole body was on fire.

She moaned, twisting against him, trying to ease the throbbing between her legs, as his free hand came up to cup her breast, tease her nipple that strained toward his fingers.

In seconds they were both gasping for breath. Desperate to make him understand what she was feeling, she tried to tug him toward the bedroom, but he resisted.

"Matt, please. I need you. I love you so much."

He looked down at her, stunned. "You love me?"

"Yes. I should have said it before. Now I want to show you. You have to let me show you."

He gently stroked his hand against her cheek. "Wham-bam-thank-you-ma'am wasn't what I had in mind for our wedding night."

"I know. But I need to make love with you now." She made the plea more urgent by reaching between them and boldly finding him, stroking him sensually, making a strangled sound rise in his throat as he fumbled for the zipper at the back of her dress.

Panting, they tore at zippers and buttons, stripping each other within seconds, then touched, caressed and kissed in a wild rush of feeling.

With a deep growl, Matt pulled her down to the carpet right where they had been standing, pressing his back against the rug and pulling her on top of him.

"We'd better do it this way, or I might be too rough," he grated as he drove her wild with his skillful hands. With a low sound of need, she brought him inside her, moving frantically, driving for release.

She climaxed so quickly she barely had time to catch her breath, and Matt joined her within seconds. Then she collapsed on top of him, her chest heaving and her body trembling with little aftershocks.

His arms came up to circle her, hold her to him as his lips stroked her damp cheek.

She raised her head and looked down at him in wonder. He looked just as dazed, his hand lifting to gently touch her lips, her cheek.

She couldn't hold back a grin she was sure looked like a cat who had just stolen a slice of roasted chicken.

He pulled her back against his chest and held on to her, rocking her possessively. But she knew that they couldn't stay here.

"We have to go," he told her, his teeth nibbling at her ear.

"I know." She forced herself to break the contact of skin against skin, then let him help her to her feet.

Looking around, she was abashed to find herself standing naked with clothing strewed in a circle around her and Matt.

"You don't have time to be embarrassed. Go get into some traveling clothes."

"How do you know I'm embarrassed?"

He laughed. "The look on your face. You're wondering how you're going to walk all the way across the room naked."

He was right, but she didn't give him the satisfaction of admitting it as she stalked into the bedroom, grabbed her clothes and disappeared into the bathroom to clean up.

In fascination she stared at herself in the mirror. She was thirty years old and almost five months' pregnant. When she'd been a teenager with those boys who wanted to get what they could from her, she hadn't felt anything except shame—and sometimes discomfort—when their hands groped her body.

But every time Matt touched her, she felt the need to meld herself with him.

She continued to stare at her reflection, trying to determine if she seemed different—beyond the obvious bulge at her middle. All she could see was that she was the same basic person. The sensuality must have been there all the time, but she hadn't known it existed until she'd fallen in love with Matt Forester. Loving him made the difference.

"Are you awake in there?" he called through the door.

"Sorry." Hurriedly she pulled on a pair of the slacks he'd brought her, and one of the flowered tops.

When she emerged, she found he'd packed their clothing in the duffel bag he'd bought—including their wedding outfits.

He looked at the plastic bag and washcloth she was carrying. "I want to put some ice on your jaw."

"I don't need it."

"Yes, you do. Stop being macho."

He gave her an exasperated look but allowed her to make a stop at the ice machine before they took the elevator to the lobby. There were no other patrons in line at the reception desk, and Matt paid cash, talking about how he'd hit it big at the craps tables.

A few minutes later they were in the truck again, with her holding an ice pack to his jaw as he drove.

She expected him to head straight for the highway. Instead he made a detour to what looked like the low-rent part of town, then pulled into a gas station where the lot was littered with cars in various states of repair.

"What are we doing?" she asked as he parked the truck in an empty space.

"Getting a set of wheels that will be more comfortable for you."

Apparently he'd already made the arrangements, because a mechanic came trotting over and handed him a set of keys.

When he saw Amanda, he gave her a once-over, then kept his eyes averted from her middle. "Your boyfriend ordered this baby—'' He stopped, flushed. ''This sweet little number special for you,'' he told her, rushing around the side of the building to a big boat of a late-eighties Cadillac that gleamed from a recent washing.

''For me?'' she asked innocently, playing along with whatever story Matt had fabricated. Not so long ago, his stories had made her nervous. Now she was kind of enjoying them. But when they were safely in the car, she asked, ''What *exactly* did you tell them?''

''The truth. That I was desperate to marry you. Only I invented a father who was standing in my way. And I thought this car would impress him.''

''Oh, Matt.'' With the new insights she'd acquired, she realized something she'd been too dense to figure out before. She'd been fearful of the silver-tongued devil. But every time he'd made up a story to explain why they were together, it was about how much he wanted her. Or that she was carrying his child.

Gently she touched his cheek as he headed for the highway. ''You're sweet,'' she murmured.

''Am I?''

''Very.''

''That's not a great recommendation for a tough security man.''

''It's a great recommendation for my husband.''

''Your husband,'' he said in a husky voice, and she could tell that the reality was just sinking in. Reaching over, he squeezed her fingers, then brought his hands back to the wheel. ''We didn't get that doctor's appointment for you,'' he said. ''We'll do it as soon as we get to L.A.''

''Thank you.''

They had cleared the outskirts of the city. Turning, she looked back at the bright lights behind them. Ahead was only the darkness of the desert, broken by an occasional pair of headlights coming toward them.

When he couldn't suppress a yawn, he turned his head toward her. "You should get some sleep."

"I want to stay awake—with you. This is our wedding night."

"Yeah."

She thought for a moment. "Tell me about the drug guy, Dexter Perkins."

He laughed. "Not a very romantic subject."

"No. But maybe it will keep me awake."

"Okay. Let's see... He was from a middle-class home, but his father ditched the family when the kids were teenagers and got himself a younger wife. Dexter had some minor brushes with the law. Then he cleaned up his act and went to UCLA. He was a brilliant student, but he clashed with some professors in the chemistry department and quit."

To her chagrin, that was all she remembered, because she fell asleep before they were fifty miles outside Vegas.

THEY SPENT the first night in the L.A. area in a motel in the Valley. Then Matt found them an apartment in a small residential hotel in Santa Monica where Amanda could see waves breaking on the beach from their third-floor window. She'd never seen the ocean before, and the sight of the endless waves rolling in fascinated her.

Matt rented the place for a month, explaining that they would probably leave before the time was up. She didn't tell him how tired she was of changing residences. Instead she enjoyed the small freedoms he judged were safe—like walks on the beach when he came home in the afternoon and trips to shopping centers to buy baby clothes and some softly feminine maternity dresses that he insisted on getting her. She'd never been much for dresses, but she found she was enjoying the way they made her look. And she definitely enjoyed the warmth in Matt's eyes when *he* looked at her.

She had just popped a pan of biscuits into the oven one

evening when she heard Matt's exclamation from the living room, where he was relaxing in front of the TV.

"What?" she asked, sticking her head around the archway that separated the two rooms.

"Another one of those Las Vegas guys bought the farm," he said, gesturing toward the TV screen.

Amanda settled on the couch beside him. This time the dead man was Chet Houston, who had apparently walked into his office in the middle of a robbery attempt. He'd been shot in the head.

"I don't like it," Matt muttered.

"Now, you really don't think it's a coincidence," she said, not bothering to make it a question.

"That's two people who were involved with Colin in the casino deal who are also dead."

"What do you think it means?"

"Maybe that somebody who was excluded from the group is making his displeasure known. Maybe that Roy thinks these guys were responsible for Colin's death and he's following through with his revenge threat."

Their attention shifted to a more personal topic as the announcer continued. "Authorities are looking for a tie-in to the hit-and-run death of Chris Tallwood, an associate of Houston's. A man who made inquiries at the offices of both men last week is wanted for questioning." It was followed by a description that matched Matt—the way he'd looked last week. Then he'd been in a white shirt and a business suit. These days he wore jeans and T-shirts.

He swore under his breath, and she reached to clutch his hand. When he felt the pressure of her fingers, his reassurance was instantaneous. "They don't have my name. But they've figured out someone who looks like me was nosing around both offices."

"What are we going to do?"

"Sit tight. There's no reason to think the guy they're looking for has gone to L.A.," he said, stroking the dark mustache that he'd been growing on his upper lip. He was letting his hair grow, too. Once it had been conservative in length. Now it was brushing his collar in back.

The buzzer in the kitchen rang, and she jumped up to get the biscuits out of the oven before calling him to the table.

He took a big portion of the stew she'd made and two biscuits. But she watched as he ate, looking for signs that he was more worried than he was letting on.

"This is the best cooking I've had in years," he said as he used a biscuit to sop up some of the rich gravy.

"You said that yesterday."

"It was true yesterday, too. That Middle Eastern chicken dish you made was fantastic. If I'd known what kind of cook you are, I would have proposed as soon as I saw you." He grinned, but she was pretty sure he was forcing the good humor.

"Are you going to cancel my appointment with Dr. Stalton tomorrow?" she asked, trying to keep her voice steady.

He'd gotten her an appointment with an OB/GYN in Monrovia, telling the receptionist that his wife had accompanied him on a business trip to California. Now she watched him weighing pros and cons in his mind.

"I know it's important to make sure everything's okay," he finally said. He thought for a minute. "I gave a false address. And with the fake ID, it should be okay."

Relief swept over her, and she reached across the table for his hand, stroking her thumb across his knuckles.

"We'll get through this," he said, his voice strong with conviction, but she wasn't sure whether he really believed it now or whether he simply wanted it to be true.

ONE THING SHE DID KNOW was that he was very cautious when he drove, staying strictly within the speed limit and making frequent checks in the rearview mirror.

At the doctor's office, she sat with Matt in the waiting room, filling out an insurance form, trying not to feel as if she had

intent to defraud as she wrote down the false information she
had memorized.

Then the nurse took her back to one of the exam rooms,
asking her to take off all her clothes and slip into some of
those absurd paper garments that were only a little better than
being naked.

"I didn't have to undress when I went to my own doctor
last," she objected.

"Dr. Stalton always does an internal exam with new OB
patients."

"Oh," she answered. When she was alone again, she
reached for the buttons at the front of her dress, then stopped
as a sudden feeling of vulnerability swept over her. What if
Logan had found out about the appointment? What if he was
planning to come in and scoop her up when she was least able
to flee? For a paranoid moment, she thought about leaping out
of the cubicle, running back to the waiting room and grabbing
Matt's hand.

Closing her eyes, she ordered herself to get a grip. But her
hands were still shaking as she undressed herself and climbed
onto the exam table.

When she heard a knock at the door, every muscle in her
body clenched. Then Dr. Stalton walked into the room and
introduced himself.

"Thank you for seeing me," she managed to say.

"You're a little tense. Is something wrong?" he asked as
he listened to her heart.

"I'm always nervous with a new doctor," she answered,
willing herself to calm down.

The doctor was both gentle and thorough, telling her that
she was still a bit small for her due date but it was nothing to
worry about. After that, she got to listen to the baby's heartbeat, which was reassuring after such a long time without a
doctor's visit.

Still, when she came back to the consultation room, she was
alarmed all over again to find Matt talking to Dr. Stalton.

"Is there something wrong?" she asked, hearing her voice rise.

The doctor looked at her in surprise. "No. Mr. Cunningham asked to be included."

Mr. Cunningham was Matt. Ralph Cunningham, which she was having trouble remembering, since she'd never met a man who looked less like a Ralph Cunningham.

"In any case, I like to bring the husbands back if they've come here with their wives. Doesn't your regular physician do that?"

Amanda opened her mouth to answer, but Matt was already speaking. "I wasn't able to come with Susi on any of her earlier visits to her regular doctor. So I appreciate getting to be here today."

He held out his hand to her, and Amanda joined him in the other chair facing the doctor. He kept his strong fingers curled around hers.

"I was telling Mr. Cunningham, everything is fine. Your blood pressure is normal. No protein in your urine, no abnormal water retention, and the baby is developing normally. Do you have any questions?"

She felt Matt's fingers tighten on hers. "Well, my wife and I have a pretty active sex life, which neither one of us wants to curtail because of her pregnancy. I'd like to make sure that there's no problem with that."

Her cheeks reddened, but Dr. Stalton seemed to take no notice.

Briskly, he said, "I always tell couples sexual relations during pregnancy are good for their emotional well-being. You just want to make sure not to put any undue pressure on the uterus."

Matt stretched out his legs, crossing them comfortably at the ankles. "And oral sex is all right?" he asked, making her go a shade redder.

"Yes," the doctor answered, keeping his voice even as he

recited a few clinical details that made her sink lower in her chair.

As soon as they were in the elevator, she turned to him, her eyes flashing. "Were you trying to embarrass me in there?" she demanded.

"No. I was trying to make sure that the things I've been wanting to do with you are okay for you and the baby. So now I know," he whispered, his lips playing with her mouth as his hand slid over the roundness of her tummy.

They reached the parking level, and the door opened again, exposing their activity to a mother with two little girls in tow.

"Mommy, that lady's pregnant," one of the girls remarked loudly.

"And he's kissing her," the other one added.

Amanda barreled out of the elevator. Matt followed at a more leisurely pace, and she could hear him laughing behind her.

As soon as they were in the car, he pulled her close again, explaining in very erotic terms exactly what he was going to do with her when he got her back to the apartment.

LATER, AS THEY LAY IN BED, sated, she figured there wouldn't be a better time to bring up a topic she knew was going to be explosive.

"You've been investigating Dexter Perkins. And I get the feeling you haven't found out too much," she began. "Like whether or not he could have ordered a hit on Francetti."

"Perkins is pretty circumspect about his business and his personal life. He's shut down his drug lab and he's running scared—of someone. If I had to guess, I'd say he was too much of a wuss to go after Francetti."

"Well, I was thinking about a more direct approach to getting information out of him. Kind of like what you did in Las Vegas, only you can't be the one to do it, because your face is known."

"What exactly did you have in mind?" he asked cautiously.

"What if I go to him and tell him that I'm carrying Colin's baby, and I'm desperate to know what happened to the father of my child?"

Chapter Thirteen

Matt's face contorted. "Absolutely not!"

"You said I was a good actress."

"That has nothing to do with it. I'm not going to let you do anything dangerous."

"But we both know it's dangerous to stay here in L.A. while you investigate Perkins. We need to be away from the city—somewhere we won't see too many people."

He scowled at her again, but she saw he'd taken the point.

Fluffing up the pillows, he propped himself against the headboard, his toes playing with her knee under the covers. "Okay, let's hear your crazy idea so I can point out the flaws."

She gave him a steely look, moved her knee away, then fixed her own pillows, pulling the covers over her breasts as she sat up.

"Still modest?" he asked, his voice silky. "We're going to have to do some more training exercises."

She ignored his blatant attempt to change the subject and said, "You told me that Perkins eats in public places—a half-dozen different restaurants near his apartment. What if we find out which one he's at tomorrow for supper? I can go in, let him see my belly, make him feel sorry for a poor woman with no father for her child."

Matt considered the idea. When he said, "All right," she almost rolled off the bed in shock.

"All right? Just like that?"

"Yeah, 'cause the only way you're going into any restaurant with Perkins is if I'm with you."

"That will spoil the whole thing!"

"I don't mean we need to be holding hands. You can walk in alone. If Perkins is there, I'll already be sitting at a table nearby."

"Thank you."

"Don't thank me yet. We're going to go over some scenarios and contingency plans so you'll be prepared for anything that comes up. If I tell you to get up and duck out the back way, I expect you to do it without argument."

She saluted. "Yes, sir."

He gave her a considering look. "Are you taking me seriously?"

"Yes."

"Then let me fill you in on everything I know about his background. Then we'll start going over some ground rules."

BUD LOGAN WAS TIRED of waiting around Las Vegas. He'd dropped a thousand dollars in the casino downstairs and come up to his room in disgust. He was lying on the bed in his hotel room drinking vodka and orange juice and watching a porno movie when the phone rang.

"What do you want?" he barked.

"We have the information you sent."

Instantly his attitude changed. "Good."

He glanced at the clock. It was ten-thirty in the evening. But that wasn't late for a Las Vegas business deal—not in the city that was open twenty-four hours a day. "When do I get the money?"

"Right now, if that will be satisfactory."

Bud let the air slowly ooze out of his lungs so that the man on the other end of the line wouldn't hear his relief. He'd been hanging around for days, wondering what the hell was going on, trying not to worry that his delicate negotiations were going to fall apart. Now he knew that everything was coming up roses.

"We have a man down in the lobby. Can you meet him?"

"Of course," Bud answered. Standing up, he jammed his feet into his loafers and looked down at his knit shirt. The color was dark, so it would probably do. Besides, this wasn't some kind of social call.

"How will I know your guy?" he asked.

"He's got your description. He'll find you."

"Oh. Right."

He was in the lobby in ten minutes, looking around as a man in a chauffeur's uniform marched up to him.

"Mr. Logan?" he asked deferentially.

"Right here."

"Follow me. I have a car waiting."

As Bud stepped outside, he thought that it still felt as if it was over ninety degrees, even this late in the evening. But the air-conditioned white Mercedes immediately eliminated any discomfort.

Leaning back in the seat, he watched the brightly lit hotels flash by. "Where are we going?" he asked as they headed up the strip toward the outskirts of the city.

"My employers want this meeting to be private."

"Understood," Bud acknowledged crisply.

They cleared the city limits, then headed into the desert. Bud watched Joshua trees and cacti drift past in the moonlight, wondering where the rendezvous would be.

When the car turned off the highway, he sat up straighter, straining his eyes to see at the farthest edge of the headlight beam. But there were no other cars in sight.

"Hey, where are we going?" he asked, his voice suddenly querulous. "Did my brother Roy send you? Are you working for him?"

"No" the driver assured him, pulling to a stop beside the unpaved track.

A lie? He looked wildly around, assessing the desolate setting. It would be just Roy's style to set up something funny out here in the desert.

His eyes flicked back to the driver and saw the man had a gun in his hand.

Frantically Bud reached for the door handle, but he never made it out of the car.

IT WASN'T JUST WORRY about the confrontation with Perkins that had Amanda's nerves twanging as she waited outside a restaurant called La Mesa, on La Mesa Road. Matt had laid down so many rules that she was having trouble remembering them all.

He'd warned her that it might take a couple of tries to get the restaurant location right, since he couldn't stake out all of them by himself. But they'd hit it lucky on the second try. Perkins had pulled into the parking lot and gotten out of his car fifteen minutes after they'd arrived.

He was in his early twenties, already starting to bald and apparently as nervous as she was, Amanda noted.

"If he's so jumpy, why does he go out at all?" Amanda asked as they watched him cross the parking lot.

"I guess he can't stand being cooped up all the time. And he probably figures that nothing can happen to him in a public restaurant—he's not going to be executed mob-style."

"Let's hope not," Amanda murmured.

Matt waited five minutes, then followed Perkins in. Five minutes after that, Amanda sat down at one of the outside tables where diners could eat under a wooden arbor shaded by flowering vines. Picking up a greasy corn chip, she dipped it in the bowl of salsa, feeling her stomach roil with indigestion. But she needed to do something to occupy her hands and mind.

It was still early for dinner, and through the arched window she could see that the place was about a quarter full. Matt sat about ten feet from her, at a heavy wooden table for two. Their quarry occupied a similar table about eight feet from Matt. Most of the rest of the diners were farther back in another section.

Muscles tensed, she waited for Matt to give her the signal to come inside. He'd been in there forever, and she was still on the outside looking in.

Then he dropped his napkin on the floor and reached to pick it up. That was the sign they'd agreed on. Laying down the corn chip, she pushed back her chair so quickly that it clattered backward, and she had to grab it to keep it from tipping over.

Nervously she smoothed out her dress. It was cornflower-blue, with a high waist that accented her pregnancy, making her look both vulnerable and pretty. She'd never thought much about trying to look pretty until Matt had started picking her clothes. Now she was starting to enjoy her femininity.

Would pretty and vulnerable do anything for Perkins? she wondered as she watched the hostess approach her.

"I'm meeting a friend here," she said, "and I thought we were supposed to wait for each other on the patio. But I finally realized that he's already here—at a table." She gestured toward Perkins, who was sitting with his back to her. "So I'll just go join him."

The hostess nodded, stepping aside, and Amanda started toward the dining area, heart pounding. She kept her eyes away from Matt, who appeared to be looking down at his plate, although she knew he was recording her every move.

Stopping beside the chemist's table, she waited while he bit off a piece of taco and chewed. His looks defined the word *nerd* down to the plastic pocket protector filled with pens adorning his dirty white shirt, which looked as if he'd been sleeping in it for the past week. Although the body odor coming off him in waves almost made her gag, she kept her place.

He looked up at her inquiringly, his eyes focusing on her

face, then her bulging middle, then her face again. "You want something?"

"May I sit down? I feel so tired when I have to stay on my feet these days," she said. Without waiting for permission, she pulled out the chair opposite him and plopped down.

"You're interrupting my dinner."

"I know. But I'll only take a minute of your time," she answered, putting an undercurrent of desperation in her voice, but not pushing too hard, lest he complain to the management.

He was already looking apprehensive as she added, "It's a very delicate matter."

"Yeah?"

"My boyfriend and I were going to get married. But he was killed before he could make me his bride. Now—" She stopped and sighed deeply. "Now I want to find out what happened to him."

"What does that have to do with me?"

"I think you knew him."

Perkins looked at her warily.

"His name was Colin Logan."

From the instantaneous change in Perkins's expression, she knew she'd hit a delicate subject.

"Lower your voice! I don't know anyone named Colin Logan," he replied in a strangled whisper.

"I understand why you don't want to admit the connection," she said, trying to breathe through her mouth to lessen the odor as she leaned across the table. "But Colin and I had a very close relationship. He was doing a lot of things to raise money so the two of us could buy a little ranch. I know he had business dealings with you."

"The hell you do! What are you up to?" He glanced around, looking relieved that nobody was paying them any attention.

"Just what I told you."

"Are you trying to shake me down for money? Did that

uncle of his send you—Bud Logan?'' he asked, punctuating the question by jabbing his fork in her direction.

"Uncle Bud?'' she managed to say. "No, I met him a couple of times, but I haven't seen him since before Colin died.''

"So you're trying to get money out of me on your own?''

"No, Colin left me well off,'' she replied with one of the answers she'd rehearsed. "We had a joint bank account. And there's enough to take care of me and the baby.''

"I had nothing to do with your boyfriend's death,'' he snapped. "So you can stop having me followed around.''

"I'm not having you followed.''

He snorted. "Oh, yeah? Then who is?''

"I don't know. But please hear me out. After what happened to Tim Francetti, I'm scared.'' She paused, but his facial expression didn't change. So she went on. "I don't think it was a coincidence that Colin ended up dead in a Denver alley. And I don't want anybody to come after me and my child. So any hints you can give me about what happened to him would be most appreciated.''

"I don't know what happened to Colin. And I don't know this Francetti guy. I'm just praying that what happened to Colin doesn't happen to me,'' he muttered. "That guy was poison. I'm sorry I ever got mixed up with him. And you will be, too. If you don't—''

Before Perkins could finish, Matt was at her side. "Come on, we're leaving.''

She and the chemist both stared at him as if he'd just beamed down from the *Starship Enterprise*.

"Come on,'' he said, pulling her to her feet and steering her toward the back door just as a man in a business suit entered the restaurant.

"That's one of them!'' Perkins gasped, pushing himself up and looking wildly around.

Matt yanked on Amanda's arm, propelling her toward the rest rooms. Perkins streaked past them, pushing open the emergency exit and setting off the alarm.

As the bell clanged, Matt hurried Amanda into the parking lot and toward his car.

"Stop!" a voice rang out above the din of the alarm.

Ignoring the command, he opened the passenger door and handed her inside.

She thought she heard a cracking sound as he ducked behind the wheel and ground the key in the ignition. Backing up with a squeal of tires, he careened out of the parking lot and into the flow of traffic, narrowly missing a small car that was speeding toward them.

"What's happening?" she gasped.

"I don't know. But that guy was Will Marbella, one of the syndicate members I was investigating in Las Vegas."

"You said he's a solid citizen."

"That's the image he projected. But he was shooting at us— him or somebody with him." Matt took a corner on two wheels, then made another lightning-fast turn.

Twisting around, Amanda scanned the street in back of them. It was empty. "You lost him."

"I hope so," Matt answered, putting distance between themselves and the restaurant before finally taking a freeway on ramp.

"What was Marbella doing coming after Perkins?"

"Perkins or us," Matt informed her. "If somebody was looking for us, they might have staked out the chemist."

"Us or me?"

"I don't know."

A small noise bubbled in her throat as she suddenly realized the implications.

Matt swung his eyes toward her for a moment. "Are you okay?"

"Yes. Thanks to you. I didn't think somebody would stake out Perkins to get to me."

"That may not be what happened. We may just have walked in at the wrong time again."

"Maybe. But I get the feeling we're not keeping our apartment in L.A. any longer.'' When Matt nodded gravely, she continued, ''Where are we going now?''

''I'm still considering a couple of options.''

It was a measure of her changed behavior that she didn't press him.

''I need you to tell me what you found out from Perkins.''

She repeated the conversation as best she could, giving him both the words they'd spoken and her impressions of the chemist.

''Well, we know he's afraid of someone,'' he said. ''Maybe Bud was hassling him. Maybe he's lying about Francetti. Or maybe he's tied to the Las Vegas syndicate—in some way that I haven't figured out.''

Amanda nodded, trying to come up with a connection, but it was like having pieces from two different puzzles mixed together. And she'd never been good with puzzles.

They pulled into the parking garage under the building. Before he opened the door, Matt turned to her. ''Are you up to helping me pack?''

She was weary of packing and unpacking, weary of having no place to call home. But she made her voice strong as she answered, ''Yes.''

He squeezed her hand. ''This is our last move until after the baby is born. I promise.''

She nodded, hanging on the words yet afraid to believe them.

They held hands in the elevator and in the hallway. Then Matt unlocked the door and stepped into the entryway. When he turned the corner into the living room, he stopped and swore.

''What? What's wrong?'' she asked, trying to see around his broad shoulders.

It wasn't Matt who answered the question. Instead a low, steady voice commanded, ''Raise your hands slowly.''

Wordlessly Matt complied.

"Now step in here. You, too," the voice said, speaking more loudly, including her in the order.

As Matt moved out of her way, she saw a man sitting in one of the two easy chairs, a gun trained on Matt's chest.

She stared him with blank-eyed shock. My God, who was he? One of the Las Vegas businessmen still looking for Perkins? Or had Logan finally found her?

"You wouldn't shoot me," she heard Matt say, his voice seeming to come from a great distance.

"Don't give me a reason." The man's dark, assessing gaze swung to Amanda. "I know he's wearing a gun. Take it out of his holster and put it on the end table beside my chair. And don't try anything funny, because we could have a bad accident if you do." The man's gaze came back to Matt. "Tell her to do it," he commanded.

"Do what he says."

Amanda felt cold, naked fear seep into her bones. Fear for Matt. If this gunman worked for Logan, he wouldn't shoot her, she told herself as her hand unconsciously flattened against her tummy. He wouldn't harm the baby, because Logan wanted Colin's child. She had to cling to that conviction or go mad.

But Matt didn't have the same protection. He was the one who had snatched her out of Logan's clutches.

When she touched his shirt, she could feel his warm skin through the fabric. That helped—almost as much as it made the task of retrieving the gun all the harder. Somehow she managed to get the pistol out of the holster at the back of Matt's waistband and onto the little table, where it hit the wood with a thunk that reverberated through the room.

"Sit down," the stranger said. "We've got some talking to do."

Chapter Fourteen

"Can I sit beside her on the couch?" Matt asked, his gaze fixed on the man who had broken into their apartment.

The stranger nodded, and Matt wove his fingers with Amanda's, bringing her down beside him. When he felt her hand tremble, his grip tightened reassuringly. She pressed her body to him, drawing strength from his hard frame.

"How did you find us, Hunter?" he asked.

"Hunter Kelley?" Amanda whispered as the name registered. "You mean the man who was in the helicopter, calling to you on the bullhorn?" That seemed like a lifetime ago.

"Yeah, from Randolph Security," Matt said, his voice tight "I thought he was my friend."

"I am," the security man answered. "That's why I came here alone, to get some answers."

"Let us go," Amanda pleaded. "We haven't done anything."

"I need to evaluate that for myself."

"Tell me how you found us," Matt said again.

Hunter lifted one shoulder. "That would be giving away trade secrets. And also letting down my friends at 43 Light Street."

"Are you here because of the Light Street organization? Or as a Randolph agent?" Matt snapped.

"Neither."

Amanda stared at him. Matt had told her about his group of friends, many of whom worked at 43 Light Street in Baltimore, who often unofficially helped out the Randolph agents. "Then would you mind explaining why you're holding us at gunpoint?" she asked.

"I want to find out what's going on. Personally—not for any organization." Hunter gave her an appraising look, and she felt as if his dark eyes were penetrating to the very depths of her soul. "Matt saved my life that morning in Wyoming," he continued. "He told me not to land the helicopter. If I had, I would have been killed when the cabin blew up."

"I didn't know that," Amanda murmured.

"It's not the kind of thing he'd work into the conversation," Hunter said.

"What do you think you know about our situation?" Matt asked, changing the subject abruptly.

Hunter considered the question. "I was able to obtain access to Tim Francetti's computer. Although he erased information from his hard disk, I reconstructed the content of many of his files."

"That computer is in custody of the Denver police," Matt pointed out.

"I was able to get access to it," Hunter answered without missing a beat. "I also saw the police report on Francetti's murder. There is mention of a blond woman and a dark-haired man escaping from the office. I gather that was you two."

"We didn't kill him," Matt growled.

"I assume you did not. But I also assume that you obtained a copy of the detective's files. In fact, while I was waiting for you, I confirmed that," he said, gesturing toward the laptop sitting on the dining-room table. "So I've concluded that you're in Los Angeles because of Dexter Perkins and Colin Logan."

"Right," Matt answered. "And while Amanda was talking to Perkins in a restaurant, we were spotted by one of the men involved in the Las Vegas casino deal."

Hunter quirked an eyebrow. "How do you connect Perki▯ to the Las Vegas killings?"

"I can't," Matt answered.

Amanda looked from him to Hunter. They were having ▯ perfectly civilized conversation, except that the uninvited gue▯ was still holding the gun on them. Unable to keep silent, sh▯ blurted, "Why are we talking about Perkins and the Las Veg▯ men? Aren't you here because you think Matt and I did some▯ thing…underhanded to Roy Logan?" Without letting him a▯ swer, she plowed on. "What really happened was that Ma▯ heard Logan talking to his foreman, Al Hewitt. They wer▯ making plans to capture me and hold me against my will. Ma▯ came to rescue me. And he's been keeping me safe eve▯ since."

She could see the information—or maybe the emotion i▯ her voice—had had an effect on Hunter.

"I listened to the tape of the phone call Matt made to Jed,▯ he said slowly. "It directly contradicts the facts Logan pr▯ sented to us."

Amanda squeezed her eyes shut, then opened them agai▯ focusing on Hunter. "I don't know exactly what Matt said ▯ Jed. Or what Logan told you. But I know Logan thinks th▯ I'm pregnant with his son Colin's child. And he wants to tak▯ the baby away from me."

"He's probably planning to kill Amanda after the baby ▯ born," Matt added. "That way he won't have to get into ▯ custody battle with her. Of course, his other alternative is mak▯ ing it look like she's insane or a criminal. Then the courts wi▯ have to give him the child."

Hunter looked from one of them to the other. Slowly h▯ lowered the gun and set it on the table beside Matt's weapo▯

Amanda watched the play of expressions across his fac▯ "He had proof that Miss Barnwell stole a considerable amou▯ of money from his son."

"That's bull," Matt spit out.

"He had proof that the two of you were involved in a r▯

lationship before Matt arrived in Crowfoot, that the two of you are responsible for his son's murder.''

"He concocted all that the night Amanda and I ran for our lives?" Matt prodded.

Hunter shook his head. "He made plausible claims before the incident at the cabin. Then he supported the claims with documents.''

"They're fake," Matt growled.

"Randolph Security is pursuing that theory," Hunter said. "But we can't turn against our client without proof. If we do, we risk losing our license.''

"I told Jed to check out the Highton clinic. Didn't he do that? Didn't you see the report on the clinic in Francetti's files?" Matt demanded.

Hunter shook his head. "We were unable to verify that information. The clinic increased its security after someone broke into their records. And I found nothing about the clinic in Francetti's computer. The police may have destroyed that data when they tried to recover the files. Please fill me in.''

"Amanda became pregnant through artificial insemination," Matt said. "At the Highton clinic in Cheyenne. It must have been Francetti who broke in to get their records, or someone working for him. His report verified that Colin Logan had been a donor there. The information is coded, but Francetti told Logan that Colin is the father of Amanda's child. That's why Logan went after her and the baby.''

Hunter focused on Amanda. "Why did you choose artificial insemination?''

She answered without thinking, "Because I hadn't met Matt Forester yet." As soon as she realized what she'd said, she felt her face grow hot. Matt's fingers tightened on hers.

"Is that true?" he asked, his eyes so intensely focused on her that she saw nothing else in the room.

"You must know it's true. You must know I wish I'd met you before I made the decision.''

She saw him swallow convulsively. "Would you have let

me get close enough to you to give you a child?'' he asked in a gritty voice.

"I hope I would have been smart enough," she whispered, her chest so tight that she could barely draw in enough breath to speak.

Moisture shimmered in Matt's eyes. "Thank you for telling me that."

In response, she felt her own vision blur. She was about to throw herself into Matt's arms. But a throat-clearing sound reached her from across the room, and the rest of the world snapped back into focus. With a start she realized that there was a witness to their private conversation—a man who had been holding them at gunpoint a few moments ago.

The gun was on the table now. And the man was proving to be quite different from her initial impression. "Apparently Logan wants the baby at any cost—and he was willing to manufacture evidence to support his story," he said.

"Are you going to tell that to Randolph Security?" Matt demanded.

"I can tell them, yes. And try to prove your version of events."

"It's not our version. It's the truth," Amanda insisted.

Hunter nodded. "I think I can persuade Randolph Security to help protect you against Logan. Covertly, I mean."

"No," Matt said.

Amanda's gaze shot to him. Hunter was offering them protection, and Matt was turning it down. "Why not?" she breathed.

"Because there are still too many variables, and they can't guarantee our safety," Matt answered. "Nobody can." He turned to Hunter. "If you want to help us, do some digging for me. Try to find out who killed Tim Francetti. Find out how Perkins and the Las Vegas syndicate are tied together. See if the computers at Randolph can decode the Highton clinic records so we can find out if Colin really is the father of Amanda's child. I'll give you those records."

Getting up, he went to a drawer in the dining room and pulled out a floppy disk. Sticking it in the laptop, he transferred the information from Francetti's files, then slipped the disk into an envelope and handed it to Hunter. "And while you're doing all that research, the safest thing for us is to stay hidden where nobody, including Randolph, can find us. Because, every time we surface, someone else comes after us."

Hunter nodded gravely. "I needed to hear for myself what you had to say about Logan. I needed to see from your eyes whether you were telling the truth. I hope I haven't compromised you by coming here."

"We were coming home to pack," Matt told him, explaining more fully what had happened in the restaurant this evening.

"How will I contact you?" Hunter asked.

Matt thought for a moment. "Another ad in the *New York Times*. Another Pierce Arrow. How about a 1933 model?"

"That will work. Will you call us on the secure line if you see the ad?"

Matt thought for a moment, then answered, "Yes."

Hunter stood, reached out his hand toward Matt, and the two men shook. "I am glad I came," he said. Then he turned to Amanda. "I have a background that would have frightened most women away. But Kathryn Kelley wanted to become my wife. And now the two of us have a child, a little boy named Ethan. He's fifteen months old. Being with Kathryn when she carried the baby, seeing him born, watching him grow and develop into his own person means more to me than you could ever know. I would do anything to keep him safe. Anything. And Kathryn, too," he added, his voice surging with emotion. "Without her, I would be...nothing."

The deeply felt emotions in his voice propelled Amanda off the couch and across the room. Reaching out, she embraced Hunter, and he hugged her back.

"Thank you for understanding," she told him.

"I do. Better than you know," he answered, then eased

away, looking from her to Matt. "I'd better go. You two will want to be out of here soon."

"Yes," Matt agreed.

When the door had closed behind their surprise visitor, Amanda turned to her husband. "The way he said it—Kathryn Kelley 'wanted' to marry him. Did he take her name?"

"Yes."

"Why?"

"You can ask him when you get to know him better."

"You trust him not to turn us in?" she asked.

"Don't you?"

"Yes."

She moved toward Matt and embraced him as she had Hunter—except that she held him more fiercely. They clung together, and his head dipped so that he could cover her lips with his. But before things could heat to flashpoint, he lifted his mouth away.

"I'm not going to take a chance on someone else catching up with us because we're fooling around."

She nodded, forced herself to move away from him and start packing the few things they had accumulated.

Twenty minutes later, they were in the Cadillac and heading for a residential neighborhood, where Matt made a quick change of license plates with some unsuspecting home owners.

Then they headed east.

"So, have you figured out where we're going?" she asked as they left the L.A. smog behind.

"The Shenandoah Valley of Virginia—or rather the mountains flanking the valley."

"Aren't there too many people around?"

He laughed. "You Westerners have a distorted picture of the eastern seaboard states. And that's part of what I'm counting on, that Logan will make the same assumption you did— that there's not enough room in Virginia to hide. More importantly I know the locale because I did undercover drug-enforcement work there, trying to cut the marijuana crop. So

I know some good areas where we can look for a small house and where I can put defensive measures in place.''

"Like what?''

"An alarm system, some kind of defensive perimeter and other stuff. But I won't be able to decide what will work best until I see the property.''

She turned to him, studying his profile in the illumination at a freeway interchange. He looked different from when she'd first met him. His hair was a lot longer, creating a distinct contrast to the crisply dressed security agent who had first caught her eye in Crowfoot. Now he looked as if he could have stepped off a mountain stronghold.

But she could see that the intelligence behind his dark eyes was the same. She knew his mind was busy working, his attention absorbed by contingency plans. She'd been lucky to hook up with a professional protection specialist. The knowledge that he loved her—that guarding her wasn't just an exciting episode in his life—made her heart swell.

She reached over to lay her hand possessively on his arm.

"Do you want to lie down in the back?'' he asked.

"No, I want to stay here with you,'' she answered, switching the point of contact to his thigh.

"Don't get too personal with that hand.'' He laughed. "Or we may have to pull over.''

"You're kidding.''

"Yeah.''

The darkness made her bold. "Are you always so… uh…interested in sex.''

He laughed again. "No. It's the company I'm keeping.''

"Oh, sure.''

"Do I have to pull over and prove you're turning me on?''

"No,'' she murmured, her gaze focusing on the bulge at the front of his jeans.

"I told you I was attracted to you as soon as I saw you.''

"Why?''

"You're fishing for compliments again, Mrs. Forester. How

many times do I have to repeat that I like your looks? I like the qualities you projected. Then finding out how responsive you are was a major turn-on.''

She made a small sound in her throat. ''You think I'm going to be responsive when I'm as big as the back of a barn?''

''We'll find out, won't we?''

''Are you going to be disappointed if I'm not?'' she asked in the darkness.

''Yeah. But I think I'm adult enough to handle it.''

''What about when I'm getting up in the middle of the night with a crying baby?''

''I'll help you with that.''

''You can't nurse her.''

''But I can bring her to you. And I can change her.''

''You're volunteering to change diapers?''

''I told you, I volunteered for the whole shebang. Marriage, baby tending, kid raising, the empty nest, growing old with you.'' He paused. ''Maybe you'll be disappointed in my waning sexual prowess when I'm seventy.''

''I'll believe that when I see it.''

MATT ALLOWED five days for the trip from Los Angeles to Warrenton, Virginia, with Amanda doing about a quarter of the driving. She suspected that he could have made it across the country on his own in far less time, but she knew he was taking her advancing pregnancy into consideration.

In Warrenton, she bit back her objections when he left her in a secluded motel on the outskirts of town while he crisscrossed the valley with a rental agent. On the third day, when she was about to go stir crazy, he told her there was a property he wanted her to see.

It turned out to be a small cottage built of natural stone, perched on the edge of a cliff and commanding a spectacular view of hazy blue mountains in the distance and a pine-filled valley below. It wasn't the kind of mountain setting she was used to back home with tall peaks towering over the landscape.

But it had a natural beauty that stirred her senses, and she could tell Matt was enthusiastic as he ticked off the advantages.

"It's secluded but close enough to town so that we could make trips in easily. It occupies high ground. There's a clear view of the approach. Anybody who comes in has to come up the access road—or go the long way around. And I can rig an alarm system for the back way in."

She appreciated her husband's attention to security, but she was equally interested in more domestic concerns. Inside, the furnishings were plain but comfortable, and the colors were neutral, she noted, so that adding her own decorative touches would be easy.

The kitchen was large and inviting, and there was a room she could fix up as a nursery. Yes, she could make the place into a real home—for as long as they stayed, she silently added.

"What do you think?" he asked.

"I like it."

"Good. Come on outside," he urged, his voice telling her that there was at least one more surprise he wanted to share. He took her out a rear door to a shaded patio, then down a steep trail to a lookout point. As she puffed along behind him, she wondered what was so special about this part of the property.

When he disappeared around a bend, she caught her breath, because it looked as if he'd plunged off the side of the cliff.

"Matt!"

"Right here." His head popped up, and he offered her his hand.

"You don't expect me to climb down there, do you?" she asked.

"It's easier than it looks. I swear."

She clenched her teeth and let him help her down an incline to what looked like a blank wall. Then he swept aside a patch of vines to reveal a metal door in the rock face.

"What's in there?"

"Bears."

She jumped back, and he laughed, keeping a tight hold on her hand.

"Just kidding," he admitted as he unlocked the door with a key, and pulled it open, the hinges squeaking in protest. Then he produced a flashlight from his hip pocket and shined it inside. "It must have originally been intended as a bomb shelter. It's secure and it's hard to find, which makes it the perfect stronghold for you," he added, ushering her inside. It was cool, but there was no musty smell as she had expected.

"How did you find it?" she asked as he shined the light into the farthest corners.

"It was mentioned in the real-estate description of the place. But I still had to do some scouting around to find the location."

"Why do I need a stronghold?"

"In case somebody shows up."

"You said Logan wouldn't find us here," she protested, a sudden chill traveling over her skin.

"That's what I think. But I have to be prepared in case," he answered in the darkness.

She nodded, knowing he was right. He took her hand, leading her outside again and up the hill, walking slowly to keep pace with her. "What do you think? Can we make a home here?"

"If we stay here, can I get a doctor in town?" she pressed.

"In the next town," he corrected.

"Okay, the next town. And what about if I need to call him?"

"I don't want to take the chance on installing a phone line in the house, but I can get a cell phone in another name," he told her.

"Okay. And I want a sewing machine."

"That's a top priority?"

"Yes."

"You want to make baby clothes?"

"And curtains and pillows."

He smiled indulgently. "Sure."

Weaving his fingers through hers, he led her back up the trail, pausing often as he saw her struggling to keep up.

She was excited about the prospect of making a home for Matt, of getting ready for the baby. But it wasn't until they'd gotten back to the house that she realized they were both avoiding the big question: How long were they going to be hiding out here?

Chapter Fifteen

Matt took a year lease on the property, using another one of the identities that he'd bought during the weeks he'd been away.

Amanda's first thought was that the real-estate agent wouldn't be able to track them down when they skipped town in the middle of the night. Then she told herself they weren't going to pull another vanishing act. They were staying here until after the baby was born—and by that time Randolph Security would have called with the good news that their problems with Roy Logan, the Las Vegas syndicate and the Denver police were solved.

Most of her waking hours she could make herself believe that—except when the grim reality of Matt's siege preparations intruded.

Still, life in their mountain stronghold settled into a routine, and much of it gave Amanda great joy. Each morning when she woke, she felt happier than she ever had in her life. Matt was beside her in their big, cozy bed, and when he felt her stir, he moved his hand, gently touching her fingers or her cheek, or laying his palm on her abdomen, making a connection with their child. For she had come to think of the baby as his as much as hers—in all the ways that counted. In her mind, and in her heart, the child she carried had become

Matt's—the product of the physical bond of love that they'd forged.

It wasn't just in bed that she felt fulfilled as a woman for the first time in her life. In their own way, her days were as precious as her nights. She and Matt might be living as fugitives, but she had turned their mountain hideout into a cozy refuge, with print curtains and matching pillows, a nursery full of stuffed animals and her own landscape paintings, which Matt had framed for her.

The first time she'd set out a vase of Queen Anne's lace, chicory and goldenrod she'd gathered from the hillside, Matt had stood beside the table looking at the arrangement from several angles.

"Do you like it?" she asked anxiously.

"It's beautiful."

"You seem a little doubtful," she murmured, trying to see the centerpiece through his eyes.

"No. I'm just marveling at the effect you've gotten with...weeds."

"They're wildflowers!" she corrected.

He crossed the room, bent to skim his lips against her neck. "You're enjoying all the things that go into making a home, aren't you?" he asked, and she could hear the smile in his voice.

"Very much."

"And the things you make yourself are better than anything you could buy."

She flushed with pleasure, because she'd never been with anyone who was so taken with her abilities—or so totally committed to her welfare. She felt the same about him. He was the perfect mate for her, the perfect father for the child she carried.

Yet she knew Matt wasn't simply enjoying being a husband and getting ready for a new member of their family. He was her bodyguard, too. So the next day she sat tensely with a book of baby names, trying to focus on the words while her husband was out laying a series of explosive charges that could be set off by a radio transmitter.

That afternoon he carefully pointed out the locations to her and explained how the transmitters would set off the charges. Then he made her practice what she'd do if the house were under attack.

When he wanted her to go over it again the next week, she bit back a protest and demonstrated her new knowledge of explosives for him, then brushed up her marksmanship skills on the shooting range down the hill. Actually the target practice brought out her competitive instincts, so that on several occasions she did better than he did.

The two-way radio he purchased was another safety precaution. Whenever he went out of the house, he kept in touch with her, checking in regularly.

Another ritual was his daily scan of the *New York Times* so he could check the car ads. At first he didn't seem too concerned that there were no Pierce Arrows on offer. But as the weeks wore on, she could see that the lack of a message from Randolph Security was getting to him. And so was being cooped up on this little patch of mountainside.

He'd committed himself to guarding his pregnant wife. And that meant he couldn't do any investigating of Roy Logan or Will Marbella and the other syndicate members from Las Vegas—because he was afraid that even an Internet connection might give away their location.

She could see there weren't enough activities to fill his days. There were only so many times he could check his perimeter security. Only so many TV monitors and supplies and fortifications he could add to the bomb shelter. Only so many hours he could allot to target practice.

As they lay in bed one evening in late September after making love, she studied his profile in the semidarkness. Although he'd been tense earlier in the day, he looked relaxed now. But she knew that if the light were on, she would see fine lines around his eyes that hadn't been there when they'd met.

Turning to him, she nestled her head against his neck.

"You know how much I love making a home for you and the baby," she murmured. "But I know this whole thing is getting to you."

"Which whole thing?" he asked, his voice cautious.

"Staying holed up here. Not working at your profession. Being cut off from your friends at Light Street and Randolph Security. You've told me enough about them so that I know they mean a lot to you. They're not just the people you work with—they're friends who help each other when the chips are down. It's different for me."

When he made a sound of denial, she hurried on. "I realize now that I was staying in Crowfoot because it was what I was used to. Now that I'm gone, there's nobody I really miss."

It was a long speech for her. But his answer was clipped. "I'm fine."

"Okay." Shifting her bulky body, she rolled to her side, her back to him, because the last thing she wanted to do was put pressure on him.

He put his hand on her shoulder, then moved behind her so that his chest was pressed against her back. His hand came up to circle her abdomen, resting there.

"It's been a long time since I didn't have a job to go to every morning," he said in a low voice.

"I know," she answered, laying her hand over his.

"I don't like to think that the only way I can support my family is as a gambler."

"We won't have to hide like this forever," she told him, praying that it was true, because she knew that the way they were living was going to tear their marriage apart if it went on much longer.

"Yeah," he answered, settling more comfortably against her and making a show of acting relaxed. "You want to talk about baby names?" he asked.

She'd been thinking a lot about girls' names, but she'd been worried about whether he'd like her selection.

"What about Bethany, if it's a girl?" she whispered.

"Bethany. My sister."

"Would you mind?"

She waited, her breath shallow, while he thought that over.
"I think that would be fine," he said, his voice thick.

"Good."

"What about for a boy?"

"Do you think Hunter would like having a baby named
after him?"

"I think he'd be flattered," Matt answered.

THREE MORE WEEKS SLID BY, and nothing had changed except
that Matt was more restless and she was more uncomfortable—so uncomfortable that she felt herself stiffen when he
reached to fold his arms under her breasts as she stood at the
bathroom sink. Holding her like that was one of the ways he
had of letting her know that he was thinking about making
love. Usually she responded with enthusiasm. Tonight was different, and he sensed her reluctance at once.

"It's okay," he told her as he bent to kiss the back of her
neck.

She turned in his arms, pressing her head to his shoulder.
"I...guess I'm not feeling all that great," she admitted.

His posture tensed. "Do you want me to call the doctor?"

"My regular visit is in a couple of days. I think I can wait
till then. I guess feeling draggy is to be expected this late in
the game."

"You didn't eat much dinner. Do you feel sick? Does anything hurt?"

"Well, my lower back is kind of achy."

"Want me to rub it?"

"I'd love that," she told him.

Slipping into bed, she moved awkwardly to the side, then
shifted her heavy body so that he could reach her spine.

He came down beside her, his hands working the muscles
of her back, relieving some of the tension. When he pulled

er into his arms and held her, she snuggled against him, finding a position that accommodated her bulging middle. But she
suspected it would be a long time before she got to sleep.

In fact, when Matt stirred at six-thirty, she was still lying
there—uncomfortable and unsure whether she'd gotten any
sleep at all.

"How are you?" he asked when he realized she was awake.

"Okay."

"You don't sound too positive. Do you want me to get you
something?"

"I'd better not take anything."

"I meant something like a cup of herbal tea?"

"Okay. Wild blackberry," she agreed, thinking that the hot
liquid might feel good in her throat.

Matt shrugged into a polo shirt and went to fix the tea. Five
minutes later he was back with a mug for both of them. He'd
given up coffee when she'd complained that the smell made
her sick.

While he was gone, she made a quick trip to the bathroom,
then fluffed up the pillows. When he returned, they sat together under the covers, shoulders pressed together as she took
small sips of tea.

"Better?" he asked.

"Mm-hmm," she allowed, not sure that it was actually true.
"What are you going to do today?"

He thought for several moments, and she was sorry she'd
asked, since it seemed he hadn't had any particular plans.

"Check the explosives," he finally said.

In the next moment, the portable phone he'd left on the
dresser rang, and they both jumped. The phone was only for
emergencies. Nobody knew their number, nobody had ever
called.

"Are you going to answer it?" she asked in a voice she
couldn't quite hold steady. "Or are we going to pretend we're
not home?"

"I think I'd better find out who it is," he answered tightly.

Crossing the room, he pulled up the antenna, then came back to her side before pressing the receive button.

He was close enough so that she could hear a man say, "Mr. Forester."

"There's no one here by that name," Matt answered.

"Nice try."

"Who is this?" he asked, pressing another button to put the phone on speaker. Then he was off the bed, reaching for his pants.

"This is Will Marbella. You were poking into my business in Las Vegas. Then I came looking for you in L.A. I'm afraid we just missed each other that time."

Amanda went rigid with shock. Will Marbella was the man they'd seen in the restaurant when she'd been sitting at the table with Dexter Perkins. The man who had shot at them.

Matt clamped his fingers on to her arm, then mouthed the words, "Get dressed."

"What do you want?" he said aloud.

"Ms. Barnwell."

"That's Mrs. Forester," Matt shot back.

Amanda heaved herself off the bed, feeling heavy and stiff—and terrified. Opting for the easiest thing she could find, she pulled a knit maternity dress over her head, then felt under the edge of the bed with her toes for the shoes and socks she'd been wearing the day before. She found the shoes, but the socks eluded her.

"Whatever."

The casual unconcern of the answer raised goose bumps on her arms.

"What do you want with her?" Matt asked as he checked the gun that had been lying beside the phone. From the closet he pulled out a backpack and tossed the gun inside. It was followed by one of the walkie-talkies.

"We'd like her to help us get Roy Logan off our backs. He's been killing members of our syndicate. And we feel that we can use Ms.—Mrs. Forester for leverage. We let Roy know we have her, and he leaves us alone.''

"Why would Logan be after you?" Matt growled.

"He thinks we had something to do with his son's death."

"Did you?"

"That's irrelevant."

"You're not laying a hand on my wife!"

"I'm afraid you don't have much choice. We have your road blocked. The house is surrounded. Your best bet is to come out quietly. That way, nobody gets hurt."

"Your best bet is to get the hell out of here," Matt answered, then pressed the off button.

Panic rising in her throat, she stared at him. "What are we going to do?"

He rounded the bed, sat her down and knelt in front of her, slipping on her socks and then her tennis shoes. "You have to be very strong for me. Very brave. You have to get to the shelter. They won't find you there. And if they figure out where it is, they can't get in. So you and the baby will be safe. Can you lock yourself in there for me?"

"But they're right outside." Her gaze darting toward the window, she half expected to see armed men rushing toward the house.

"They can't be as close as he says, or they would have set off the alarms. I'm going out first—"

"No!" Her fingers clamped around his sleeve.

"Let me finish. I'll go through the woods—down the other side of the mountain. If they follow me, so much the better."

"No," she gasped out. "They won't kill me. They'll kill you."

"They—" He stopped short, changed the direction of his comment. "As soon as I'm out of range of their communications equipment, I'm going to call Randolph Security. They'll come through for us when I tell them what's going on."

"For all we know, they're working with these guys," she said. "Like they were working with Roy."

"No," he answered quickly. Too quickly. As he tried to untangle her fingers from his shirt, she felt everything that they'd built together over the past months slipping from her grasp. "Amanda, let go. I have to get the controllers for the explosives."

She forced her fingers to go limp, then watched with her heart pounding as he dashed into the living room. Every moment that he was out of her sight was an eternity. Then he was back, holding up two sets of controls and the two-way radios. "When I get back with reinforcements, I'll call you," he said, stuffing equipment into the backpack.

"Don't be frightened if you hear me setting off some charges in the woods. It's just a diversion."

She could only stare at him numbly, trying to take it all in. All along he'd been preparing her for this moment, but she had never really believed that it was going to happen.

With his free hand, he pointed to a row of buttons on the other controller. "Remember, these are the ones near the entrance to the shelter. And these are for the grounds around the house. Do you remember the sequence?"

"Yes," she wheezed.

He opened the top dresser drawer, took out a pistol and set it beside her on the bed. "Keep this with you. There are more weapons in the shelter."

He bent and pressed his lips to hers—the kiss a flare of intense emotions burning between them. "I love you. Never forget how much I love you. Get to the shelter, so I know you're safe. Promise me that!"

"Don't say it that way. Don't make it sound like you're saying goodbye," she gasped.

"I'm not. I can take care of myself. But I have to know you're safe."

"All right. I promise," she managed to reply although it wasn't what she wanted to say. She wanted to beg him to stay with her or take her with him. But she held the plea back, because she knew it wouldn't do either one of them any good. He gave her arm a quick squeeze, then turned and slipped out of the room.

She kept her eyes glued to his broad shoulders as long as she could see them. When she heard the back door close, she knew she was on her own.

"Matt. I love you, Matt." The words were a choked whisper on her lips. She wanted to burrow under the covers. Instead she listened for sounds of activity outside the house. But she could hear nothing.

They'd long since traded in the Cadillac for a couple of sport utility vehicles that could negotiate the rough roads leading to their fortress. One was always parked near the house so she wouldn't have to walk far in case they needed to get away fast. The other was on the far side of the mountain, and she reasoned that Matt must be heading there.

Which meant she should duck down the path to the shelter while he was leading them in the other direction. But before she could push herself off the bed, a pain gripped her abdomen.

It lasted half a minute, and when it was over, she sucked in a breath, then let it out in a rush. Suddenly a passage from one of her maternity books flashed into her mind. Persistent lower-back ache could be a sign of labor. And her lower back had been hurting since the day before.

But she hadn't considered the onset of labor last night or this morning, because it was too early. She still had three weeks to go, and there was no doubt about her due date. That had been established with exact precision at the Highton clinic. *Please, God,* she begged, *Not now. Don't let this be the real thing. Just let it be false labor. Just let it stop.* Her silent prayer was rudely interrupted by a sound from outside—the sound of gunfire.

On a moan of terror, she pushed herself up and rushed to

the window, her eyes straining to catch sight of her husband. But he was already out of view, and she could see nothing besides the sun shining down on the splendor of the fall foliage.

Chapter Sixteen

Matt heard the crack of weapons fire, felt a bullet whiz past his ear, heard the impact of another as it plowed into a tree not far from his right shoulder.

Terror for Amanda banded his chest, making it hard to draw a full breath as he ran. He'd forced himself to leave. Now he didn't even know if he'd done the right thing. Should he have stayed with her and tried to hold them off? What if she couldn't get to the shelter? What if they didn't care about what happened to her? What if they thought that the baby was far enough along so that they didn't need the mother?

He almost turned around. Then reason asserted itself. He had to be out of the area to call Randolph Security; otherwise Will Marbella and his friends would hear the transmission. And then, God knows what they'd do.

Without slackening his pace, he pulled the transmitter from his pocket and pressed the third button on the right. Seventy-five feet behind him there was a satisfying explosion. The next button brought similar results—this time closer to his escape route. Maybe that would give them second thoughts about following him.

Still, images he didn't want to see spun in his head. And all he could do was keep running, dodging into the protection of the trees, his breath searing his lungs as he tried to get away so that he could come back with reinforcements and save his wife and child.

THE GROUND SHOOK, and the sound of an explosion hit Amanda's eardrums. Moments later it came again. Even as she cringed against the wall, she realized what must have happened. That was Matt, using the transmitter. Drawing the bad guys away from her.

She had to take advantage of the time he was buying her. For him. For herself. For their child.

Summoning every drop of inner strength she possessed, she crossed to the closet and found the kit Matt had helped her prepare in case she was in labor and they didn't make it to the hospital in time. Snatching it up, she slipped the walkie-talkie and the transmitter inside, then slung the strap over her shoulder. Grabbing the revolver, she waddled toward the back of the house.

Only by force of will was she able to step into the sunshine—arms stiffly extended as she held the gun in front of her like a character in a TV cop show. Except that she'd never seen a cop with her shape, she thought wryly as she pictured what she must look like.

Seeing no one in the immediate vicinity, she lowered the gun, then started down the trail to the shelter, moving as fast as her advanced pregnancy would permit.

Matt had disguised the path, but there were rock stepping stones hidden among the tree roots and pine needles. She'd gotten only a couple of dozen yards from the house when another pain hit her, and she stopped, clamping her teeth together to keep from crying out.

The contraction held her immobile—a big round target—and she knew with terrible certainty that if one of the intruders came upon her now, there was nothing she could do to defend herself.

When the pain eased, she started off again, almost losing her footing as she missed a stone and slid on a patch of pine needles. But she managed to keep herself upright by grabbing on to rough tree bark, managed not to drop the gun or the pack.

Sucking in a breath, then another, she waited until she was feeling steady on her feet, then started off again. Finally she emerged from under the trees and rounded a rock outcropping that would block her from view, unless someone was stationed on the other side of the mountain valley.

Pausing, she took several deep breaths, half-amazed that she had made it this far without being apprehended.

Now came the hard part—the steep slope down to the entrance to the shelter. She had come this way more than a dozen times before. But not in the past two weeks, she realized with a sudden pang. In her condition, two weeks was a long time. She was larger, bulkier and a lot less steady on her feet.

As she moved cautiously forward, the sun hit her in the face, and she lifted a hand to shade her eyes. It was then that she felt a tugging sensation inside her—and a gush of liquid between her legs.

With a gasp she stopped, reached to steady herself against the rock wall. Her water had broken. If there had been any doubt that she was in labor, that doubt was removed.

Frantically she looked around. Exposed, out in the open, vulnerable, she knew she had to get to safety. But the trail to the shelter seemed to have gotten steeper as she stood there.

Still, there was no choice now but to go forward. Gingerly, one step at a time, she started down. Half a yard onto the slope, she felt her foot sliding again, and stopped, managing to hold back a sob of frustration as she stood with her chest heaving. It was bad enough trying to do it when her center of gravity was so off balance. The fear of another contraction made it all the more terrifying.

Opting for caution, she eased to a sitting position, and moved herself along on her bottom, gripping the rough rock for support.

Finally the door was in sight, and she felt a rush of relief.

Then, just as she was about to attempt the most dangerous few yards of the journey, two things happened simultaneously. Another pain gripped her and the sound of distant gunfire cracked the silence of the mountaintop.

MATT MIGHT HAVE PELTED headlong into the thicket where the SUV was hidden, but his training had made him stop behind a tree, pick up a rock and toss it about twenty feet from where he stood.

Immediately a spray of bullets erupted from the underbrush.

Pulling his arm back, he made a groaning sound as if he'd been hit and waited with his pulse pounding, wondering if he'd fooled the guy assigned to guard the vehicle.

"Forester?"

The voice was unfamiliar. The tone was hard and unforgiving.

Matt waited, feeling each second tick by. When a patch of leaves rustled, he dodged around the tree and fired at where he judged the other man was hiding.

This time the groan was genuine—he hoped. For good measure he pumped four more shots into the area, then dodged to the next tree, encouraged by the lack of movement from the opposition. But he wasn't going to be fooled by the same trick he'd used.

Instead of a direct approach, he made a wide circle around the area, moving as quietly as he could through the underbrush, approaching from behind. When he reached the vehicle, he saw a pair of legs. They belonged to a man dressed in fatigues lying face down in a pool of blood.

He paused to disengage the machine gun from the limp hand, latch the safety, and add the weapon to his own arsenal.

Moving with economy, he opened the driver's door of the vehicle, started the engine, and pulled away from the screen of foliage, ducking low as he roared onto the dirt track. Taking the first curve at dangerous speed, he arrowed toward the road on the other side of the mountain, praying that he wasn't going to run into a roadblock before he reached the public highway.

WHEN THE SOUND OF GUNFIRE had faded and her heart rate had slowed to a manageable pace, Amanda inched along the side of the cliff, coming to a stop in front of the shelter door.

Matt had changed the locking mechanism to a keypad, and she carefully pressed the numbers, giving a little prayer of thanks when she heard the lock click. But just as she started to pull on the heave door, another pain grabbed her. This time she tried to do the breathing exercises she'd practiced with the childbirth video she'd bought. Matt had watched with her, coaching her. But he wasn't here now. The memory of the gunfire and the thought of him out there fighting for his life choked off her breath, and she went through the remainder of the contraction in a state of rising hysteria.

By the end she was sobbing, the tears coursing down her cheeks as she pulled open the heavy door, threw herself inside the shelter, then turned to push the barrier closed.

The lock snapped behind her, and she tumbled into the darkness. She and the baby were safe. But what about her husband?

Fresh tears filled her eyes, and she swiped her arm across her face. She couldn't fall apart, she told herself sternly. There were still things she had to do—things that might make the difference between life and death.

Feeling along the wall, she found the shelves where Matt had stacked supplies. A large flashlight was supposed to be within easy reach, and she found it after only a few seconds of fumbling in the dark. Switching it on, she moved to the back of the cavern, where the generator was located and started it going.

As it came on, the overhead lights kicked in, and she could hear the fan for the ventilation system, as well.

Turning off the flashlight, she looked around, getting her bearings. Matt had filled the refuge with state-of-the art equipment. There were four television screens on one wall, and she switched them on, giving herself views of the surrounding area.

The second two screens made her gasp. Ordinarily they showed only a view of rocks and trees. Now she was treated to the sight of ten hard-faced men, wearing camouflage outfits and carrying machine guns, moving stealthily from tree to tree, sneaking up on the house.

As she watched, she saw something move in the bushes near one of the groups. The men saw it, too, because they turned and sprayed the underbrush with machine-gun fire.

Then one moved forward, pushed the underbrush away with his foot and revealed the body of a doe.

Sick with horror, she watched them laughing and gesturing toward the limp body. Maybe they'd thought it was Matt in there. Maybe they simply liked to kill for the pleasure of it.

When Matt had showed her how to set off the explosive charges, she'd wondered if she could really push the buttons if she were under attack. Now she felt her anger solidifying as she watched the cruel men start off again, thinking they were closing in on *her*.

She knew the area, knew the exact location of the cameras and could relate the images she was seeing to the explosives that Matt had set around the property. The transmitter was in her bag, and she pulled it out. Her hand shook only a little as she studied the buttons, then watched the screen intently. Her bottom lip clamped between her teeth, she pressed one of the buttons, then another.

The response was immediate. The ground shook, a shower of earth and stone erupted on the screens, and a wave of sound reached her, reverberating through the rock above and around her.

But before she could find out if she'd stopped any of the invaders, another contraction hit her—longer and fiercer than any that had come before, and she pressed her shoulders against the rough wall of the shelter, this time unable to hold back a moan as the pain caught her in its vise.

IN THE DISTANCE Matt heard two explosions. He hoped that was Amanda, setting off the charges from inside the shelter. But there was no way he could be sure and nothing he could do besides keep going, his eyes glued to the odometer. He had told himself he had to be ten miles from the house before he called Randolph Security.

The phone rang when he still had two miles to go. Will Marbella again, he thought with a curse, planning to fill him in on the latest developments up on the mountain. Or, more likely, trying to unnerve him with a pack of lies.

Teeth clenched, he let the shrill ringing of the phone curdle the air inside the car as he sped toward New Hampton, his hands clenched on the wheel.

AMANDA ROUSED HERSELF to do what she knew had to be done.

Pulling off her ruined dress, she kicked it into a corner, then used some of the bottled water and soap to wash the dirt off her legs from when she'd come down the incline on her bottom. Once she'd cleaned herself off, she pulled out another maternity shift from the supplies on the shelves and slipped it over her head.

She had just finished when a flash of movement on one of the TV screens caught her eye.

It was a man, coming down the incline toward the shelter—limping, but carrying a machine gun. She sucked in a breath as she studied his face. It was the man they had seen in the L.A. restaurant. The man who had called them on the phone. Marbella.

She peered at the screen, trying to judge his position. But another contraction caught her, capturing her full attention. And when it was over, her pursuer had disappeared from view.

MATT SQUEALED around another curve, then floored the gas pedal on a relatively straight stretch of road. A whirring noise filled his head, growing in intensity until he realized that it wasn't something manufactured by his brain. It was coming from above. His heart stopped, then started up in double time as he recognized the beating of blades above him. Helicopter blades. Again!

"God no," he shouted into the interior of the SUV, pressing his foot on the accelerator, even as he knew there was no hope of escape. He and Amanda had outfoxed the sheriff the first night at the ranch, but that had been in the dark—not in broad daylight. Not when the pursuers already had him spotted.

Well, he amended, he could pull onto the shoulder and drive into the woods. Ditch the truck. Maybe he could even get away—if the cover was thick enough. But that strategy wasn't going to do Amanda one damn bit of good.

Still, he wasn't going to simply give up. So he kept driving until the chopper swooped low, circled the truck and set down where the woods thinned out along the road in front of him.

Stamping on the brake, he squealed to a stop on the shoulder and drew his gun as he leaped from behind the wheel.

A dark-haired man was already descending from the chopper, both hands raised above his head. He was unarmed and holding a white handkerchief in his right fist and shouting something Matt couldn't hear.

A flag of truce? It must be some kind of trick. Marbella trying to get him to drop his guard. Still with his own gun trained on the man's chest, Matt waited, his finger poised on the trigger.

Then the face registered. It was Hunter Kelley. With a sick feeling, Matt realized he had come within millimeters of mowing down his friend. He also knew that Hunter must have realized that chance he was taking.

Overwhelmed, he lowered his gun, hardly able to believe his own eyes as the Randolph Security agent ran toward him, shouting. As he got closer, the words began to make sense.

"We're here to help you. We've been keeping current on your status. We found out about Marbella's assault plans a few hours ago. Is Amanda with you?"

"No. I couldn't take her on a fast hike through the woods," Matt answered, then asked his own question. "Why didn't you let me know you were joining the party?"

"We were going to call you tomorrow night, but that plan got superceded."

"They surrounded the house this morning. I had to send Amanda to the bomb shelter," he answered, a choked feeling clogging his throat. God, what if she hadn't made it? What if something had gone wrong?

He tried not to let his thoughts flash in that direction as Hunter motioned him toward the open door of the chopper.

Matt ducked low and followed him inside. "Glad to see you," he shouted above the noise of the blades.

Sitting in the back was Miguel Valero, the doctor who was closely tied to Light Street and Randolph Security. Good idea, Matt thought.

Jed Prentiss, who was at the controls, pitched his voice above the noise of the rotors and shouted, "Is there a good place to set down near the house?"

Matt laughed, then leaned forward and shouted, "I made sure there wasn't."

"Then where?"

"About a quarter mile before you reach the house, there's a bare patch of rock."

As the helicopter came over the ridge, someone on the ground opened fire, and Matt heard bullets pinging off the landing gear.

Beside him, Dr. Valero swore. Matt was thinking the physician hadn't figured on going into combat, until Dr. Valero pulled up the machine gun that had been shoved out of view, opened the window and aimed in the direction of the unfriendly fire.

He got off several rounds before they moved out of range, swooped low and set down on the flat rocky area Matt had indicated.

Jed cut the engine, and they all scrambled out.

"We know there were twelve in the assault team," Hunter informed Matt as they started up the hill toward the house, moving cautiously, using the trees and rocks for cover.

"How did you pick that up?"

"We've been monitoring their communications. We would have been here before they arrived, but they suddenly moved up their timetable."

They reached one of the blast sites, and Matt counted four bodies. Already, the odds were looking better, and he was pretty sure they had Amanda to thank.

The odds improved at the next crater, where three more of the attackers had fallen.

That left four, counting the guy who'd guarded the SUV. Or maybe fewer, depending on what else had happened in his absence.

Still, Matt's tension increased as they approached the house. Bracing for a hail of bullets, he crouched low and moved from rock to tree. He made the final dash across the patio in seconds and burst through the door, gun drawn. But nobody challenged him.

Running from room to room, he called Amanda's name, but there was no answer. The other men were searching, too, but they found no one. Stopping by the sewing machine, he picked up the pieces she'd been sewing into a baby quilt, his heart blocking his windpipe as he touched the fabric that she had handled the day before.

Then he snapped himself out of his trance—it wasn't helping Amanda. Looking up, he saw that the closet door was flung open. As he scanned the contents, he sucked in a sharp breath.

"What is it?" Hunter asked, coming up behind him.

"She took the pack we'd put together for when we drove to the hospital."

"In case she was in labor?" Miguel asked.

"Yes." Matt stared at the doctor, trying to contain his panic. "But she's only a little over eight months."

"She could have gone into labor early," Miguel said. "But she may only have been taking precautions," he added as he read the panic on Matt's face.

"We have to get to her. She's all alone down there. She needs us!"

"Which way?" Jed asked.

Matt led them out the front door, then down the path to the shelter.

They reached a spot where the ground was wet. Miguel stooped down, felt the dirt, then brought his fingers to his nose.

"Amniotic fluid," he said

"Her water broke?" Matt asked.

"Yes."

"What does that mean?" Matt was afraid he already knew the answer.

"She's probably having contractions."

"She might not be?"

"They might hold off for a while."

Matt breathed in a little sigh, hoping that was true. Amanda was alone. In the shelter—he hoped. Maybe in pain. Certainly terrified.

"How much time does she have if she's in labor?" he managed to ask.

"I don't know. With a first child, it could go slowly," Miguel said. "Was she having pains when you left?"

"She didn't say so." He stopped. "She said her back hurt. That started last night."

He could see from Miguel's face that the information wasn't good news. "We've got to get her out of there."

"Yes," the doctor agreed.

Picking up his pace, Matt started down the incline—and saw the scrape marks in the dirt, and the wet streaks.

"She came down the hill sitting down," he said, knowing the other men could read the trail as well as he could.

He was about to charge around an outcropping when Hunter pulled him back, in time to avoid a stream of bullets.

They came from the rocks above the shelter. Matt curse
as he scanned the position. Whoever was up there had th
advantage.

"Can we go around?" Jed asked.

"Not unless we climb up the cliff. And he can pick us of
That's why I rented this place. It's a damn fortress."

Matt cupped his hands around his mouth. "You up the
with the machine gun. We can take you out with the helicop
ter."

"You're going to have to go and get it," a voice calle
back. "And by that time, your wife is going to be dead."

Chapter Seventeen

A stab of fear pierced Matt's throat, but he managed to get a few words out. "You're lying."

"No. I've got a special microphone pickup. I can hear her down there. She's in bad trouble."

This time he recognized the voice. It was Marbella.

"Let us pass," Matt shouted. "It's over. You've lost."

Jed had already turned and started back up the incline at a trot—going for the helicopter, Matt knew.

"Give it up!" he shouted again, trying to angle himself into position to get the bastard. He was stopped by a spray of bullets.

Cursing, he ducked back around the rock.

"I never give up," Marbella spit.

"Even when you've lost?" Hunter asked.

"Especially when I've lost! If I don't get her and the kid, neither will you. And neither will Logan. If I have to go out, I'm going to take some satisfaction with me."

Raw acid churned inside Matt, eating away at his vital organs. Amanda was only a few yards away—but she might as well be at the center of the earth. Then a surge of hope coursed through him drowning out the acid. His own transmitter might be back in the SUV. But Amanda had one.

Dodging back several feet, he crouched low and pressed the transmit button on his walkie-talkie. "Amanda. Can you hear

me?'' he asked urgently. ''Sweetheart, listen to me. Don't
waste energy answering me right now. You just have to help
us out here. We're at the entrance to the shelter. We're coming
in to get you. But Marbella is in the rocks above the entrance
with a machine gun. He's got us pinned down. We can't get
past him to get in there to help you. So you need to set off
the charges above the shelter. That's buttons eight and nine.
Can you do that for me, sweetheart? Can you press buttons
eight and nine for me?''

He waited with his heart pounding. Then, unable to stand
the silence, he pressed the transmission button again.
''Amanda. Please. Help me. Amanda, what's going on in
there? Over.''

She didn't answer, and he closed his eyes, a prayer tumbling
from his lips. ''Please, God, please. Help her. Help her do it.''

Seconds ticked by, each one a year of his life. ''She's too
far gone to do it.'' Marbella taunted from his hiding place.

Matt tensed, ready to make a run around the boulder. But
he felt Hunter's fingers tangle in his shirt—holding him back.

''Let me go,'' he shouted.

''No. He's got a clear shot if you go out there. You won't
be doing your wife any good by getting yourself killed.''

In frustration, Matt jammed the transmit button again.
''Amanda, for God's sake, help me. Please. Press the buttons.
Eight and nine.''

He had given in to despair when the sound and shock wave
of a blast hit him, knocking him back into Hunter, who
grunted as he was flattened against the side of the cliff.

Debris was still raining down as Matt dashed forward. A
chunk of mountainside hit his shoulder, but it didn't stop him
from leaping to the door. Frantically working the keypad, he
cursed when he got the combination wrong. Then he forced
himself to slow down and press the right sequence. When the
lock clicked, he pushed the door open and bolted inside.

''Amanda?'' he called. ''Amanda!''

The only answer was a low moan. Fear grabbed him by the

throat as his eyes swept the dimly lit room and found her lying on one of the mattresses on the floor, her body rolling back and forth as she whimpered in pain. The walkie-talkie was three feet away. The controller was clutched in her hand.

Running forward, he knelt beside her, carefully prying her fingers loose and moving the detonator out of the way—removing the danger of more explosions.

"Sweetheart. We're here. We've got you."

She looked up at him, her face contorted with pain, her eyes glassy. "Did I do what you wanted?" she whispered, raising her hand toward him. Like a piece of deadwood, it flopped back on the mattress.

"Yes!"

"The baby's coming. I tried to push," she went on, her voice so low he had to lean forward to hear. "I kept pushing, but…but…something's wrong…"

Miguel came down on the other side of her. "Amanda, I'm Matt's friend. Miguel Valero. I'm a doctor. I'm going to deliver the baby."

"Thank God," she breathed, relief flooding her features as she turned the responsibility over to someone else.

Matt reached for Amanda's hands, feeling her fingers clamp down on his so hard that he thought his bones might crack.

He talked to her, his voice low and reassuring, telling her everything was going to be okay. Miguel knew what to do.

From the corner of his vision, he saw the physician slipping on gloves. "I'm going to examine you now."

Matt held his breath, waiting to find out what was wrong. From the expression on his friend's face, he knew the news wasn't good.

When Miguel listened to Amanda's abdomen with a stethoscope, his expression grew even more grim, and Matt felt the world contract around him. By an effort of will, he kept his own face from showing any of his fear.

Miguel put his hand on his shoulder and drew him away.

"It's bad, isn't it?" Matt asked urgently.

"Yes. Bad." Miguel spoke rapidly. "The baby's in a transverse lie. There's a foot sticking down. If we were in the hospital, I would do a cesarean section immediately. But I don't have any anesthetic."

"The helicopter," Matt gasped. "We can get her to the hospital."

Miguel shook his head. "That will be too late for the baby. His heart beat is slow. He's in distress."

"My God. What are you going to do?"

"She's fully dilated." He swallowed. "I can grab the foot and do a breech extraction. That's not going to be any picnic for her, either. I have morphine. That's the best I can do for her."

"Do it!"

Miguel's face was drawn as he cupped Matt's shoulder again, his fingers digging into the flesh. "I may not be able to save them both," he said. "If I have to choose between Amanda and the baby, what do you want me to do?"

Matt stared at him, hardly able to make his mind function. He'd heard stories of how the whole life of a drowning man flashed before his eyes. The same thing happened now. Only it wasn't his whole life. It was the past few months—the precious minutes and hours he'd spent with Amanda. Falling in love with her. Watching her personality change and blossom as she outgrew the abuse of her past. Feeling the bond they'd forged strengthen every day. And his own bond with the unborn child, who had become as important to him as if he'd been the biological father.

Choose one of them?

The very thought made him physically ill.

"If I can only save one of them, tell me what to do!" Miguel's voice penetrated his numb state of shock.

"Save them both," Matt ordered, knowing he might be asking the impossible.

Miguel nodded tightly, then looked around the shelter. "Let's get her up on the table so I have room to work. Position her with her hips a little over the edge. And you can support her feet with the chairs.''

Matt bent over Amanda and picked her up, hearing her groan as he cradled her in his arms.

"That hurts," she gasped out.

"I know, sweetheart. I know," he told her, wishing he could take the pain into his own body. "You've been so brave. You only have to hold on for a little bit longer," he added, hoping he was telling her the truth. "We're getting you up where the doctor can work," he explained as he laid her on the table, where Miguel had already spread a blanket.

Miguel was at her side then, talking to her. "The baby is turned sideways inside you," he said. "That's why you can't deliver him. I'm going to try to turn him. I'm sorry; it's going to be painful. But I can give you morphine."

"Please, don't worry about me. Just save my baby," she gasped, the plea choking off as a contraction seized her.

"I'll do my best," Miguel said, then reached into his bag and brought out a hypodermic.

Matt clenched his teeth, holding back the agony of fear that he knew he must not let Amanda see. He would give his heart's blood for this woman. But all he could do was grab her hand and let her fingers dig into him again as the doctor administered the injection.

"Hold on, sweetheart. Hold on to me. Give the pain to me," he whispered, knowing his voice would break if he tried to speak any louder. And knowing that what he was offering her was not nearly enough.

When he looked back at Miguel, he saw the doctor's lips moving, heard low, rapid words in Spanish and knew that he was praying. Then he made the sign of the cross.

Until that moment, Matt truly hadn't comprehended what he was asking of his friend. Now he felt his heart leap into his throat, blocking his windpipe.

The next few minutes were the longest of his life. He was afraid to watch what was going on, so he kept his eyes focused on Amanda's face, wincing as her features contorted with pain. Every time she made a low, whimpering sound, he felt as if his heart were being torn from his chest.

Please, God, help Miguel do this. Please, he silently prayed, the words running together in his mind as the endless seconds ticked by.

When he heard a new sound, at first he didn't understand what it was. Then he realized it was a baby's tiny cry. When he turned and saw the perspiration on Miguel's forehead and the look of relief on his face, Matt understood he had been present at a miracle.

"Is the baby all right?" Amanda gasped out, her words slurred from the morphine.

"Yes. You have a daughter. She's good," he answered as he suctioned the baby's nose and mouth. When he laid her on Amanda's chest, she cradled the tiny body and Matt circled them both while Miguel cut and clamped the cord.

"Bethany." He whispered the name that Amanda had chosen. His sister's name.

"Thank you," he breathed—to God, to Miguel, to Amanda.

"We need to get both of you to the hospital," Miguel said.

"Her Apgar score?" Amanda asked, referring to the tests that were used to evaluate a newborn's condition. Her words were slurred from the drug.

"Six."

Her face contorted with anxiety. "That's not good," she whispered.

"Give her five minutes. We'll try again," Miguel said.

Matt felt Amanda's whole being focused on Miguel as he worked on the baby.

Finally, he delivered his verdict. "She's up to eight. That's good!"

"Thank you, oh, thank you," Amanda breathed, and Matt saw that she was at the end of her resources.

"Just rest," he whispered, watching her eyelids drift closed.

He stared down into her face, relieved to see that the pain and the fear were over.

The sound of someone clearing his throat made Matt's head jerk up. It was Hunter, who still guarded the doorway.

"Is everything all right?" he asked, his face anxious.

"Yes," Matt told him, praying that it was true.

"Good. The rest of the invaders fled in their SUV," Hunter said, then added, "Jed's here. He can't land, but we can lift them into the chopper."

Matt nodded, grateful that his friends were doing some of the thinking for him now. He helped Miguel wrap mother and child in blankets.

Miguel took the infant. Matt carried his wife, cradling her protectively against his chest, turning his head to give her a quick kiss on the cheek before carrying her outside.

Minutes later they were on the way to the hospital.

TIME WAS DISTORTED so that Matt wasn't sure whether a million years had passed or only hours. But the clock on the wall said five o'clock, so he knew it must be early the next morning as he stood beside the bassinet gazing down at the tiny hand curled around his index finger.

He hadn't left the hospital, but sometime during the night, his friends had brought him a change of clothing. Then they'd made him shower and get a few hours' sleep, pointing out that he wouldn't do himself or Amanda any good by falling on his face from exhaustion.

Now he marveled at the perfectly formed little fingers clamped around one of his. His daughter's fingers. The child who belonged to him—because he claimed her as his own. As much his as any flesh of his flesh could be.

Mesmerized by the contact, he felt his eyes mist as he thought how easily he could have lost this precious new life. Or lost Amanda—the woman he'd fallen in love with before he knew what was happening to him.

He turned his head toward his wife, watching her sleep,

wanting to take her in his arms and hold her close. He needed
that contact. But he wasn't selfish enough to wake her. She'd
been through an ordeal that would have killed her and their
daughter if he and Miguel hadn't gotten to her in time.

So, much as he longed to tell her how much he loved her
and how awed he was by her bravery, he stayed beside the
bassinet, talking in low tones to Bethany, telling her all the
good news he desperately wanted her mother to hear.

"The Light Street Detective Agency came through for us,"
he said. "Randolph Security turned the Logan case over to
them, with Hunter working as a liaison to one of their new
partners, Hannah Dawson. She's really something. One of the
best investigators I've ever met.

"Thanks to her, Roy Logan's in jail. And so are the members of the Las Vegas syndicate—the ones Logan didn't knock
off. It was the syndicate that raided Tim Francetti's office,
stole his records and had him killed. The Denver police have
proof of that now. So we're in the clear.

"Marbella was the head of the organization. He kept up a
lily-white front, but he and his buddies were the ones who had
Colin killed, too, because his L.A. drug connection would
have contaminated their squeaky-clean operation—and the Nevada Gambling Commission might not have given them a license. So when Uncle Bud came to them trying to trade you
and your mom for their safety, they thanked him for the information—then got rid of him, too."

He swallowed hard. "But the best news of all is about
you."

"What?"

It was Amanda who had spoken, of course, and Matt's head
whipped around. His heartbeat quickened when he saw that
his wife was awake. Her eyes softened as they focused on him
and Bethany.

"How long have you been playing possum?" he asked,
carefully pushing the baby's bed so that he maintained the
contact with his daughter while he moved closer to his wife.

"I woke up when you started talking to her."

"I didn't mean to disturb you."

"I know. But I don't mind. I got to hear the news report."

"All good news."

"Yes." She reached out a hand, and he linked his fingers with hers, so that he was holding on to the two people who mattered most to him in the world—the two people he had almost lost. Moisture stung his eyes, and he blinked to clear his vision.

"You said the best part was about Bethany?"

Matt cleared his throat. "First of all, she's fine. And second, she's not Colin's child."

Amanda's face held a mixture of relief—and skepticism. "How could that be true? How do you know?"

He began enumerating the facts he'd been bursting to tell her. "Colin's blood type was A positive. We got that from the records of the Highton clinic. The hospital did blood work on you and Bethany after they admitted you. Your blood type is O positive. Hers is AB positive." He felt his throat tighten painfully. "Like mine," he finished.

Amanda stared at him. "Like yours," she repeated softly, her features suffused with wonder.

"Yeah. So she can't be Colin's. Francetti made a mistake. Or he made it up, so he could offer you and Bethany to Logan."

"Oh, my God," she breathed, her eyes shifting to the baby, who must have sensed that her mama and papa were talking about her, because she stirred, turned her head and started to cry.

"I think she's hungry. Would you give her to me?" Amanda asked.

Matt carefully lifted the tiny bundle from the bassinet and placed her in his wife's arms.

"Can you crank up the bed a little?" she requested.

He complied, then watched Amanda open the front of her

gown, and lift the baby to her breast. After a few moments Bethany found her mother's nipple and began to suckle.

Matt moved closer, awed by the connection between mother and child—so simple yet so complicated.

"She knows how to do it," he whispered.

"Our daughter is a smart little girl."

"Our daughter," he repeated. "I can still hardy believe it. AB is the rarest blood type. And hers, too."

"I'm glad," Amanda answered, holding out her free arm. "Come up here and hold me."

"Do you think it's allowed?"

"I think I earned the right to have my husband's arm around me."

"God, yes!" he answered, easing onto the bed beside her and cradling her close, stroking his lips against her cheek as she nursed the baby. "I'm in awe of you."

"It's not that hard to nurse a baby."

"I'm talking about holding off an invading army."

"I think I had a little help."

"Don't be modest, sweetheart." He let his fingers slide through her beautiful blond hair. "I love you," he murmured. "Have I told you that recently?"

She snuggled against him. "You can tell me anytime you want. As long as you're willing to keep hearing the same thing from me. Matt, I love you so much."

He felt his eyes mist again and struggled to get control of his emotions, aware again of how much this woman had given him—of how much he needed her and their child. Without them, he'd been living only half a life.

She turned her head toward him. "Is everything you said really true? Are we safe?"

"It's all true!" He laughed. "And Randolph Security has been holding my back pay, so we can use it for a down payment on a house outside of Baltimore. All the Light Street women are chomping at the bit, waiting to meet the woman who snared the notorious bachelor, Matt Forester. They've already started organizing a baby shower. And Hannah Dawson, the P.I. who worked on the case, is anxious to fill you in on the details of the investigation.'' He stopped, realizing that he was babbling. ''I mean…I guess I'm getting ahead of myself,'' he amended. ''We never talked about where we're going to live—whether you want to go back to the ranch.''

''I want to live in Baltimore, where your work is,'' she answered promptly. ''Where your friends are. You've told me so much about them, I feel like I know them already. I'm going to sell the ranch. Then we'll have enough money for an estate. Unless you're too macho to let your wife help out with the finances,'' she amended.

''I'm not too macho.'' He swallowed. ''But do you really want to sell the property that's been in your family for generations?''

''Living with you convinced me I don't want to go back to Crowfoot. I want to be where it's convenient for you. Because I can be happy anywhere. She looked down at the child nursing at her breast, then back at Matt. ''Being Bethany's mom and your wife, making a home for the two of you…'' She paused, and her voice softened. ''And…and maybe a sister or brother for her.''

''I'd like that,'' he answered.

''One more or two?''

''You're ready to go through that again?'' he asked remembering the agony on her face when he'd burst into the shelter and then when Miguel had turned Bethany so he could deliver her.

''No.'' She managed a small laugh that ended in a wince of pain. ''I figure nothing can top that. A nice normal delivery in a hospital will be a piece of cake.''

''Oh, yeah.''

''And the next time I think I'm going to have a lot more fun getting pregnant,'' she whispered, dipping her head.

He crooked his finger under her chin and brought her face back to his. ''You can't be thinking about *that*.''

"Well, it's a little soon…but I know I will be." The flush he loved so much spread across her cheeks. "See what you did? You turned a little virgin country girl into a woman."

"My woman." His arm tightened around her.

"Your woman," she agreed. "For as long as you want me."

"Forever. Definitely forever," he answered as he tightened his arms around his wife and child, thanking God for the twists of fate that had brought them both into his life.

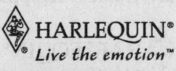

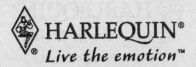

HARLEQUIN®
INTRIGUE®
BREATHTAKING ROMANTIC SUSPENSE

Shared dangers and passions lead to electrifying
romance and heart-stopping suspense!

Every month, you'll meet six new heroes
who are guaranteed to make your spine tingle
and your pulse pound. With them you'll enter
into the exciting world of Harlequin Intrigue—
where your life is on the line
and so is your heart!

THAT'S INTRIGUE—
ROMANTIC SUSPENSE
AT ITS BEST!

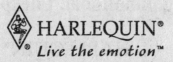

HARLEQUIN®
Live the emotion™

www.eHarlequin.com   INTDIR06

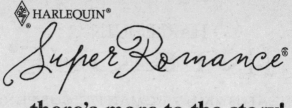

HARLEQUIN®
Super Romance®

...there's more to the story!

Superromance.
A *big* satisfying read about unforgettable
characters. Each month we offer *six* very different
stories that range from family drama to adventure
and mystery, from highly emotional stories to
romantic comedies—and much more! Stories
about people you'll believe in and care about.
Stories too compelling to put down....

Our authors are among today's *best* romance
writers. You'll find familiar names and talented
newcomers. Many of them are award winners—
and you'll see why!

If you want the biggest and best
in romance fiction, you'll get it
from Superromance!

Exciting, Emotional, Unexpected...

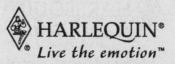

HARLEQUIN®
Live the emotion™

HSDIR06

HARLEQUIN®
Presents

**The world's bestselling romance series...
The series that brings you your favorite authors,
month after month:**

Helen Bianchin...Emma Darcy
Lynne Graham...Penny Jordan
Miranda Lee...Sandra Marton
Anne Mather...Carole Mortimer
Susan Napier...Michelle Reid

and many more uniquely talented authors!

Wealthy, powerful, gorgeous men...
Women who have feelings just like your own...
The stories you love, set in exotic, glamorous locations...

HARLEQUIN®
Presents

Seduction and Passion Guaranteed!

Harlequin® Historical
Historical Romantic Adventure!

*Imagine a time of chivalrous
knights and unconventional ladies,
roguish rakes and impetuous
heiresses, rugged cowboys
and spirited frontierswomen—
these rich and vivid tales will
capture your imagination!*

*Harlequin Historical...
they're too good to miss!*

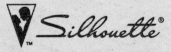